W9-AQG-361

OPEN
ROAD
SUMMER

OPEN ROAD SUMMER

EMERY LORD

WALKER BOOKS
AN IMPRINT OF BLOOMSBURY
NEW YORK   LONDON   NEW DELHI   SYDNEY

First published in the United States of America in April 2014
by Walker Books for Young Readers, an imprint of Bloomsbury Publishing, Inc.
www.bloomsbury.com

Bloomsbury is a registered trademark of Bloomsbury Publishing Plc

For information about permission to reproduce selections from this book, write to
Permissions, Walker BFYR, 1385 Broadway, New York, New York 10018
Bloomsbury books may be purchased for business or promotional use. For information on
bulk purchases please contact Macmillan Corporate and Premium Sales Department at
specialmarkets@macmillan.com

Library of Congress Cataloging-in-Publication Data
Lord, Emery.
Open road summer / by Emery Lord.
pages   cm
Summary: Follows seventeen-year-old Reagan as she tries to escape heartbreak and a bad
reputation by going on tour with her country superstar best friend—only to find more
trouble as she falls for the surprisingly sweet guy hired to pose as the singer's boyfriend.
ISBN 978-0-8027-3610-9 (hardcover) • ISBN 978-0-8027-3611-6 (e-book)
[1. Best friends—Fiction.   2. Friendship—Fiction.   3. Love—Fiction.
4. Country music—Fiction.   5. Singers—Fiction.]   I. Title.
PZ7.L87736Op 2014   [Fic]—dc23   2013025427

Book design by Amanda Bartlett
Typeset by Westchester Book Composition
Printed and bound in the U.S.A. by Thomson-Shore Inc., Dexter, Michigan
2 4 6 8 10 9 7 5 3 1

For Janelle, who has always held on tight

OPEN ROAD SUMMER

CHAPTER ONE

Nashville to Charlotte

The fans scream for her, but they don't really know the girl on the magazine covers—the girl with the guitar and the easy smile. Her given name is Delilah, and they think she goes by Lilah. But anyone who really knows my best friend calls her Dee. They think she's seventeen, and she is. But she never acts seventeen. She acts either thirty years old, like a composed professional, in record-label meetings and interviews, or twelve years old, with me—giggling like we did back when she still had braces, back when our summer plans were nothing more than sleepovers and swimming at the pool. They think she wrote the songs on this album while getting over a breakup. But they're wrong. She's not over it. Not even close.

On the side of her tour bus, there's a ten-foot-tall picture of Dee surrounded by a field of wildflowers. The shot captures her hand midstrum against a twelve-string guitar.

Next to the picture, "Lilah Montgomery" is scrawled in a cursive font meant to mimic Dee's handwriting. Fans wait in line for hours to get that same signature on posters and T-shirts. The newest album is called *Middle of Nowhere, Tennessee*, and the title song has been number one for two weeks already. It's an upbeat song—a happy one, but it was written more than a year ago.

> *Middle of nowhere, Tennessee,*
> *Exactly where I want to be.*
> *Our initials carved in the old oak tree,*
> *And every road takes me back home.*
> *Middle of nowhere, Tennessee,*
> *Dancing on the porch, you and me.*
> *This is where I was born to be,*
> *No matter how far I may roam.*

The song, like so many others, was written for Jimmy.

I feel out of place here, in the expansive parking lot behind Muddy Water Records, outside Nashville. This is the starting point for Dee's summer tour, and all three passenger buses are lined up, waiting to take us on our way. Dee wafts within the crowd, making cheerful introductions between the families of her band and crew, all here to say good-bye before the buses depart. I'm hanging back, waiting for her, when I sense someone in my peripheral vision. Someone who is not so subtly staring at my legs. There's plenty to see, since my hemline is pushing the limits of public decency.

"Hey," the guy says, eyeing me in an overeager way that makes me feel embarrassed for him. "Are you part of the backup band?"

"Sure." This is a lie. I smirk, but it's forced. I'm not in the mood, not after the month I've had. Besides, he's not my type. Neatly trimmed hair, tucked-in polo shirt. One glance at him and I'm repressing a yawn.

"I'm Mark Tran," he says. "I'm the assistant lighting director for the show."

"Reagan O'Neill," I reply. Then I launch the grenade. "I'm seventeen."

It lands. Boom. My new friend Mark pinkens as he mutters something about it being nice to meet me. You can only have so many guys hit on you before it gets terribly, almost insultingly boring. My appearance and collection of tiny clothes are like flypaper, drawing in good boys and bad boys, boys younger than me and men old enough to be my father. Their reactions make it easier to tell the difference between the harmless guys and the ones who are venomous—the ones who will make it sting. But sometimes they fool me.

Dee greets her violinist's mom with an enveloping hug. The woman looks startled, her eyes widening over Dee's shoulder. My best friend is a hugger, with arms like an unhinged gate. At the mere thought of embracing strangers, I cross my arms, which triggers a splintering pain in my left wrist. I'm wearing my leather jacket despite the early June humidity, hoping that no one notices how tightly the left sleeve fits over my blue cast. The persistent ache feels like a reminder that I can't keep making bad decisions without breaking more pieces of myself.

"Reagan," Dee calls, waving me over. "You ready?"

I walk toward her, my tall shoes thudding against the asphalt. This sound is my touchstone, and it follows me anywhere I go. Unless I'm sneaking out of the house. In that case, I use my bare feet to dodge the creaky stairs. Today I chose my heeled motorcycle boots to go with a summer dress made of thin floral-print cotton. Contradiction suits me.

Dee signs a few more autographs for the family members of her band and crew as we try to move toward our tour bus. One girl looks eleven or twelve, and she's trembling like she's had espresso injected into her veins.

"I think you're the prettiest person in the whole entire world," the girl says as Dee signs a photograph of herself, "and I listen to your music, like, every single day."

Though I've seen emotional fans with Dee before, my first thought is: *This is so weird.* Dee doesn't think it's weird. Without a moment of hesitation or a look of confusion, she squeals a thank-you and hugs the girl, who clutches on to her, stunned.

To her fans, Dee is the best friend they've never had, and I guess that part isn't so weird. Dee's the only real friend I've ever had—the one who comes running even though I'd never admit I need someone by my side. She jokes that she keeps bail money in her nightstand; I joke that she'd be my one phone call. Only I'm not joking. She would be.

Dee hooks her arm through mine as we walk toward her family. I already said good-bye to my dad, standing on the porch of our farmhouse before Dee's mom picked me up. I didn't want to do the drawn-out, forlorn farewell, because neither of us is forlorn. We both know we need a break. He needs a break from my causing trouble and bickering with my stepmom, and I need a break from . . . well, from my whole life, really.

I stay back, crossing my arms again, as Dee hugs her dad—a long, clinging hug that reminds me that leaving isn't so easy for her. Mrs. Montgomery is hugging Dee's aunt Peach, who is our summer chaperone. After Peach boards the tour bus, Mrs. Montgomery waves me over, and I uncross my arms. The casted one aches, of course, but I don't let myself linger on that anymore.

"You girls are going to have such a fun summer." She clasps her hands against my shoulders. "I can't wait to hear about it."

To her credit, Dee's mom doesn't admonish me to behave or warn me not to get Dee in trouble. No, Mrs. Montgomery has never been like that, even though I probably deserve it. She hugs me as she always does, like I'm her own daughter.

"You call if you need anything, okay?" Dee's mom whispers as she releases me. This is such a mom thing to say when leaving a daughter at summer camp or at college or, I suppose, on a concert tour. It's nice to have someone say it to me.

Beside me, Dee crouches down, pulling both of her little brothers into one big hug. She whispers something to both of them, and they nod obediently in response. When she stands back, her eyes are glistening with tears.

"None of that," her mom says. "We'll see you opening night. You won't even miss us."

That's not true. Dee would love to have her family on tour, but her parents think it's important for her brothers to stay grounded in reality. They're in elementary school, and they should have summers of cannonballs into the pool and makeshift lemonade stands. They should have a childhood that's based on more than their sister's fame—a childhood like Dee's.

Now Dee's mom holds her close and says something in her ear. Advice, I suppose, or an affirmation of how proud she is. Mrs. Montgomery is a songwriter for a big label on Music Row, but she's never been a performer. She filled their house with Emmylou Harris and Johnny Cash, and she showed Dee by example that she could make her very own music. Dee's parents never pushed her toward this career, but her DNA twists into bars of music instead of double helixes.

With one last squeeze, Dee untangles her arms from her mom's neck. She exhales deeply, linking her pinkie with mine. "Let's do it."

So, with Dee glancing behind us one last time, we step into our home for the next three months. My laptop and camera bag are already on board, and my one massive suit-case is packed in the undercarriage of the bus. Dee designed the interior of the bus herself. Both sides are lined with long leather couches—cushy and deep like the one in her parents' living room. One couch sidles up to a retro dining nook while the other ends near the compact kitchen area, which is complete with a sink and a well-stocked refrigerator.

I plop down on the right-side couch, cozying against the throw pillows. Dee had them made with a floral fabric to look like the wildflowers on her album cover. There's a full-size bed in the back, where Peach is already lying down, and two bunks tucked into the bus's side wall.

Dee nestles into the couch across from mine, turning so she can look out the tall windows at her family. They can't see her, but she presses her palm against the glass. Her other hand rests on the couch, lingering near her two ever-present cell phones: one for personal contacts and one for work calls. The personal phone holds only a few numbers.

Everyone in the crowd waves as the bus lurches forward. Dee waves back even though no one can see her but me. The bus driver honks the horn a few times, and just like that, we're on our way to everywhere. Dee keeps looking out the window, watching as the scenes of downtown slide into images of our small town on the east side of Nashville. The snapshots of home pass us by—the wide trees and fields of crops and little houses, each with its own American flag. Outside, the sky is darkening, and so is Dee's mood. She's wringing her hands absentmindedly, smoothing a fingertip over her polished nails.

Real-life Dee doesn't have shiny pink nails. She has dirt under her fingernails from playing with her little brothers. She's still in full makeup from the press conference earlier, and, with false eyelashes too dark for her fair complexion,

Dee looks like a higher-contrast version of herself. Her blond hair is in loose waves that end exactly at her shoulders, the same cut and style as my own. The only difference is that Dee's natural coloring looks like an American landscape—country-sky-blue eyes and hair the color of Tennessee wheat fields, golden strands with darker undertones. My hair is nearly black, and I have jealous green eyes. In a fairy tale, she'd play the good fairy. I'd be the evil witch's screwup second cousin.

Dee's working through something in her mind, hugging herself as one hand toys with her necklace. The necklace is her trademark talisman—a thin chain with a tiny horseshoe that rests right on the hollow of her throat. Jimmy gave it to her for her fourteenth birthday, and she's never played a show without it. The necklace suits Dee so perfectly—the gold color and the simple, delicate charm—that it seems intrinsic, as much a part of her as the tiny scar on her chin or the freckles across her shoulders.

"Hey," I say, finally figuring out why she's so preoccupied. "That reporter from earlier . . . she doesn't know anything. I think her hair was proof of that."

Dee tries not to smile, but she can't help it. I like to think of myself as the devil on her shoulder, happy to say the things that she's too polite to think. "I don't want it to be like this, you know. Missing him makes me feel weak and pathetic."

"I know." When she talks about Jimmy, she almost never says his name. She doesn't have to. He's the "him" in every sentence that really matters; he's the "he" in every song.

She shakes her head. "I brought this on myself by writing the songs that I wrote. Of course they were going to ask. I just have to take it."

Thinking back to this afternoon's press conference, I bite down on the insides of my cheeks—a habit I've developed since I quit smoking last month. The media session, held in the event room of the record label's building, was mostly uneventful, but one reporter got pushy.

"Your first album was all about falling in love," the reporter said. "This album seems to be mostly about heartbreak. Can you speak to that?"

Dee's smile stayed glued on, but I know sadness swelled in her lungs. In interview prep, Dee's publicist quizzes her with painful questions like they're multiplication flash cards. I knew she could handle this question, but she looked so diminutive up on the platform, sandwiched between her bulky manager and her towering publicist at a long table.

"Eh," Dee answered smilingly, trying to sound casual. "I didn't want to be seen as a one-trick-pony songwriter, so I focused on something other than falling in love—falling *out* of love."

That's another thing the fans have wrong about her. They think she's a celebrity, and she is. But she's also a real girl, one who fake-smiles until she can close her bedroom door and sob.

"Did you recently end a relationship that caused you heartbreak?" It was the same reporter, butting in without being called on. My noncasted hand gripped into a fist. "Perhaps a long-term relationship with a high-school boyfriend, as it's been rumored in the tabloids?"

Behind the microphone, Dee caught her smile right before it dropped to the floor. "The only relationship I'm in is with my guitar. We're still very happy together; thank you for asking."

Laughter spread through the crowd of reporters. Even Dee's sour-faced publicist, Lissa, almost smiled. Dee moved on with press-conference pleasantries, but my edges are harder than hers and always have been. She forgives, forgets, moves on; I smolder quietly like embers, waiting for just enough fresh air to rage into a wildfire. Needless to say, that reporter better hope she never comes up against me. I grew up in a minefield of mean girls, and their snarky shrapnel made me bionic. Now I've got a stockpile of verbal ammunition and a grudge against anyone who crosses Dee.

Dee sighs and slides over to my couch, still with the same solemn look on her face.

"Reagan, I can't tell you how much it helps to have you here." She's the only person I know who can say sentimental things and still sound completely real. She glances toward the back of the bus and says in a quieter voice, "Peach is great, but it's not the same."

Peach is Mrs. Montgomery's youngest sister. When Dee was little, she couldn't say her aunt's real name, Clementine. She called her Peach instead, and now everyone else does, too. Dee takes after Peach, with her fair skin and naturally blond hair. But Peach is taller, with straightened hair and feathery bangs.

I smile at her. "I wouldn't have missed it."

Actually, I almost did miss it. My dad was reluctant to let me spend my summer traveling the country on a tour bus with only Dee's twenty-six-year-old aunt as the chaperone. He isn't much for parental mandates, so I assume that my stepmother was pulling his puppet strings. Fortunately, they both hated Blake, the guy I was dating at the time, and would have done anything to put distance between us. They finally agreed to the tour when I mentioned college applications. I plan to use the tour as a way to add to my photojournalism portfolio. By summer's end, I should have shots from all over the country.

For me, this summer is more than a pleasant detour; it's a necessary diversion. For the past year, I've been stuck in the life of a normal junior in high school, passing the time with people I don't especially like at parties that aren't especially fun. So I made my own fun, and it did not go very well. Meanwhile, Dee has been performing at award shows, shooting magazine covers, and completing the *Middle of Nowhere* album.

Peach emerges from the bedroom area in the back of the bus. When Dee opened for the band Blue Sky Day last year, she needed a guardian to accompany her on tour. Dee's parents couldn't come because of her brothers, so Peach volunteered. She wound up dating Dee's banjo player, Greg, which explains her eagerness to join up on this tour as well. Dee requires very little supervision, so Peach spends her time hanging out with her boyfriend and fielding phone calls from Dee's management team.

True to form, Peach is holding a magazine. She keeps up with all the gossip websites, too, checking for articles about Dee. I'm always tempted to read what people say about Dee, but my temper can't handle it.

"Thought you might want one." Peach smiles as she hands me the open magazine. "It's not out till next month, but we got a few first-run prints for approval."

"Thanks," I reply before she retreats to the bedroom. I examine the front of the magazine, which happens to be a favorite of mine. I never would have thought Dee could land the cover of *Idiosync*; she's the first country artist ever deemed cool enough for it. The magazine's aesthetic is edgy and urban, which is how I'd describe my own sense of style— but never Dee's. In the picture, she's wearing red ballet flats and a tight navy blazer over a white collared shirt and jeans . . . while riding a mechanical bull at a Nashville saloon. Instead of some trying-to-be-sexy rodeo-girl pose, Dee's holding on with both hands, head tilted back and laughing. She looks taller than her petite stature—only one inch taller than me—and it makes me wonder if other people in magazines are smaller in real life. *BUCK THE MAN*, the title screams. *Dixie darling Lilah Montgomery talks prep-school style, small-town roots, and bucking off pop music.*

Dee grins at me, pointing at the bold-font headline. "Lissa

is *not* happy, so, naturally, I'm thrilled. She's making them change the title of the article."

Most of Dee's "look" has been a bickering match with her publicist at some point or another. The wardrobe battle raged on for months. Dee has a very specific sense of style, which is inspired mostly by the old movies she watched with her mom when she was little—shrunken blazers; girlie skirts or modest, colorful dresses; and delicate ballet flats. When Dee was starting out, Lissa fussed that her style was "too collegiate for our target demographic." The record label wanted her in cowgirl boots, but Dee refused. After her first album, Dee was offered a promotional deal for J.Crew's new teen line. Lissa's eyes spun like a slot machine landing on dollar signs, and she never mentioned Dee's clothing choices again.

I skim the article, hoping the interviewer played nice. *Idiosync* mocks clichés, which is why I like it, but if they made fun of Dee, I'll have to cancel my subscription and send anonymous hate mail.

Country chanteuse Lilah Montgomery is everything you expect and a whole lot more that you don't expect. She is a giggly blond gamine, she is affably coy about her personal life, and she is unpretentious to the point of eating a messy cheeseburger in my presence. In the two hours I spent with Lilah Montgomery at Smokin' Pistols Saloon in Nashville, she proved sweet as pecan pie. But this rising star will raise her voice, all right. Just ask her if she plans to veer her upbeat country-gone-folksy songbook toward the pop music scene.

"Never," she insists. Her voice carries vehemence, a resounding finality that defies the usual public-relations doublespeak. "No, let me rephrase that. I won't change the way I write music; I won't change my subject matter or add bass beats or refrain from using a banjo and harmonica in my backup band. But if people who enjoy pop music also enjoy my music, wonderful. I'm thrilled. But I won't compromise who I am as an artist or songwriter."

Industry critic Jon Wallace calls her a "musician's musician"— an artist focused on instrumentation, on perfecting complicated harmonies and pioneering her own sound. Lilah cites Patty Griffin, Joni Mitchell, and Dolly Parton as her biggest musical inspirations, though her music is pointedly more cheerful than her inspirations suggest. Where does that extra spark come from? Her mother—songwriter Laura Montgomery.

While I read, Dee's spinning her work phone in the palm of her hand without looking at it. Instead, her gaze shifts around the tour bus as if she's tracking the flight pattern of an aimless gnat. When Dee's mind darts around, her eyes do, too.

"Hey," I say. "Relax."

"Yeah, yeah." She waves her hand at me. "I'm relaxed."

This would be a lie no matter when she said it, even in her sleep. The first time I saw a diagram of nerve endings in my biology book, I thought they looked like tiny, splayed-out hands or the bird's-eye view of a leafless tree. I'm pretty sure Dee's nerve endings look like coiled springs.

"Terry texted me again. He won't give it up." Terry, her manager, is relentless.

"Which 'it'?"

"Performing 'My Own.' Not gonna happen." She taps her fingers on her phone, standing her ground.

The song is an upbeat powerhouse, complete with hand claps in the chorus.

On my own, you'll see,
This ain't no Les Miserables.
I'm wild and free and I'm seventeen,
And I'll make it my job
To show you how good my life can be;
Ain't no pain in my alone.
I'm happy to be just little ol' me,
And I'll make this world my own.

She thought if she could write a song about being happy without Jimmy, maybe it would become a self-fulfilling prophecy. That plan didn't work, but her label loved the song enough to put it on the record. Dee cares deeply about honest performances, and she can't make herself prance around stage while singing a lie to her fans. When Dee refused to include "My Own" in the tour set list, Terry's face looked like an oven-baked ham—pink and almost steaming.

The sky is nearly dark now, smudges of clouds across an inky sky, and the bus window reflects my image back to me— the sharp collarbones that have long been my least favorite feature, the wavy hair that's hard to manage without the use of my left hand. But, worst of all, behind thick black eyeliner, my eyes look tired. And I *am* tired—weary, even—but at least I'm here, hiding in Dee's life until I can handle my own.

As we barrel toward North Carolina, I take in the last glimpses of Tennessee that I'll have till late August. I don't think I'll miss Nashville, except maybe the country sky at night, the way every centimeter is flecked with stars. It's something I could never capture in a photograph, the hugeness of the universe and the smallness of everything else. When Dee and I were little, the world seemed so vast—so impossibly, frighteningly vast that we could never make it our own.

Does the sky go on forever? Dee asked me the summer we met. We were lying on our backs in the cool grass, facing up. She'd gotten a book of constellations for her eighth birthday, and we were using it to search the sky.

Yep, I told her. *It's called infinity.*

Infinity, she repeated. There was a pause as I traced Ursa Minor with my finger, and I could feel her looking over at me. *Do you think we could be friends for infinity?* she asked.

After a moment, I said, *Yeah. I'm pretty sure we could be.* She linked her pinkie with mine, our secret signal, and the planet spun on beneath the starlight. These days, the world doesn't seem nearly big enough to outrun our problems.

My eyes follow a blinking airplane light, and its steady path leaves me thinking about how far we've come. It's no secret that Dee has come a long way from the middle of nowhere, Tennessee, but, as the cast on my arm reminds me, I have, too. The difference is: I still have a lot farther to go.

CHAPTER TWO

Charlotte

I've been to Dee's concerts before, of course, but never like this. *Nothing* is like this. We spent yesterday at the concert hall, as Dee and the band did a final dress rehearsal, but now this place is a never-ending fun house of Dee look-alikes. Younger girls stand with their moms alongside countless girls our age in matching outfits—blazers and horseshoe necklaces and ballet flats. I even spot a decent number of good-looking guys. I'll come back for them when I'm done with my phone call.

I'm hunting for a place quiet enough to wish my dad a happy birthday because even Dee's dressing room is too noisy. When I mentioned that I was stepping out to call my dad, I pretended not to notice Dee's freshly waxed eyebrows lift in surprise. She recovered quickly, though, and gave me an encouraging smile.

Of course Dee doesn't expect me to check in with my dad. My family life belongs in the lyrics of a bad country song. My mom walked out on us when I was eight, and my dad took it badly. He moved the two of us from Chicago to his hometown of Nashville, presumably to be closer to the Jack Daniel Distillery. Even though he quit drinking when I was twelve, enough damage had been done. I was mad at my mom for abandoning us and mad at him for abandoning me emotionally. Not even Dee's good influence could keep me from trying to hurt my parents the way they hurt me. At least that's what my court-appointed therapist thinks, and I hate to admit that she's probably right. I also hate to admit that she's court-appointed.

My track record started with mouthing off in seventh grade and skipping a few study halls in eighth grade. Freshman year of high school, I flirted with senior boys and made out with them in their cars, just to feel that rush of it all. I snuck out of the house to parties, where I smoked, drank bad beer, and needed Dee to help me home. After Dee left on her first tour, I lost my virginity to a guy I barely knew, which was an experience that's barely worth remembering.

An underage-drinking charge sent me to court last fall. I tried to laugh it off when I told Dee, who sighed into the phone from whatever city she was in at the time. I hardly said a word during the sentencing, but somehow the judge dubbed me a charity case. She gave me a community-service requirement and mandated therapy to rehab my attitude. I set myself back on the straight and narrow, or I tried, at least. But then I met Blake during my community service. He made everything worse.

My list of offenses runs long, and I'm not proud of any of them—except maybe the time I outran a cop while wearing stilettos. But things changed in April, and so did I. I'm trying to get my act together, but I can't be someone I'm not. I still flirt with boys to get what I want, and I still crave the occasional cigarette. I'm just not as bad as I used to be.

I turn another corner, only to find even screechier girls at a merchandise counter. This is getting ridiculous, so I stop dead when I spot a door that says AUTHORIZED PERSONNEL ONLY. After glancing around for security guards, I decide to authorize myself. I look official enough; I have my most expensive camera and my tour pass around my neck. The latter identifies me as ALL-TOUR VIP REAGAN O'NEILL, complete with a grim-faced picture. I wasn't ready when the guy took the photo, the hallmark of someone who is better behind the camera than in front of it. Turning the doorknob, I see that it's the back end of an empty conference room. Perfect.

"Hey, Dad," I say as soon as he answers the phone. "Happy Birthday."

"Thank you, darlin'." He sounds surprised that I bothered to call. "How's everything goin' so far?"

"Good."

"Good," he says after a moment. "You sound tired. Are you tired?"

"Yeah. We've been up since five o'clock this morning."

He chuckles. "Well, now, I don't think you've been up that early since you were a baby."

I want to say that I'm often still up at 5 a.m. without his knowing it, but I trap the words inside my mouth. That was the old me, and the new me is still learning.

"Is she nervous?" My dad adores Dee—of course he does. Any parent would.

"A little. Mostly excited."

"Good. Can't wait to hear about it." There's a pause, and he asks, "You stayin' out of trouble?"

"Yes, Dad." I can practically hear Brenda feeding him the questions. "So far I'm hanging out with Dee or sitting around. That's it."

"Well," he says, "thanks for checkin' in."

"I'll call in a few days," I promise, and then he says a hello from Brenda. I swallow hard. "Hi back."

After I hang up the phone, I'm surprised to find that I actually miss my dad. I have no siblings and no mom, so he's my only real family. We've had our rough spots, but he's worked hard to change. He'll show his sobriety chip to anyone, and he turns down drink offers with a smile and a "No, thank you— five years sober." He's always wanted people to know, to keep him accountable and understand that they could talk to him if they were having the same kind of struggle.

I sneak back out the door I came in and make a beeline for the nearest group of hot guys. They're standing in line for Lilah Montgomery merchandise, although one guy is already wearing Lilah apparel of his own—a homemade T-shirt that reads: MARRY ME, LILAH!

Making sure my press pass is front and center, I make my way toward him. The shirt will make Dee laugh, maybe even ease her nerves. His gaze bounces from my cleavage to my face, as if he noticed but won't let himself look—a decent guy.

"Hey," I say coolly. "Mind if I get a shot of your T-shirt?"

"Not at all." He looks pleased. With his arm around one of the girls in his group, he puffs out his chest and gives me a big grin. He's a clean-cut blond, medium height, with an easy smile. If Dee had a type other than Jimmy, this guy would probably be it.

"Thanks." I rest my camera back around my neck. "She'll like it."

"You know her?" he asks. All his friends quiet down, watching my face. One of the girls glances at my tour pass. "Wait. Are you *'riding top down with Reagan'* Reagan?"

I shrug, nodding.

Dee penned my name into the lyrics of her first single, "Open Road Summer." She wrote it when we were freshmen, daydreaming about our summers once we turned sixteen. No offense to her dad's old convertible and the back roads of our hometown, but the reality of our open road summer is better than Dee could have imagined. The song means a lot to me, even if it's weird that thousands of people sing my name.

"What's she like?" another guy asks.

I don't know how to answer that, so I smirk and tell him, "She's all right. Enjoy the show."

They call after me as I walk away, asking if they can meet her. I ignore them and flag down a little girl dressed up as Dee, complete with a short blond wig and a plastic toy guitar. I'm not much for kids, but this one is cute. The little girl poses next to her mom, hand on her hip.

"I'm going to show her these pictures before she goes onstage," I tell the girl after snapping a few shots.

She gasps, wide-eyed. "Will you tell her my name is Olivia?"

"Sure."

Over Olivia's head, her mother mouths, "Thank you."

"No problem." They both squeal as I walk away. If I'm being honest with myself, I'd probably wish for a mother like that—a mother who could have taken me to concerts, gotten excited about the things I was excited about. That would have been nice, though I'd settle for any mother who didn't leave.

After a few more pictures of beaming fans, I make my way backstage. Everyone rushes around, pushing past one another in a frenetic blur. I find the greenroom door, where a woman with a panicked expression and a walkie-talkie nearly plows me over. Dee's family is on their way out, and her youngest brother has a poster board tucked under his arm.

"Hey, sweetie," Mrs. Montgomery says, swiping my cheek with a lipstick peck as she passes by. "How ya doin'?"

"I'm good. Is she okay so far?"

"She's great. You gonna stand in the front row with us?"

"Yeah, but I'll watch the first few songs from side stage for the camera angle," I say, lifting the camera from my neck. "Let me get a picture before you go."

Her brothers hold up the poster—WE LOVE YOU, SIS in big block letters—while her mom and dad wrap their arms around each of the boys. They beam as I capture the image, but one second later, Mrs. Montgomery dabs her knuckle at the corner of her eye, intercepting a tear.

"Sorry," she says, laughing. "Allergies."

Dee's youngest brother chimes in. "She's very emotional about this concert."

"You, hush." Mrs. Montgomery laughs. "He repeats everything he hears, I swear. See you out there, darlin'."

Inside, Dee's wrapped in a robe I bought her two Christmases ago, in full makeup, hair done. People buzz all around her at a speed that feels like fast-forward, but she sits still in a director's chair, looking at her reflection. Her expression is quizzical, as if she's searching for something in her own eyes and can't quite find it.

I walk up behind the chair and touch her shoulder. She startles, glancing up at me.

"You okay?" I frown at her, unsettled by the expression I just saw.

She smiles, but her chest is rising and falling too fast. "I feel like I'm floating outside my body, like this isn't really happening."

Her hand is at her throat, twisting at her necklace. She's not blinking enough, panic prying her eyelids open. Either that or she's concentrating all her energy on holding up thick false lashes. "They're all here to see me."

Most of the time, Dee seems in awe of her own life, as if she's tripped and fallen into it. But it isn't randomness or luck that got her here, and I wish she knew that.

"Hey," I say. "You've done this a hundred times."

"Not as the headliner! I'm *it*!"

I have to stifle at laugh. "Do you think all those people were trying to buy tickets for a Kira King concert, but—oops—how did they wind up at this Lilah Montgomery concert?"

She rolls her eyes, but the absurdity of my comment must have resonated because the creases in her forehead relax.

Looking at Dee, I can't hear the din of the people bustling around us. The world goes quiet as I watch her face, moments from one of her biggest dreams coming true. I lift my camera and take a picture before she can swat me away.

"At least take one of both of us," she says. I hold the camera up with my good arm—a total photographer no-no—and grin as it clicks. When we survey the final product, it looks like two normal best friends. And we are, I guess, outside of my police record and her superstardom.

"Frame-worthy," Dee decides.

"Hey." I click back to the picture of the little girl in the Dee costume, posing next to her mom. "You have to see this."

Dee laughs and presses the zoom button. "Oh my gosh. So cute."

"Her name's Olivia."

"Lilah," a production assistant says. "It's time. The local opener's on in five."

Dee nods, glancing at me. "I guess this is it."

"Guess so," I say as she stands up, taking another deep breath.

She slides off her robe to reveal her first outfit of the night—a bright-red dress with cap sleeves. Dee hugs her arms around my neck, channeling all her nervous energy into an uncomfortably tight squeeze. Quietly, she says, "Infinity?"

"Infinity," I agree as she releases her grip on me.

"See you after," she calls, and then the assistant whisks her away. I put my camera back around my neck and glance around. Nearby, Peach is talking to one of the venue managers, explaining something that requires counting on her fingers so he'll understand. I click a few more pictures of the bustle backstage, capturing images of the backup band tuning their guitars and performing their preshow cheer.

I see it all through the lens of my camera—the flurry of movement, the venue staff in black T-shirts, giving orders into their headsets. As I take it all in, my mind weighs the texture, the composition, the possibility of each changing scene, and I struggle to hold back, to keep my finger from pressing too soon. That's my biggest flaw as a photographer. I'm impatient—trigger-happy. I want the shot now, now, now, click, click, click, and if I could just wait a second more, the moment would really flourish.

From the wings, I watch as Dee's band begins the first

song. Even though I know the exact moment she'll enter, it still makes my skin prickle. The opening chords break into the first verse, and her silhouette rises from a hidden compartment in the stage. At the sight of Dee's outlined form, the audience erupts. Screams and whistles lift toward the high ceiling, so powerful that the roof could pop off like a champagne cork.

Dee struts to center stage, singing into a handheld microphone. Now the crowd starts singing along and clapping. Behind Dee, the huge screen bursts into an image of blue sky. She throws her whole body into the music, tossing her hair around. Despite the enormous stage, she looks tall, this tiny girl who can fill a venue with thousands of people and her own music. You'd never know that her nerves are zapping like electrical wiring gone wrong.

Halfway through the concert, I sneak out to the VIP area, which is the floor space right in front of the stage. While I wait, I snap a few pictures of Dee's brothers, who are wearing big headphones to protect their ears from the huge amps. Mrs. Montgomery catches me lurking and waves me over with a wide grin. Dee reenters the stage—this time in a different dress, and the crowd reignites.

"Isn't this amazing?" Dee's mom yells to me over the cheers.

Dee takes a seat on a stool in the middle of the stage with her guitar and starts strumming chords. Her horseshoe necklace glints in the light of the stage.

"This song is called 'Old Dreams.' It's for my mama, and

for all the girls who came here with their mamas tonight—especially Olivia."

This is what I could have told the guy from earlier, the one who asked what she's like. Amid the jitters of her first opening show, Lilah Montgomery remembered the name of the little girl who dressed up like her for this show—*that* is what she's like.

I wish I could see Olivia's face, wherever she is in the crowd. I imagine her shrieks of joy, how she'll run into school to tell her friends. I wonder if her mother feels the same joy, watching her daughter. The same joy all over Mrs. Montgomery's face. I wonder if my mother thinks of me at all, wherever she is.

For the rest of the concert, I'm rapt as though I've never heard these songs before. The first ending comes quickly, and then an encore. When Dee returns to the stage, the background screen changes to a field of wildflowers. Guitar in hand, Dee sings about where we met all those years ago— *the middle of nowhere, Tennessee.*

With a full house and a full heart, my best friend strikes her final pose—arms raised high, head thrown back. She's doing it, like she always said she would.

The memory comes barreling back to me, from three years ago. I wasn't surprised that the school counselor called me down to her office to "check in" only a few days into freshman year. Gossip had been following me around since I was in middle school, when a gaggle of mean girls started a rumor that I was anorexic. By the time I hit a C-cup in eighth grade, they were saying that I'd gotten implants, that I was an aspiring porn star, that I was a slut. Any time I missed school for a dentist appointment, I returned to rumors that I was cutting class to fool around with a senior. I was the girl who had no mom, the girl whose dad was not so anonymously in Alcoholics Anonymous. Even the school counselor believed the rumors about me might be true. I could tell she was fishing around for information about the gossip du jour—that I'd hooked up with a teacher. I was *fourteen* and had only kissed two boys ever. Plus: ew. A teacher?

I sighed, shaking my head at the counselor. "Look, Mia Graziani started that rumor to deflect attention from her own problems. I don't want to gossip, but . . . frankly, I've seen her throwing up in the bathroom twice this past month, so . . . either pregnancy or bulimia. Poor girl."

It was a total lie, and I almost felt bad about it. But I *hated* Mia. I hated her for choosing me as the subject of her cruelty. I hated her more for bringing out the viciousness in me. This wasn't who I wanted to be, but how many times can a dog get kicked before she bares her teeth in return?

I retreated to the girl's bathroom as the bell rang. I went into the stall where "Reagan O'Neill is a whore" was written on the back of the door. In black Sharpie, I spelled out exactly where Mia Graziani could shove it. It wasn't long before I heard the creak of the door and soft footsteps.

"Reagan . . ." Dee always sounds like her mom when she uses her calm voice. "C'mon. Come out."

I complied by kicking the stall door with all my might.

Dee winced at the sound of the metal door slamming against the wall and then surveyed my vandalism. She was holding the bathroom pass from the class we were both supposed to be in.

"They're just jealous."

"Why would they be jealous?"

"Because you're beautiful and smart. They know it. You make them insecure."

"Yeah, right." I scowled, kicking the door again, though with less force this time.

Dee caught the door with one hand before it could hit the wall.

"They're mean to you, too, you know," I said. They called Dee "Frizz" behind her back and talked about her songwriting contract with air quotes, like they didn't believe it was real. But it was still unkind of me—attempting to drag Dee along the low road with me. Her cheeks flinched, trying to frown, but she wouldn't let them. Even then, Dee was strong. Not in the loud, brassy, I-am-woman way that some girls are. She was strong then the way she's strong now, in a quiet but irrepressible way.

"Yeah, I know," she said finally. "But my mom says the best revenge is living well, and I believe her."

And now—arms high and pyrotechnic sparks showering the stage beside her—she's proving her point. I believe her, too.

CHAPTER THREE

Charlotte

It's after 2:00 a.m. by the time we return to the hotel. I didn't drink any champagne at the show's after-party, since I'm still on the sober wagon. And now I know the reason why they call it "the wagon"—because not drinking at an after-party is about as fun as bumping along in a wagon on the Oregon Trail. Don't get me wrong—I'm not an alcoholic or anything. I'm just an all-or-nothing kind of girl, and I've done "all," so now I'm trying "nothing." Dee didn't drink, either, of course, because Dee doesn't drink and never has.

The show was an undeniable hit. Now Dee's family is on a red-eye flight back to Nashville, and I'm here with Dee on her own personal cloud nine.

Once inside our hotel room, Peach moves straight to her bedroom. Dee is a hurricane of adrenaline and triumph, twirling around the lobby of our room. I drop my purse on the floor and plop down on the couch next to my laptop. I want to upload my pictures from tonight before I go to bed so I can clear them off my camera for tomorrow. I type in my password and, before I can even hit Enter, something in the room changes. Dee's excitement was pulsing like a current through the air, but now the energy in the room has flatlined.

Sure enough, her face is pale, frozen as if she's been slapped. Hard. She's staring down at her work phone.

"Reagan." Her voice sounds choked. "Search my name."

My fingertips clack against the keyboard, and for once I hardly feel the cast on my left hand restraining me. The search returns for "Lilah Montgomery" appear, and my throat sinks into my stomach. Dee sits down—or her knees buckle—so that she's next to me on the couch.

From the last half hour alone, there are twelve news stories linked to her name, each with equally horrifying titles: *LILAH MONTGOMERY: NUDE PIC SCANDAL, COUNTRY PRINCESS DETHRONED?, THE BOY SHE LEFT HEARTBROKEN.*

"What the—?" I gasp, my eyes speeding over the screen.

Of *course* there are no nude pictures of Dee floating around. It's the last article that scares me, the one that hints that they found out about Jimmy. This is the nightmare, the worst-case scenario, and I can't believe it could be a reality. Dee and Jimmy were such homebodies, even before Dee's first record. They were always so careful to not be photographed together.

Dee keeps her hand over her mouth, her eyes wide as she breathes, "Click one."

I open the first link, bracing for the worst. With the story, a picture pops up—one that I recognize.

They cropped it. They cropped out the pool in the background and the few people who are standing around Dee and Jimmy. The magazine also edited the picture so it's only their upper bodies, embracing in a lip-lock. His swim trunks aren't visible, nor are her bikini bottoms. To make matters worse, Dee's then-long hair covers her bathing-suit straps. From the angle it was taken, with Jimmy's arms around her, the bathing-suit top is totally hidden.

"No," Dee whispers. "*No.*"

With some clever editing, an innocent snapshot taken at his birthday pool party last year looks like a naked, full-on make-out picture. This photo undermines Dee's squeaky-clean image and all but exposes Jimmy as the boy all those songs are about.

The story begins: *Teen country star Lilah Montgomery is the subject of the most recent nude photo scandal. This shocking photo surfaced the same day as the first show of her sold-out headlining tour. Montgomery has been a media darling for the past two years, known for her Southern manners and good-girl reputation, but this photo does beg the question: how much of her sweet-as-iced-tea personality is an act?*

"Those *assholes.*" My voice sounds gravelly, a primal anger surging inside me.

Dee sits perfectly still, eyes staring at the screen. The

web page reflects back in her irises, which are as wet and blue as pool water. I know this feeling of paralysis, when you realize that the hot pain in your back is a knife.

"You could show them the real picture," I say stupidly, grasping for a solution.

"It's already out there." Her words are strained, almost a whisper. "There's a picture of Jimmy all over the Internet, and they'll find him now."

She's right, and I can't deny it. The media circle Dee's life like vultures, waiting until their prey is weak enough to attack. This is their moment.

"Peach!" I yell toward her bedroom door. "Peeaaach!"

This is the same instinct as screaming for your parents when you're sick in the middle of the night—that somehow, a grown-up can fix it. Peach hurries into the room, panic replacing the sleepiness on her face.

"What is it?" she asks, rushing to us.

I turn the computer screen toward her.

"Oh no," she mutters, covering her mouth. "No—they didn't."

Dee swivels, facing Peach. "Did you know about this?"

"Lissa told me that it was a small possibility," Peach admits, her face wrenching with guilt. "She told me not to say anything to you, because the label was trying to pay off the magazine so they wouldn't run it."

"You could have at least warned me!" Dee cries. "I'm not a child! I had the right to know about this!"

I chew the insides of my cheeks, desperate for a cigarette.

You quit, I remind myself, but my mind travels to the emergency pack I have stashed in my suitcase.

"I'm sorry," Peach says. "I'm so sorry."

Dee hangs her head in defeat. She turns back to the computer, staring again at the headlines.

"This is so unfair. It's a *lie!*" Her voice cracks. "This could ruin everything—my new record, the whole tour . . . *everything.*"

I can't stand it anymore, and I slam my laptop shut. "This is *bullshit.*"

Normally Peach would reprimand me for my language, but instead she says, "I know."

Another tear slips down Dee's cheek, and I reach my hand over to hers. "Can we sue them? She's a minor. Peddling something as a nude picture has to be illegal."

"Probably," Peach mutters. "Lissa said a bunch of mumbo jumbo about emergency meetings and legally pursuing responsible parties and media redirection."

"My brothers," Dee says, her thin shoulders shaking with absorbed sobs. "They're so little. How are my parents supposed to explain this to them?"

She stands up, smacking her palm repeatedly against the closed laptop, like the computer itself is to blame.

"Delilah . . . ," Peach says in a soothing voice, but Dee holds up one hand to stop her.

"Don't," she snaps. "I need to call my mom."

She closes our bedroom door behind her with a slam, and I let her go, praying that her family's flight home has landed by now. Peach retreats to her own bedroom, and I have a staring contest with the minibar. I've always thought of myself as an enthusiastic but purely recreational drinker. It disturbs me that I'm drawn to it now, in a moment of crisis.

I stand up and pace, moving toward the freestanding rack that holds Dee's wardrobe. My mind wanders as I run my hands over the fabrics, the summer dresses and fitted jackets. These are outfits for interviews, press meet and greets, sound checks, and basically any photographable circumstance. Dee's whole life is carefully chosen, fitted, and pressed, but imperfections sneak in all the same—a missing button, a rip in a hem, a vicious rumor.

When Dee signed with Muddy Water Records, its media staff scrubbed her personal presence off the web. Though a few kids in our grade have ponied up pictures of Dee, only two have ever included Jimmy—a picture of them at sophomore-year homecoming and a picture from a football game where people in our class were crammed into the bleachers, arms slung over one another's shoulders. But in those pictures, Dee and Jimmy were among a big group of people. And frankly, neither of those pictures is interesting.

This picture is interesting, so I shouldn't be surprised that someone sold it. People will do anything for money. But we're from a small town outside Nashville—a small town where people take great care to protect Dee and, for that matter, Jimmy. They moon over the time Jimmy pulled over to help them change a tire and about how proud they are of the example Dee sets for their kids. Others have stories about the time Jimmy's dad came into his vet clinic in the middle of the night to care for their sick dog or the time Dee's mom showed up with a casserole after someone's grandmother passed away. It's the unwritten law of small-town folks: we guard one another. That Southern brand of trust is stronger than whiskey, and, when broken, it burns even more.

After half an hour of mindlessly pacing the suite, I knock on our door. Dee's lying facedown on the bed, blond hair splayed out on a pile of hotel pillows. I sit down beside her, and she rolls over to look at me. Her face is a smeary mess of mascara. I reach for a tissue, and I wet it with the bottled water on the nightstand.

Dee sits up and leans forward, tilting her chin toward me. I swipe the tissue across her cheeks, clearing the charcoal trails of makeup. I know how to do this—how to take care of someone—only because of Dee. If I had a tissue for every time she's cleaned me up, I'd have enough to suffocate the person who sold that picture to the media.

"What can I do?" I ask. I almost never see her without mascara anymore, and I'd almost forgotten how her golden eyelashes disappear against her pale skin. I toss the tissue into the trash can, and it lands with a soggy thwack.

"Just sit with me." She scoots over to make room for me. "I have to do something."

So I climb onto the bed next to her, with our legs stretched out on the white comforter in front of us. Dee cradles her personal phone in her hands.

"I talked to my mom," she says. "My brothers don't know yet. She said not to worry about it; she'll explain, but . . ."

She trails off, and I glance over to see fresh tears forming.

"But . . . ," Her voice breaks. "Apparently the reporters found Jimmy's house."

I wince as I imagine Mrs. Collier, Jimmy's mom, asking hordes of reporters to leave. Jimmy closing the blinds in his bedroom, leaving through the garage, becoming the subject of attention he never wanted.

"It's exactly what he was worried about." Dee covers her face with her hands. "I feel so terrible. His family . . . I can't even . . ."

"Hey," I say. "Look at me."

She peeks out at me from between her fingers.

"This is not your fault—do you understand?"

Dee buries her head again and moans, "What will my fans think of me?"

"Hey." I clear her arms from her face. "They know who you are."

She bites her lip. "I hope so. Okay."

"Okay."

Dee lifts up her cell phone and taps her finger against the screen. For the first time in ten months, she finds Jimmy's number and types a message: *I am so, so sorry about this.*

After she clicks the Send button, I wrap my arm around her. I know how hard it is for her, composing such a short message. Dee has so much more to say to Jimmy. In fact, she has six songs on her new album full of things she has to say to Jimmy. It only takes a moment for the phone to beep with a return message: *It's not your fault, Dee. Don't worry. It'll blow over.*

We both look at the text for a moment. Dee blinks rapidly, like she's surprised that, after all this time, he's still a few clicks away. There's an invisible barrier between them, and it follows Dee no matter where she travels. Dee and Jimmy's history is as wide as a river, and they can't simply skip across it to get to each other. It's too treacherous, too easy to get caught up in, too huge. Jimmy feels the same impassable distance. I see it all over his face at school, where we're so careful not to mention her directly.

But here they are, crossing a rift that has been mutually imagined this whole time. A pained look crosses Dee's face, and she tosses her phone off the bed—maybe out of frustration, maybe as an attempt to keep herself from telling him how she feels. Instead, she tells me.

"I miss him." She sighs, leaning into my shoulder. "So much."

"I know," I tell her. "I know."

Maybe it would be easier if Dee hated Jimmy, but even I can't hold the breakup against him. Dating Lilah Montgomery meant fame and bragging rights—and Jimmy wanted none of it. He only wanted Dee and a simple life in our small town. Jimmy plans to attend college and then move back home to be a veterinarian like his dad. He can't drop his goals to follow Dee around any more than she can drop her career to go to college with him. And without dropping her career, Dee's life will never be simple. Their dreams are too different. That's why he cut her loose after four years together, right as her career hit its stride. *I'm so happy for you*, he told her. *I can't hold you back. I have to let you go.* In his mind, he was freeing her.

Dee told me that he wiped at his eyes as he said those words. She flung herself onto him, crying into his lap. He wouldn't change his mind.

She glances over at me, eyes bloodshot. "Do you think he still thinks about me?"

"You don't have to ask that. You *know* he does."

When we were younger, hardly anyone noticed Dee. She was shy, a quiet shadow to my loudmouthed troublemaker. Dee was also sort of stout, with braces and frizzy hair. She's always been beautiful, though not everyone saw it then.

But Jimmy Collier did. In sixth grade, he sat next to her in math. Jimmy was always nice but quiet, like Dee. Girls were starting to notice him since he'd grown almost six inches in as many months. He could only see Dee. He slid her silly notes and drawings during class, and she giggled into her hand.

One afternoon, they got sent out to the hallway for laughing in class. I gawked from my desk as they scampered out the door. Dee had never even gotten a warning look from a teacher before. While they sat on the tile floors of the middle school hallway, Jimmy asked her to go over to his house for dinner with him and his parents.

They became a couple at age twelve—a puppy love that

turned into something more over the years, something solid and real. Falling in love with Jimmy boosted Dee's songwriting to another level. She and her mom recorded a few songs, and the record labels went nuts. Then, before high school, Dee grew into her body. She got her braces off and learned how to tame her hair. This transformation gave her enough confidence to get up onstage and sing.

There are thousands of guys who'd duke it out for a single date with Dee. But all she wants is her cowboy—the same boy who rides horses, helps his family with their business, and always gave her homemade valentines. The boy who loves her too much to keep her.

"Oh, Reagan," she says, sighing. "I just don't know what to do."

I climb under the covers of the king-size bed we share. The record label offered to find me a separate room for our hotel stays during the tour, but we declined. I'm here because she needs me here and because I need to not be alone.

"I wish I could go back to yesterday, before the world knew about Jimmy," Dee whispers. "He's a part of my life that I never wanted them to have."

"I know. But they'll forget it soon enough."

"Yeah. But I won't." She's going to cry again. When I reach for another tissue, she whispers, "I'm sorry. I don't know why I'm still crying."

"Are you kidding me?" I pass her the tissue. "If I were

you, I would have had an all-out diva fit. I would have broken lamps, and, let's be honest, probably wound up in jail somehow."

This gets a small smile.

"You wait." I'm pillaging my brain for a convincingly positive outlook. "By August, we'll look back on this and think, 'Oh yeah—remember that? That sucked.' And that will be the end of it. One bad memory in a whole summer of good ones."

"You're a really good liar, so I'm not sure if I believe you," she says, and a laugh breaks through. "But I want to."

We lie in the quiet for a while, Dee staring into nowhere. When her eyes finally close, there's such heaviness to them— like they should click shut with the weight of a door. I turn off the lamp and stare up at the ceiling, settling my head against the starched hotel pillow. I use my good arm to pull the comforter so that it covers Dee to her shoulders. The girl on the magazine covers looks so small and helpless, curled up with a crumpled tissue still in her palm. A thought hits me like a pang, as it occasionally does—where would I even be without her? I've taken so many side roads and built so many walls that I created my own labyrinth, trapping myself inside. When things went too far in April, and even I knew it, Dee pulled me out and directed me straight into her world. She's letting me hide, sliding her life over mine.

I owe Dee for so much, for the pinkie links and kindnesses and phone calls and bail-outs. This is the currency of friendship, traded over years and miles, and I hope it's an even exchange someday. For now, I do what all best friends do when there's nothing left to say. We lie together in the darkness, shoulder to shoulder, and wait for the worst to be over.

CHAPTER FOUR

Charlotte to Richmond

Dee didn't sleep well last night. Though her mumblings were nonsense, she sounded troubled. Her restless movements jostled me from sleep, which is one of many detriments to bunking with another person. Still, I can't fall asleep next to anyone but her.

So far, this morning has been a special kind of hell. Dee woke up, realized that the photo leak wasn't a bad dream, and started crying all over again. We wait in the suite area of the hotel room until Dee's publicist bustles in, looking prepped for scandal damage control. Dee sits on the couch, stony-faced, with her arms folded tightly over her chest. Peach greets Lissa, then goes back to toying with the ends of her hair, while I attempt to drown myself in hotel coffee. I'm still two cups away from being caffeinated enough to summon language—not that my opinion will matter in this forum.

The first time I met Lissa, she reached one hand out to shake mine while using the other to grab a nondisclosure contract. Next thing I knew, there were several pages of legal text in front of me, much to Dee's mortification. She reached her hand over mine to keep me from signing, all the while explaining to Lissa that she trusts me completely. Lissa looked like she felt sorry for her, like she'd seen too many starlets sold out by their best friends. I scratched my signature onto the page before Dee could stop me. Legal document or not, I'd never sell her out.

Now, Lissa wears the same pitying expression on her otherwise inexpressive face and a skirt suit that is the sartorial equivalent of a stern talking-to. Standing in front of us in the hotel suite, she clasps her hands like she's about to begin a formal presentation.

"Obviously, we have a situation here," she begins.

This complete understatement gets an eye roll from me. I hate her pandering, brusque tone, as usual.

"The Muddy Water management team had an emergency conference call late last night," Lissa says, folding her hands primly in front of her, "and we all agree that the key here is going to be reputation rebuilding."

I make a snorting noise to convey the ridiculousness of Dee having a bad reputation.

"While we will likely pursue some course of action in regard to damages, the fact remains: the picture is out there, and we have to direct attention away from it. Although I will note that in the past twenty-four hours, your name has been searched for online more than it ever has been before. As they say, no press is bad press."

That's it. I'm done. "Oh, you have got to be *kidding* me, lady."

Lissa looks miffed that I've interrupted her prepared soliloquy, but she presses on. "We agree that the best course of action is to give the media another story—a positive story that will garner as much, if not more, public interest."

Dee's eyebrows furrow, skeptical. "Like what?"

"Like a budding relationship with another entertainer."

"I'm not *in* a relationship." Dee's annoyance seeps into her voice. Even if Dee were in a relationship, Lissa would have coached her not to talk about it. "And definitely not with another entertainer."

"You won't have to be. The idea is to bring on a tour opener—someone about your age who is seen by the public as grounded, likable, good-looking. Preferably someone who is already on the label, so we'll avoid paperwork and still provide an opener you're already comfortable with."

Dee narrows her eyes. "You're thinking of Matt Finch."

Lissa gives a nod, and Dee stares off into nowhere, rocking herself a bit as she considers the idea.

Matt Finch is a former member of the Finch Four, a wholesome teen band that included his sister and two brothers. When we were in middle school, the band was a phenomenon. All three boys were sweet-faced, and they had hordes of screaming preteen fans. All the girls I knew wanted to *be* Carrie Finch, and they all wanted to marry Matt, the youngest and closest to our age. The group disbanded when the oldest Finch got married, and I've hardly heard of them since. At least, not until Dee befriended Matt Finch at a record-label party last year. Like Dee, he's known for being well-adjusted and well-behaved. I have to hand it to Lissa; if Dee was ever going to consider this idea, Matt Finch would be the only person worth bringing up.

"No," Dee says, finally. "No, I would *never* ask Matt to lie for me."

"Again, there would be no lying. He'll simply be joining the tour, and the media will draw their own inferences." Lissa says this like she's trying to communicate with someone who has only recently learned basic English.

"No," Dee repeats. "I won't even put him in that position by asking."

"Well, the record label has already contacted Mr. Finch, and he's agreed to come aboard as the opener for your tour."

My jaw drops, and I can't quite get my lips to form the words that Lissa deserves to hear. Fortunately, Dee doesn't seem to need my help.

"You contacted Matt on my behalf without asking me?" she shrills. She jumps to her feet, running her fingers through her hair as if she's tempted to pull it all out. "This is just . . . *humiliating.* He's my *friend,* and he gets contacted by my publicist?"

Peach is noticeably quiet, staring at the carpet. She's supposed to be the grown-up, but even she has no idea what to do. It's not reassuring.

"This is a business arrangement facilitated by the label, which you share with Mr. Finch." Lissa's calmness isn't soothing or mature. It's robotic. "The label had hoped to find a suitable opener for the entire tour, instead of the local acts we currently have booked for each show, but we couldn't work out the logistics. Now we can. So we did."

Dee's mouth hangs open, but no words of protest come out. My turn, I guess. "He doesn't even play country music, does he? Besides, when's the last anyone's heard of him?"

With unveiled annoyance, Lissa directs a look at me. "His acoustic style is in keeping with the kind of pop music audience we'd like to attract for the Lilah Montgomery brand. He'll be playing primarily from the solo album he released. Mr. Finch also writes his own music, which we believe is a fit parallel for the appeal of the *Middle of Nowhere* album."

I guess I do remember a solo album—from at least a year ago, maybe more. It never took off. How convenient. Scandal ignites out of nowhere, paving the way for a fake relationship that puts two Muddy Water Records performers in the spotlight. I glower at Lissa, suddenly suspicious that she planted the photo herself.

Peach finally chimes in, her voice meek. "How would this even work, logistically?"

"Mr. Finch is set to arrive in Richmond by this evening, where we are sending an additional tour bus to meet up with your current caravan. The backup band will learn any songs he needs them for, and he'll begin opening for the tour as soon as Little Rock."

My eyes flick over to Dee. It's supposed to be our summer—the two of us, not some tagalong who's hitching a ride on her rising star.

"Dee?" Peach asks quietly. "What are you thinking?"

"I'm thinking that I'm pissed at Lissa," Dee snaps. She glances back up at Lissa, who doesn't even react. "I need to speak with him myself."

"Very well," Lissa says stiffly. "I'll be in the hotel business center if you need anything before you leave. Mack will be up shortly to get you down to the bus, at which point I'll be returning to Nashville."

"We'll miss you," I sneer, and Peach instantly gives me a reprimanding look. Lissa doesn't even blink. I could be invisible, or naked, and she probably wouldn't notice unless it somehow made the record label money. She collects her briefcase and walks toward the door in that straight-backed, snotty way that makes me want to kick her. Dee doesn't say good-bye, which is uncharacteristically impolite of her.

"Ugh," Dee groans, beating her palms against the coffee table. "She *knows* I wanted Matt to open for me anyway but he was dealing with some family stuff, so I didn't want to ask. It would be so fun to have him along, but not like this— not with the pretend-boyfriend strings attached."

I stare down at the criss-crossed leather straps of my favorite wedge sandals. *We* were supposed to have so much fun. Well, maybe not *fun* fun, but we were at least supposed to stay together the way the two weeping willows in her parents' backyard do—standing their ground side by side, even if they're both drooping.

"Lissa made it sound like a done deal," Peach says, her voice quiet. "I haven't seen your tour contract, so maybe it's not within their rights. . . ."

"No." Dee waves her off. "Look, I hate that Lissa did all this without even consulting me, but I don't think it's worth fighting them. I just need to go call Matt and talk it out between the two of us." After Dee shuts the door to our room, I glance over at Peach. She has her elbows propped on her knees, her silky hair dangling in her face as she stares straight down at the carpet.

"Do you think Lissa leaked the picture?" I whisper.

"No!" Peach sounds indignant, but her insistence gives way to a helpless sigh. "I mean . . . I guess I don't know."

"I don't trust her."

Her eyes bear into mine with the same intensity Dee sometimes gets when she's talking about something that really matters to her. "Reagan, the last thing Dee needs is a conspiracy theory. . . ."

She's right, of course. I want someone to blame, and Lissa is an obvious choice. "I know, but if Lissa . . ."

"She didn't." She stands up, smoothing her jeans. "I have to finish packing."

Peach disappears into her room, and I pace the perimeter of the hotel room until Dee emerges from our room. "How'd it go?"

"Good." Dee nods, still clutching her personal phone in her hand. There's more energy in that single nod than I've seen since last night. All morning, her body language has been heavy—belabored movements and slogging feet. However reluctant she was at first, the prospect of Matt Finch joining us has perked her up a little. "Matt made me feel like it isn't weird at all, said he's more than happy to come on tour—that he wants to. I think it's going to be a good thing. But don't tell Lissa I said so."

"As if I would talk to Lissa."

She almost smiles but is interrupted by a knock at the door. I open it to Mack, Dee's primary bodyguard. Mack is as wide as he is tall, with a jovial smile that undermines his intimidating features. But this morning, there's no smile to be found.

"Dee, honey," he says. "You ready?"

"I guess," she says, throwing her purse over her shoulder. Mack worked the Blue Sky Day tour, and she begged him to stay on for this one, too. Mack graduated from law school in May and had planned to spend the summer studying for the bar exam and pursuing a career in entertainment law. But he couldn't say no to her, and they both knew it.

"Baby girl, I'm gonna shoot you straight," Mack's low voice rumbles. "We got some people outside."

Dee pinches her lips together. "Photogs?"

He sidesteps the question. "Usual routine, okay? Eyes ahead, no reactions."

She nods. Mack turns to Peach, who has reemerged with

her suitcase. "Can you go down now and board the band's bus? The paparazzi will assume that Dee's riding in whatever bus you get on. Maybe we'll throw a few off."

Peach squeezes Dee's arm. "I'll see you in Richmond, okay?"

Dee nods again, mouth still pressed shut. We make our way downstairs in silence, and she slides a pair of big sunglasses on her face. When I link my pinkie with hers, she squeezes so hard that I worry my bones will snap. The elevator dings open, and Mack hurries us across the lobby. The doors to the outside span before us, wide glass panels that make the bright sunlight feel garish.

As soon as we're through the doors, Mack puts his arm over Dee. Her hand slides out of mine and then it's surreal, like slow motion. The reporters and photographers are on either side of the path to the bus. Their yells blend together as they stick microphones and cameras in Dee's path. Out of the corner of my eye, I see the hotel concierge stretching his arms to keep them back. I glance at Dee, who keeps her head ducked down, eyes focused on the path in front of her.

"Back up!" Mack bellows. "Give her space."

I feel a push at my arm, and I shove back. I'm not the celebrity, and I have no obligation to be on my best behavior. Besides, my arm's already in a cast, and the hard plaster would give me the edge in hand-to-hand combat.

"*Lilah!*" someone screams near my ear. "Lilah, what do you have to say about the nude photo?"

Dee's face stays emotionless, like she's doing an impression of Lissa.

"*Lilah!*" yells a huskier voice. "Did you lose your virginity to Jimmy Collier?"

Mack keeps moving Dee forward, and I lose sight of her face. Blood rushes through my veins, too fast and too hot. This is a particular talent of mine—going from zero to livid in less than a second.

I watch in horror as a hand approaches Dee's arm, a man with a camera trying to block her from getting on the bus. Before I can even react, Mack holds his arm out, Heisman-style. The reporter stumbles to the ground, and his camera lands beside him with an awful, plastic crack.

"That's assault!" he howls from the concrete. "Assault!"

Dee climbs onto the bus, and Mack stands in front of the door. "No. You laying a hand on Ms. Montgomery is assault, under Section Four, Article B, of your state law."

"What are you, big boy—a lawyer?" The guy pulls himself to his feet and looks at Mack with his beady, weasel eyes. I sense his attempt to get a rise out of Mack, something for the cameras.

Mack's a solid foot taller as he looks him square in the eye. "Yep."

With relish, I laugh in the guy's face, and he sneers at me. "The public has the right to know that Lilah Montgomery is not a good role model for their children. She's just a promiscuous kid who—"

Before he can finish, I lunge toward him, claws out, but Mack catches me by my casted arm. His grip should hurt, but I don't feel a thing.

"Get on the bus, Reag," Mack says evenly. "Don't give them a show."

With a deep exhale, I take a step onto the bus, but I turn back, tempted. The reporter opens his mouth to say something, but I hold up my hand to stop him. Or slap him. I glance around at the rest of them—these overeager grown men and women, desperate to prey on an innocent girl—and my Southern upbringing rears like a stallion. "*Shame* on you. You're a grown man. You even being here is skeevy and pathetic."

"Reagan, enough," Mack says.

I launch myself onto the bus before I can get angrier, and the driver shuts the door behind me. Inside, Dee has crumpled to her knees on the floor, cradling her face in her hands. I drop to her side, sitting on the floor with my back up against the couch, and she slumps against me. She inhales sharply, breathing too fast, as if crying and gasping for air all at once.

I let her cry, thinking of how many times she's picked me up from the places I've fallen. She practically scraped me off the pavement after Jen McNally's Christmas party last year, drunk as I was. She's picked me up from seedy bars and bad situations, with Jimmy carrying me to the truck more times than I care to admit. Dee would drive into hell to pull me out of it with her bare hands. She may be a girlie-girl, but when it matters, she's all fight. I know she can pick herself up, even now, but she deserves to let it out for a while.

She's hiccup-crying like a little kid, but this is worse than the scraped knees of our younger days. This pain feels distinctly adult, like Dee's mom or at least Peach should be here to fix this. It's not okay, but I whisper it anyway. "It's okay. It's all right."

Dee cries against my shoulder, her tears soaking warm through my shirt.

"You've seen what's happened to those other girls," she mumbles, and I know her mind is flipping through tabloid pages. "It starts with a few ugly rumors, and then the media turns on them, and their careers are over, and they wind up in rehab, and—"

"Hey. That's never going to be you."

"You don't know that." Dee shakes her head, her hair still holding its curl from the concert last night. Even with most of her makeup cried off, she looks like a star.

"I *do* know that," I say, but she seems unconvinced.

She sits up, wiping under her eyes. "Matt will already be there when we get to Virginia, right?"

"I think so."

Dee nods, taking a deep inhale. "You know, he's been in the spotlight forever."

"Yeah. He has."

She leans against the couch, limbs melting into the soft leather. "He'll know what to do."

Somehow, this thought calms Dee as we roll toward Virginia. She falls asleep on the floor beside me, head propped up on a wildflower pillow. It's an understandable impulse, to be on the floor when everything is falling apart, like you just want to feel the solid ground beneath you. When you're on the floor, there's nowhere farther to fall.

I pull out my laptop to hunt for information on Matt Finch. Dee likes him, but Dee likes everyone. I, on the other hand, don't like him—or, at least, I don't like that he stands to benefit from a situation that has my best friend falling asleep with puffy eyes.

My online search is fruitful. Matt Finch has been off the radar for about a year, no tour dates listed on his website. Apparently he had a fairly public breakup two years ago, when he was seventeen. The girl he was dating wasn't famous until she went to the tabloids about their split.

When I'm done stalking his personal life, my investigation turns to his solo music. I survey the song clips on his website and select the first one—"Human," a title that intrigues me. Clicking Play, I adjust my headphones in my ears.

Piano chords rise above the faint drumming and then give way to Matt Finch's voice—deeper, of course, than when he was in the Finch Four. I shut my eyes to listen closer. He isn't oversinging or trying too hard. His voice slides from one note to the next with ease, like he's coming up with the lyrics just a heartbeat before singing them.

I listen closely, trying to string the lyrics together for their full meaning. Dee says that phrases in songs are like beads in a necklace—they should stand on their own, but they make the most sense together.

Oh, you know I'm only human;
I bend and fall and break.
You cut me and I bleed;
I'm a mess for you to make.
So forget the words and give me deeds;
My heart was yours to take.

In a rare moment of emotional clarity, I feel as if Matt Finch has somehow seen the events of my life and transcribed them into song. I know this feeling. I know it all too well—when the world is so callous to you that your mind screams: "I am human, I am bleeding, *stop this!*" His voice is beautiful but wrenched—like he's experiencing the pain all over again as he sings.

I sense that I'm being watched. Dee is awake and staring at me.

"What are you listening to?" she asks when I remove my headphones. She narrows her eyes at me, and I feel as if I've been caught in a personal moment.

"Um." I click out of the website as if to hide the evidence. Embarrassment clouds my brain, and I can't think of a lie. "Matt Finch, actually. His solo album."

"Oh yeah?"

"Yeah. It's . . . um . . ." I pause, picking my words carefully. "It's good."

"Yes, it is." Dee's eyes move away from me, like her thoughts are floating across the room. "I cried the first time I heard 'Human.'" After a moment of quiet, she refocuses on me. "Anyway. You'll really like him. Matt's just *nice*, you know? Not like other show-business types."

It's an inadvertent insult to her own people, which makes me smile. Dee lies back down, closing her eyes again as she repeats, "He'll know what to do."

We arrive in Richmond, Virginia, five slow hours later. As instructed, we wait on the bus as roadies "secure the perimeter" and begin to unload. I stay next to Dee on her couch, waiting for Mack to come collect us. The hotel is calm as we enter through a side door, but I shudder, reliving the memory of those reporters outside the last hotel. Dee's mouth remains in that plaintive line, and I don't even notice that she's searching something on her phone until it's too late.

"Give me that." I snatch the phone from her hands as the elevator opens. Turning to Mack, I say, "Thanks—we're good from here."

When the doors close us inside, Dee's eyes are pressed closed, tears slipping out on either side of her face.

"It's so bad," she whimpers.

I glance down at the phone I took from her. She searched her own name and, sure enough, in just a few hours, the story has spiraled downward in the way that only salacious gossip can. The results are so ugly—*LILAH MONTGOM-ERY SCANDAL: IS THERE A VIDEO??* and a story in which an "industry source" speculates on whether Dee's tour sponsors will pull out of their deals. *Stargazer Magazine*'s website published a scathingly self-righteous op-ed about Dee, even though they featured a glowing interview with her earlier this week—what a bunch of fair-weather fans. This article reinforces how steadfast I need to be for Dee. The day after the disaster is the best friend big leagues, and I'm up.

I grasp her hand as the elevator doors open to our floor because I understand now. The picture is not just embarrassing, and it's not just an invasion of privacy. Dee's professional world could implode. For two years, her rising popularity has seemed untouchable. She doesn't have a backup plan. This career is all she's ever wanted or worked for. Her sponsorship, her fan base, her future: it's all hanging in the balance between rabid reporters and judgmental mothers who will refuse to buy concert tickets for their daughters.

Peach isn't in the room yet, but our suitcases have been delivered on a gilded luggage cart. Dee darts to the nearest couch and curls into a tight circle, like a cat.

"I wish there was something I could do." I hover near her, as if my physical presence could shield her.

"You're doing it," she says. "You're here."

I sit down on the couch, and she stretches her legs over my knees.

"Imagine if I were here alone right now," she mumbles. "That would be awful."

"Was it so bad being on tour last year, with Peach?"

She shrugs. "It was a little lonely sometimes."

"We should have tried to pack me in your suitcase like we joked about." I move my knee, bouncing her legs. "Remember?"

Her head pivots toward me, her mouth almost smiling. There's a twinkle of interest in her eyes, the same spark that accompanies a new song idea, and it flickers between me and the huge suitcase by the door. I know what she's thinking, and while I normally wouldn't go along with it, I'm half past desperate to cheer her up.

"Oh, c'mon," she begs.

"*Fine*," I say with a wave of my hand.

She returns a moment later, rolling the suitcase behind her. It lands with a thud on the ground, and Dee unzips it hurriedly. We both lift, angling the suitcase until all her casual wear—old jeans and yoga pants and underwear—falls into a pile on the hotel carpet.

Though I feel completely ridiculous, I plop myself into the empty suitcase, trying to tuck my legs inside. Dee starts giggling as she tugs off my sandals, trying to make me fit. This spurs me on because Dee's real-life laughter is hilarious in itself. In interviews, her laugh is musical, a trilling sound that is completely under her control. But her true laugh is the nerdiest sound in the world. When she gasps for air, she sounds like a goose honking.

I slide my head into the corner, my own laughter shaking the padded suitcase walls.

"Scrunch your legs up more," Dee says through her laughter. "I wish you could see how hilarious this is."

I fold my arms tightly against me, cast hard against my chest, and I shift so that my knee drops into the suitcase. My jeans hug my body in all the right places, but they're not ideal for bending my legs.

"Am I all the way in?"

"Yes!" Dee's voice is hard to understand through her honking and the suitcase's insulated sides. "This is going to happen."

She tugs at the zipper, leaving an open space at the top. I poke my head out the top to see Dee, doubled over in laughter. Maybe it's funny because we're so tired, so overwhelmed and desperate to laugh. But no matter the reason, I laugh so hard that it feels like a muscle spasm in my stomach. I couldn't stop if my life depended on it. Dee's all-out raucous laugh reminds me of being eleven again, of sleepovers where we woke her mom up with our giggling. *Girls*, Mrs. Montgomery would say, *it's time to quiet down and go to sleep*, even though she seemed to be hiding a smile of her own.

"Get my camera, get my camera," I say. Dee retrieves my camera from my bag, holding it with shaking hands. She steadies herself, taking a picture that I hope won't be blurry.

I'm jolted by a rhythmic knock at the door, and Dee nearly drops my camera in surprise. I'm still too slaphappy to panic about my beloved camera's well-being. For some reason, the chance that the hotel staff will see me zipped into a suitcase is even funnier to us. Dee unzips the suitcase enough that I can wriggle an arm free, and I keep tugging at it as she runs to answer the door. On her tiptoes, Dee peers out the peephole and then throws the door open with full-body enthusiasm.

The guy at the door looks a bit older than us, with light brown hair that curls slightly at his ears. If this is a hotel concierge, he's the hottest one ever. Like, of all time. And here I sit, a barefoot jackass in an empty suitcase. I bolt up, fluffing my hair before he can see me.

"Hey, little lady," the guy says, opening his arms to Dee. He's familiar. I try to place him, but I'm too busy scrambling to my feet, tugging my sandals back on.

"Matt!" Dee wraps her arms around his neck, and he lifts her off the ground. Of course. Matt Finch. I didn't even recognize him, all grown up. Standing up a bit straighter, I curse myself for being so uncool. When Matt sets her down, Dee says, "It is *so* nice to see a friendly face. Thank you for doing this."

He shakes his head. "It's a bunch of crap, what happened with that stupid picture."

"Tell me about it." She gestures back toward me, and Matt's gaze follows. "This is my best friend, Reagan."

When his eyes land on me, something about his expression changes—like he recognizes me from somewhere, too. I look back, appraising him quickly. He's kind of beautiful, in an understated, comfortable-looking way—the kind of guy who doesn't mind seeing a rom-com with you and gives you his hoodie when you're cold.

"Hi," he says, regaining his manners. "I'm Matt."

I reach my noncasted arm to shake his hand, business-like. After all, he could be the enemy—a rook in Lissa's publicity game. "Nice to meet you."

"Reagan's hanging out with me all summer," Dee says.

"Is that right?" Matt keeps his eyes on me. "Groupie, huh?"

"For Dee, maybe." My tone is curt, even as I fight the urge to ogle him. He was cute when we were younger, but in a baby-faced way. Now he's all strong jawline and broad shoulders, his white T-shirt pulled tight across the chest and looser at his waist.

He raises his eyebrows. "Point taken."

His eyes are somewhere between gray and blue, and his hair is somewhere between brown and blond, and I am somewhere between hostile and attracted.

"She's just kidding," Dee says. "We listened to your new stuff online, and she loved it."

I bite the insides of my cheeks. Dee has a habit of putting my cards on the table without my permission, and it drives me crazy. I would have preferred that he didn't know I like his music.

"Is that right?" he asks, intrigued.

"It's pretty good. I was surprised."

"Ouch." His mouth pulls into a half smile as he turns to Dee. "She tells it like it is, huh?"

Dee nods. "Reagan's very honest."

"So." He crosses his arms as he surveys our room. "Did

you guys want to grab dinner, or were you too busy zip-
ping yourselves into suitcases?"

Dee laughs, but I feel the unfamiliar flush of embarrassment. Matt raises his eyebrows at me again, teasing me with
a single look, and something about it shakes me. Maybe it's
because I got caught doing something weird or maybe I'm
rusty after two months of living like a nun, barricaded in my
room. Either way, Matt Finch has thrown me off my game
within a minute of his arrival. At this rate—with heat still
flooding my cheeks—it's going to be a long summer.

CHAPTER FIVE

Raleigh to Savannah

Matt arrived on Monday, and, by Tuesday morning, pictures from our dinner popped up online. We sat on the patio of a local bistro, at Lissa's request. Under a wide umbrella, Dee and I sat across from Peach and Matt, enjoying bottomless iced teas and Matt's one-man show, Cheering Dee Up.

Summer Love? the online clip posed. Beside it, the picture captured Dee laughing, with her hand on Matt's arm. He'd been asking me about my camera and explaining how he really isn't photogenic. Then he regaled us with his repertoire of awkward camera faces while, apparently, a photographer crouched in the bushes of the park across the street. None of us had noticed, but I'm sure Lissa tipped him off.

Matt proceeded to show us his entire stock of camera expressions: Surprise Mugshot, Blinky McStupid, and Double Chin for the Win. Peach wiped tears of laughter from her eyes, and I pressed my lips together to keep from spitting out my iced tea. But Peach and I were conveniently cropped out of the photo, which included a suggestive caption. *SPOT-TED: Lilah Montgomery sharing a very friendly dinner with Matt Finch. It is rumored that Finch has joined Montgomery's tour as an opener . . . and maybe more.*

While those pictures sparked gossip about Dee and Matt, a radio clip from Wednesday ignited it. Dee had a call-in interview with a local radio station, so she didn't have to go to the studio. We were all sitting around in the hotel as she answered the DJ's questions. The clip featured a particularly leading moment.

"So, Lilah," the DJ said through the speakerphone, "I've been hearing some pretty loud rumors about you and Matt Finch. Care to settle a bet?"

"We're just friends," Dee said automatically. She loves that she doesn't have to lie. Sure, she and Matt are misleading everyone a little, but they aren't outright lying.

"No comment!" Matt yelled from beside her. He'd plopped down on the couch, leaning his mouth near the phone.

Dee giggled and hissed, "Shhh!"

"Was that Matt just now?" the DJ prodded, not even bothering to conceal his excitement.

"No comment!" she chirped.

From a media standpoint, the clip is totally incriminating, more than enough to prove that they're together. He watched from the wings with me during Dee's Tuesday show in Richmond, but he stood in the VIP section for last night's Raleigh show, in full view of concert-goers. I'm sure those pictures are online by now, too. The public doesn't need more than that to confirm the news of young love. These stories are all fluff, of course, but Dee's been in a better mood since Matt showed up.

"Matt's been with us for three days, and there are hardly any mentions of the *nude* photo," Dee muses as we roll farther south down the coast. There's a bitterness in her voice when she references the photo now—but at least no tears. She's perusing the forums of her website, which have exploded with comments in a blur of abbreviations and symbols and exclamation points: *OMG Finchgomery!!! So cute together!! True <3 4LM, finally!!!!*

The positive response to Matt and Dee as a couple is overwhelming, with entertainment news sites updating several times daily with any pictures or details they can find. But it doesn't change how badly Dee's been shaken. The photo showed us just how delicate her popularity is, how quickly fans could turn on her, and how many ugly words could be thrown at her from behind computer screens. She stayed up till 2 a.m. writing a post for her website explaining how much she loves being a role model for young girls, even though she knew her management team would never let her post it. Instead, she'll work it into a live interview soon, when Lissa isn't there to stop her.

"Hey, Reagan?"

"Yeah?"

"Do you think I should text Jimmy and tell him that I'm not really going out with Matt?"

She doesn't owe him anything. But it does feel, even to me, like lying by omission. Besides, Jimmy can keep a secret. "What's your gut feeling?"

"Text him," she decides. Then she nods firmly, glancing out the window as the bus veers toward the off-ramp for a fuel-up.

"I can run inside the gas station if you want something."

She perks up. "Really?"

It makes more sense for me to do snack runs alone. If Dee went, too, we'd hold up the tour caravan while she signed autographs for truck drivers and vans full of families on vacation. "Of course. I was going to run in anyway."

"Awesome." She looks relieved. "I'm dying for some trail mix."

"No problem." I reach for my purse and slide the strap over my head. It's the kind of bag that sits on my hip, with a strap that goes diagonally across my chest and settles into my cleavage. Dee says these purses are called satchels, and I say she's lived in Tennessee too long.

"Wait!" she calls, holding out some cash toward me.

"Dee," I say sternly. "Stop."

She recognizes the hard edge in my voice, the tone I take when there's no reasoning with me. I don't use that tone with her often, but when I do, it's always about who's paying.

After finding a bag of trail mix for Dee, I scan the shelves for my own snack food. Eating junk food in front of Dee is cruel, but it's never stopped me. She eats healthy most of the time—as much for her energy levels as for her weight. I'm debating between Swedish Fish and M&M'S when Matt Finch turns the corner, a family-size bag of Twizzlers tucked under his arm.

I arch an eyebrow at him. "Are those all for you or do you have a family on your bus?"

"Twizzlers are a low-fat candy," he says, indignant. "It says so on the bag."

He holds up the bag for my examination, and I smile. "Nothing is low-fat when you eat a *pound* of it."

"Are you saying I need to watch my figure?"

He really does not, but if he's fishing for a compliment, he won't find it here. So I shrug, going back to my own considerations. Finally, I choose the candy that combines my dual cravings for fruit and chocolate: Raisinets. Matt moves past me to the refrigerators, reaching in to extract a beverage. Out of the corner of my eye, I notice that his choice is a pink bottle.

"Strawberry milk," I say, eyeing him as we head toward the counter. "Really."

He turns to me. "Do you have something to say about my snack selections?"

"Nope." I fall into line behind him. "I just didn't realize you were a middle-school girl going to a slumber party."

"And I," he says, plunking his strawberry-fest down on the counter, "didn't realize you were a soccer mom justifying her chocolate craving with the fact that raisins are a fruit."

Matt Finch hits back. I like it.

"Her stuff, too," he tells the cashier.

"No," I say hotly, even though the guy behind the counter is already punching extra buttons. "Seriously, do you people think that noncelebrities can't afford gas station candy?"

"I'm sure you can." He slaps down enough money for all of it. "But see, if I pay for this now, you'll feel bad for giving me such a hard time."

I really will not. As we walk toward the exit, I smirk at him. "You obviously don't know me at all."

"Maybe not," he says, propping open the door for me. "Yet."

Beyond the gas station's overhang, the sky spans wide, an unreal blue with cotton blossom clouds. I assume we're somewhere in South Carolina, but there's no way to know based on geographical sights alone. A long stretch of highway, the blinding summer sun—it's all the same between one place and the next. The band and crew are messing around outside our line of tour buses, stretching their legs and smoking. I spot Peach in the crowd, leaning against the band's bus and chatting with her boyfriend. Dee's drummer, whose name I can never remember, glances up and gives me a long once-over, from head to open-toe heels.

From beside me, Matt says, "I think I've got your number."

"I wouldn't give you my number."

He smiles. "No, I mean . . . I think I've got you figured out."

"I knew what you meant."

"He just looked at you like he's stranded in the desert and you're a tall glass of water. That must get old."

Of course it does. "Not really."

He's grinning enough to create slight dimples—surprising on such a chiseled face. "I get it. You're like a porcupine. You've evolved spikes to keep the creeps away."

"They're called quills. And don't act like you know me."

I mean this to be my parting line, the last word before I turn away. I mean to leave him in the dust, giving my hips an extra sway for his viewing pleasure. Instead, Matt keeps pace with me, past his own bus and toward Dee's.

"What are you doing?" I ask.

"Asking Dee a question."

I walk up the steps to our bus with Matt on my heels and toss the bag of trail mix to Dee. It lands next to her on the couch, and she scoops it up eagerly.

"Thank you!" Seeing Matt behind me, she sits up straighter. "Hey!"

"Hey," Matt says. "Can I hang with you guys for the next stretch? Reagan invited me."

"No, she didn't," I reply flatly.

"Well." He flashes that wily smile. "Not in *words*. She invited me with her eyes."

I shake my head at Dee, but she looks delighted at the prospect of company. "Awesome! We can write together like we talked about!"

Matt breaks open his bag of Twizzlers. "Let's do it."

Hours later, I'm still editing photos while Matt and Dee work on their joint songwriting. They've already talked about concepts and possible main chords, with Matt pluck-ing on one of Dee's spare guitars. Now he lays reclined on one of the couches, arms stretched behind his head. Dee sits cross-legged, glancing up at Matt as she scribbles possible lyrics into a notebook.

"Okay." Matt runs his hands through his hair. "I have a song idea. We could call it 'Dee Montgomery Is a Songwrit-ing Machine and Matt Finch Is a Hack.'"

"Oh, stop." She swats his leg. "Your new stuff is beautiful."

"My new stuff," he says, using air quotes, "is well over a year old. I'm so far past writer's block. It's writer's . . . barricade. Writer's vault door."

"We'll come up with something good," Dee promises. Her smile warps into a drawn-out yawn, and she opens her eyes wide, as if forcing them to stay open by brute force.

"Did you sleep at all?" I ask. She got out of bed a few times last night, creeping out into the common room after we got home from her concert.

"Only a little," she admits. "I was in such a writing mood. I kept thinking of things, and I wanted to get them down before I forgot."

I know that, of course. She tried to play quietly in the common room, but I could still hear. Not that I minded. Hearing Dee work through a new song reminds me of when we were younger, before she even started performing.

"You'll get sick if you lose too much sleep," I warn, affect-ing a deeper tone and thick Southern accent to imitate Peach's voice.

She laughs again, but it's punctuated by another yawn. "Okay. I'll go lie down. Wake me when we're near Savannah."

"I will," I tell her, turning back to my computer screen. I'm editing the images from her Raleigh concert last night. There's one particularly good one of Dee with the mic in one hand and her other hand on her hip, sassy and midlyric. I drag it into the file I've created called Maybe Portfolio—the growing list of my favorite photos so far.

Dee moves toward her bunk, and Matt looks over at me.

"That was a hell of a Peach impression." He gives me a respectful nod.

I shrug. "Practice."

There are a few beats of silence, but I can feel his eyes on me. Finally he says, "You don't really emote. Did you know that?"

I don't like when people try to explain me. So I lift my shoulders into an exaggerated shrug. There—I'm expressing what I feel: apathy, with a side of annoyance.

Matt is undeterred. In fact, his grin widens. "See, right now, I'm not sure if you completely hate me or if you think I'm the hottest guy in the world."

"Neither." I do think he's hot, but the hottest guy in the world? I'd have to meet more guys, globally, to be able to comment on that. "I just don't really trust you."

Matt raises his eyebrows, but I can tell he's not offended. In fact, he looks almost impressed. "Well, you shoot from the hip—I'll give you that."

Crossing my arms, I glare in his direction. His presence is

disconcerting, and I've wanted to address it for a few days now. This is my opportunity to do it without Dee overhearing me. "I think maybe you're an opportunist. That maybe you were a little too eager to jump on the tour, cash in on the situation Dee is in right now."

I pause to let this sink in and, sure enough, he crosses his arms, too—defensive. But he also looks amused, as if my direct approach is a little sideshow designed specifically for his entertainment. "You've been off the radar for a few years, and you're on Dee's record label. Maybe Lissa leaked that photo; maybe the two of you planned this whole thing to help restart your career."

"Wow," he says, running a hand through is hair. He's still smiling, though, which confirms that he's as impossibly smug as I suspected. "You shoot from the hip with a machine gun."

I keep my arms crossed, and I won't be the first one to blink.

"All right." He leans over in his seat, resting his arms on his knees so that he's eye level with me. Squaring his shoulders, he says, "Here we go—in no particular order. I got out of the music business on my own accord, and I'm not even sure I want back in. Also, I've had my heart pulverized and then splashed all over the tabloids, too, so I know what Dee's going through. I genuinely care about her, and I'd never hurt her."

I'm quiet for a moment, waiting for his expression to falter, for his body language to expose any degree of untruthfulness. His usual look of amusement is gone, replaced by a solemnity that I haven't yet seen on him. "I like that you asked me."

I look at him challengingly. "I don't remember asking anything."

"If the situation were reversed—if the press were dogging my sister the way they are Dee—I'd be asking the same questions."

"I didn't ask any questions."

"You didn't have to. You're asking what I want from Dee. And the answer is nothing. I wanted to shake things up in my life, and the tour option presented itself. Complete serendipity. So here I am, and that's it."

I buy it. When someone is lying to me, I can usually sense it. Subconscious gestures and certain word choices flare up, the flickers of dishonesty. Not Matt. His whole presence is still—settled.

"Okay," I tell him, a truce.

He nods. "Okay."

We look at each other for a moment before I return my attention to photo editing.

"So . . . whatcha doin'?"

"Editing images."

"From last night?"

I nod, keeping my eyes on the screen. Now that I feel like he's as trustworthy as Dee seems to think, I can admit that there's something about Matt Finch that I like. Maybe more than one thing. I like that he makes Dee feel at ease. I like his self-deprecating sense of humor and the arm muscles that flex when he strums his guitar. The more I find myself interested by him, the more I try to seem uninterested. It's a necessary boundary that runs the perimeter of my whole being, and I've built it brick by brick. After all, my left hand is still bound by a heavy cast, resting inoperably at my side.

Matt moves from the couch and sits next to me, his leg touching mine. His sudden nearness startles me, and I turn the laptop screen away from him. Up close, he smells like plain white bar soap—the kind that you slide against your arms.

"I can't see the pictures?" He seems to be withholding a smirk, like my protectiveness is cute to him.

"Do *you* like people reading over your shoulder?"

The smirk pulls wider across his face, and he moves down on the couch, leaving a foot of space between us. In a way that is clearly patronizing me, he says, "I'm sorry. May I see the pictures from the show, please?"

"Nope."

"Please? Just one?"

If he's going to act like an obnoxious little kid all the way to Georgia, I'm going to smack him with my casted arm. But when I glance up to tell him so, he looks hopeful—like he genuinely wants to see my photos. I swear his looks are pure Darwinism. If he wasn't so cute, someone would have killed him for being annoying by now.

"Fine." I turn the screen so that it faces him.

"Wow." Matt leans closer, scanning the image of Dee I

just edited. Her little pose, the glint in her eye. "That's her, all right."

"Obviously."

He looks up at me. "I mean, this captures a particular side of her beautifully. She's this tiny girl, but she's so powerful and in control."

I glance back at the photo. It's a great shot, but I didn't realize it said all that. I turn the screen back toward me. "Yeah, well."

"How long have you been into photography?"

"Three years. Since my first photo class in high school."

"So the end career goal is . . . paparazzi?"

Asshole. I sneer. "God, no. I want to take photos of concerts, of political events, landscapes, of countries in revolution. Photos that accompany news stories. Photojournalism."

My sincerity softens his tone. "You're talented."

"You've seen one picture. And it was of your girlfriend."

He turns toward me. "Say what?"

"I know. It's a 'publicity stunt.'" I use air quotes. "But c'mon. Every guy in America is in love with her."

Matt shakes his head. "I mean, I love her. But in a sisterly way—like, she literally reminds me of my sister. I don't think I can change that, even if I wanted to, you know?"

I resist the urge to wrinkle my nose. He's only nineteen, and I hope he doesn't see me as too young for him. That would ruin my plans to flirt with him—not to start something up, of course, just to flirt for the hell of it. It's a law of nature, like a cat with something shiny; dangle it in front of her long enough and eventually she'll paw at it. Only in this case, I'm the cat and Matt is something shiny. The pawing part is the same.

"Besides," he says. "I'm more into brunettes."

To top it off, he grins at me, those dimples making parentheses beside his mouth. I feel warmth spread through my chest, but I manage to play it cool, shaking my head at him. "You're very self-satisfied, aren't you?"

"Something like that. And besides, I know Dee's still upset about . . . you know."

This is the first time that he's mentioned Jimmy. Dee told Matt every detail of the breakup, but I wasn't expecting him to bring it up.

"He sounds like a good guy," Matt says, glancing up at me. Maybe it's so Dee won't hear us, but his voice is soft. Hushed and almost reverent, like heartbreak is too sad to use your regular voice.

"He *is* a good guy." My mind flashes through images of Jimmy—helping me to his truck after a bender of a party, slamming Pete Harmon into a locker after he called me a slut in the hallway, looking at my best friend like he's never seen anything so beautiful up close. "But he really believes he's holding Dee back by staying with her. He thought she'd move on and be better for it."

Matt shakes his head. "It seems crazy to me, that they're both hurting so much by being apart. Seems like they should just be together."

"I know." I look down at my hands in my lap, at the thick

cast enclosing my healing wrist. And for some reason, unwelcome pensiveness finds its way to my mouth. "But it must be nice to have someone love you like that, you know? Jimmy cares about her more than he cares about himself, and even though they're not together, she knows that."

Embarrassment floods my stomach like straight liquor, hot and biting. I have no idea what compelled me to share such a personal longing—the deep-seated wanting, that someone would love me in a limitless, sappy way, like Dee and Jimmy love each other. Like Dee's parents love each other. I've seen that kind of unconditional love, but I've never felt it. I glance over at Matt, hoping that he's not smirking at me. He's not.

"Yeah," he says quietly. His eyes follow the passing road outside the window. "Must be nice."

As I stare back down at my photographs, my thoughts linger on a camera function called aperture, used to describe how much light is being let into the lens. It seems easy to think of myself this way—as someone who programmed herself to let in the least amount of light possible. There's space for Dee and for my dad, and that's the best I can do.

When I met Blake, I let myself click open a few millimeters, unfurling like a spiral shutter. In fact, I let in just enough to be overexposed. Burned. Maybe I should have known. It doesn't bode well, meeting someone while doing court-ordered cleaning tasks in a retirement community. What can I say? The orange jumpsuit did it for me.

I liked Blake because he was always in motion. There was always another party to stop at before heading home, a weekend on a houseboat with his friends, and any other adventure that came up. He was reckless, always the center of attention. As we made our way to the back porch at any given party, people slapped him on the back and called him by nicknames with suspicious origins.

He graduated from high school two years ago and failed out of his first year of college, so I probably should have picked up on his aura of loserdom. At first, I didn't care about Blake's future, because *we* didn't have a future. I just liked hanging out with him, having his arm slung over my shoulder at parties as he joked around with his buddies. Blake, for all his faults, was never boring. But then I got used to him finding me by the keg, smiling as he said, "There's my girl." I got used to his slow grin and the persistent cologne meant to mask the pot smell. For a minute, I thought I belonged somewhere, and for that same minute, it felt nice. Until it broke me.

My cast feels especially heavy today, edged with my desperation to scratch an itch I've had for over a month. I push my finger under the gauze, uselessly rubbing at any spot I can reach. I've suffered the thickness, the musty smell, the underlying ache as a reminder of the changes I need to make. *Let the cast be your cocoon*, my therapist said, and I rolled my eyes. But I don't have the patience for metamorphosis. I want to be free.

CHAPTER SIX

Charleston

"You have to swear," Peach says. "If you think anyone notices you, you have to leave. Okay?"

It's late on Saturday, and we're in our Charleston hotel. Earlier today, Dee played an afternoon show at an outdoor venue. The weather stayed clear, and the grassy space for the audience made the whole show feel perfect for summer. It was Dee's last show without Matt as an opener. Now that the backup band is prepped for a few of his songs, Matt will be playing a set in every city. He called a bar here in town to ask if they'd let him play a set tonight, as practice for Dee's show. They agreed, and he asked us to come along.

"And you do have to be up early to leave for Little Rock," Peach continues, now biting at her thumbnail. She's nervous about us going, but not so nervous that she'll cancel her date with Greg to come with us. Best chaperone ever. "So be back at the hotel by curfew."

"Okay, okay." Dee adjusts her wig. It's a soft brown, straight and long. Her makeup artist gave her dark eyebrows, too, and she's wearing my clothes. My low-cut tank top and skinny jeans are tighter than anything she'd usually wear. She's traded in her flats for a pair of spike heels. She doesn't look like Lilah Montgomery at all, and she certainly doesn't look like Dee.

Normally she wouldn't risk this kind of exposure, to be seen at a bar. But Matt assured us that he could get us in to watch the show, and Dee's eager to see the set he has planned to open her show. Plus, she's thrilled at the idea of outsmarting the media.

Dee rummages through a jewelry box at the bathroom sink. "Aha. Perfection."

She fishes out a necklace and clasps it around my neck without asking. It's a silver arrow, pointing straight to the right. She knows I'll love it, and I do.

"I'm so excited!" She claps her hands. "I feel so normal!"

I do not. I feel almost nervous, not quite as in control as I'd like to be. Something about Matt puts me off guard, and I don't like it. As I was picking out something to wear, I caught myself worrying that I'd look like I tried too hard. I decided on a black tank-top dress, which is tight and cotton and simple, very I-just-threw-this-on. The necklace gives it a more feminine touch. Still, I lean forward in the mirror, adjusting my bra for maximum cleavage.

Peach gives me an intentionally loud sigh, and I glance up. She makes no secret of her feelings about my wardrobe. Any time a roadie gives me a second look, Peach clucks at me like I'm on a stripper pole.

"You're seventeen," she says disapprovingly.

Dee, not realizing that Peach was directing that comment toward me, chimes in, "I know! Only young once!"

I survey Dee's heavy makeup, searching for the right word. "You look so . . . vampy."

"Vampy?" She giggles at herself in the mirror. "These are your clothes."

"I know." I laugh, too. "But they look strange on you."

She shimmies her hips in a sort of victory dance. "I like it. I feel exciting."

"You're Lilah Montgomery. Doesn't get much more exciting than that."

"Tonight, I'm Dee. The night is ours, and I'm free to be. Little old me."

Dee writes rhyming lyrics even as she speaks. With another little spin, she grabs her purse and links her arm in mine.

On our way out the hotel door, Peach yells, "Be careful. I mean it, y'all."

At the door of the club, Dee is surprisingly confident for someone who has never been in a venue underage without a record-label rep. Mack dropped us off at the front, but not before giving us a quick lecture about making good choices. He'll be just around the corner, watching TV at a local sports bar, and if Dee is exposed as Lilah Montgomery, he can pick us up in two minutes.

"Matt Finch's guests," Dee tells the bouncer, leaning to glance at his clipboard. Above us, the marquee reads: MATT FINCH LIVE—ONE NIGHT ONLY. "Samantha Alabama and Ronnie O."

Matt texted us these names on our way to the bar, and Dee cackled at such obvious pseudonyms. I have no idea how he came up with "Samantha," but I get that "Alabama" replaced "Montgomery." As for my name, "Reagan" to "Ronald" to "Ronnie."

The bouncer gives us wristbands and says, "Y'all have a good night."

Dee claps, grinning as if we're entering Disneyland instead of a dive bar, though I have to admit—it's nicer than I expected. It seems clean enough, with shiny oak bar tops, and the patrons are mostly college students. If I didn't know any better, we'd fit right in.

"I'm going to get us drinks."

Dee's grin falls. "Reag, I thought you weren't—"

"I'm not. I meant water."

"Oh." Her face relaxes. "I'll come, too. Then we can scope out seats."

We stand at the bar, and Dee glances around, taking it all in. Her eyes widen as she notices a couple engaged in a full-body make-out session, and my instinct is to cover her eyes. In this place, I feel like the devil, escorting a newly fallen angel through the underworld.

I put two fingers up and mouth "water" to the bartender. He nods, giving me the "hold on" motion. I'm not used to ordering water, but I know the bartenders take their sweet time getting it, in favor of paying customers.

Dee props her elbow on the bar, and I sit on one of the stools. The bartender hands a beer to the girl nearest us. She's pretty, but her face is flushed, her hair is nearing disarray, and she has that sleepy-eyed, I-love-everyone-in-this-bar look. Her eyes slide over to Dee's face and stay there, suspicious.

"This is so super weird," the girl says, her posture sloppy as she leans toward Dee. "But has anyone ever told you that you kinda look like Lilah Montgomery?"

"Once or twice." Dee flips her fake brown hair.

"I don't see it." Glancing at Dee, I add, "No offense."

"None taken." Dee smiles, and the girl continues to examine her. I start to plan our quick escape from the bar, but Dee looks totally calm.

"It's your face shape," the girl decides. To my relief, she laughs, sloshing a bit of beer onto the floor. "People tell me I look like Kira King, and I'm like, ew. No. That girl is a tramp, and she can't even sing."

Kira is a singer-actress-whatever, a few years older than us. Dee's friendly with Kira, but she doesn't especially like her. Dee shakes her head. "You're *much* cuter than Kira King."

The girl gestures at herself. "I know!"

"Brianna!" a voice calls in our direction. "Come on!"

"Gotta go," the girl says, turning back to us. "Don't wanna miss Matt Finch! Yum."

As she walks away, I sneer at her. Idiot. Matt's a human being, not an apple pie.

The bartender finally hands us our waters, and Dee's beaming. "This is so fun."

"Bar small talk with drunk girls?"

She shrugs. "It's just fun to have conversations that don't revolve around my work."

For a moment, I feel a twinge of sympathy. The rest of the world sees the money, the glamour, the flawless hair and wardrobe. Without seeing the inside view, they'd never realize that Dee is caged. The fame is like a dream house—it's picture-perfect from the outside, and it's something Dee built herself. But now that she lives here, a tall fence runs around the border of her life, keeping others out and barricading her in.

We settle in at a bar table facing the stage, which is nothing more than a single platform with a microphone and an amp. Behind it is a deep blue velvet curtain with a few strings of white lights draped across it. I'm not sure if Dee has ever played a venue so small and unassuming, and she cranes her head to people-watch in every direction.

I lift the glass of water to my mouth with my noncasted hand, tucking my left arm under the table. Now that we're here, I wish I had worn a jacket to cover up the cast. But it's Charleston in June, and even the inside of this air-conditioned bar is muggy. There's a group of girls already camped out in front of the small stage space, and more girls are gravitating toward it by the minute. They all look like they've tried extra hard tonight, like they're desperate to get with Matt Finch for One Night Only. Best of luck, bitches.

As I'm sizing up the newest pack of groupies, a tubby guy in his midtwenties jumps up on the stage, tilting the microphone toward him.

"Hey everyone, thanks for comin' out tonight," he says. "Although our stage is normally used for your karaoke stylings, tonight we have a last-minute and mostly unpublicized treat for you. Ladies and guys pretending to be gentlemen to get these ladies to go home with you, please welcome Matt Finch!"

The squeals rise up while girls push to find a spot near the stage. They're clapping as best they can with drinks in hand, and Matt ducks onstage from behind the thick navy curtain. Dee lets out an impressive wolf whistle, which sets off the whole crowd even louder. I wish all these skanks would just sit down so I could see. Repositioning my chair, I nearly strain my back trying to see past a tall blond in unnecessarily high heels.

Matt's guitar is strapped over his chest, covering most of his button-down shirt. After spending a few days with him, it's strange to see him onstage. This is the first time I've seen Matt Finch: Performer. In the white light of the small barroom stage, he looks less cocky than tour-bus Matt, but he's still quietly confident, with a smile that draws you in.

"Check," he says into the microphone. "Check."

More squealing and whistling. Most of the guys in the building are clumping toward the back of the bar or locking themselves into their own conversations, making it clear that they're not here for Matt. It seems that his fan base is primarily made up of adoring girls.

"Okay," Matt says, smiling. "Hey there. I'm Matt Finch."

They *woo-hoo* and clap like banshees on nitrous oxide. The people who scream for Dee are teenage girls and younger. But with Matt, the girls howl like a bunch of starving street cats about to get table scraps. It's unseemly.

"Thanks." Matt runs a hand through his hair. "Thanks for having me. You all are my trial run for a set I'm playing on tour. Have you heard of a little lady named Lilah Montgomery?"

The crowd cheers again, and this time the guys in the bar add some whoops.

"Oh, that's sweet," Dee whispers, smiling.

Matt starts strumming, feeling around for his first chords. "Well, I'm opening for Lilah tomorrow night, and this is a preview. Here we go."

He launches into his first song, a popular one from his Finch Four days. I like it better with just him. The girls sing along at the chorus, swaying like . . . well, like drunk girls. When he hits the final notes, he follows up with a cover of "Carolina in My Mind" by James Taylor. Everyone in the bar goes crazy, singing along and cheering. Dee and I seem to be the only people who aren't Carolina natives, though Dee could pass for one, enthusiastic as she is.

By his fifth song, I almost forget that Matt Finch onstage is the same guy who's been giving me a hard time for the past week. He seems more like himself somehow, more open and subdued. He's performing, but it feels like he's not performing at all. More than once, I catch myself envying the microphone, so near his mouth.

He introduces "Human," the song that had struck me before I even met him. I feel that same deep stir, the chords gushing like a tide across my insides—up and back, up and back. For a moment, the world around me blurs so that only Matt is in focus. He goes somewhere else once he starts singing, his eyes closed. It feels like he's playing the guitar alone in his bedroom, and we're all just random voyeurs.

The hurt in his voice is so real that I can feel it settle in next to my own, somewhere in that aching part of my chest. Seeing this piece of Matt makes me want to be near him—to see his scars up close and find out if he's as broken as me.

That's ridiculous, of course. But more than ever, I feel a craving—stronger than the dull buzz of nicotine or the rush of a fourth beer. I'm hungry for newness, a fresh start, a do-over. I want to reach back into my history with a grade-school pink eraser, scrubbing away my decisions like mistakes on a math test. Too bad I drew my mistakes in ink.

In my mind, the song lifts me out of this uncomfortable wooden chair, and I'm somewhere else, too. I've forgotten about all the other people in the room, until a few of the drunker girls began to sing along during the last chorus. It takes all my self-control not to douse them with my ice water.

Matt pauses to take a drink from his water bottle. "How we doing, Charleston?"

The ruckus that follows is proof that he's won them over.

"All right," Matt says, placing his hands back on the guitar. "What you're about to hear is brand-new. I hope you like it. It's called 'Yet.'"

The first chords are upbeat. Hopeful. When he opens his mouth, I run the lyrics through my mind, processing their meaning as quickly as he can sing them.

It's been the longest time
Since I've been in this place,
Where I spend my whole day
Hoping I'll see your face.
Then I script things to say,
And maybe what you'd say back.
You don't know it yet,
But, girl, it's a fact

I feel my face getting warm, and it's not the heat of the stuffy club around me. Did he write a song about Dee?

That I can see us
Staying up late,
Talking all night,
But I guess I'll have to wait.
'Cause it's brand-new,
Yeah, I know we just met.

I want to be there with you,
But not just yet.

"Just met"—so apparently not Dee. Maybe it's a purely hypothetical song. I mean, technically, Matt just met me. But he wouldn't write a song about me, much less invite me here and play it in front of me.

"This is so good," Dee whispers.

Matt shuts his eyes as the guitar gets louder, breaking into a second verse.

Girl, you've got that look,
Like you're hard to impress.
So I'm bumbling with words,
'Cause my mind is a mess.
You were out of the blue,
And you caught me by surprise,
With a slight smile, that long stare,
And a challenge in your eyes

Maybe he wrote this song to lend credence to his sham relationship with Dee. That has to be it.

I could feel all this
In that single look,
Like you could see my soul.
You could read me like a book,
And I think it's something.

Though I know we just met,
I'm gonna get there with you.
You just don't know it . . . yet.

I want it to be about me. No, I don't. He's singing a few bars of *la-la-las* while my mind races. Of *course* I don't want it to be about me. A celebrity who's in a fake relationship with my best friend? I mean, he's hot, but so what? I could go home with any hot guy in this bar if I wanted to—which, as New Reagan, I do not. Besides, Matt Finch, classifiable good boy, would never go for a girl like me. Of course he wouldn't.

"Wow," Dee says after he finishes the last chorus. "That song would get all kinds of radio time."

I'm relieved that Dee didn't suggest that it might be about me. Because it's not.

Matt announces his last song, and he plays another selection from his solo album. The crowd is still totally into him, all the girls looking at him with the same hypnotized stares.

He disappears offstage to raucous hoots and whistles, and the crowd starts to mill around again as standard bar music takes over the speakers. Across the table, Dee's face still radiates excitement. I find myself grateful for Matt, who gave her this much-needed night out.

Out of the corner of my eye, I see him ducking back into the bar, trying to make his way toward us. A group of doting bimbos sidelines him immediately, asking for pictures with cell phones and crappy point-and-shoot cameras. He smiles gamely as the flashes go off, girls wrapping their arms around him, and my gag reflex trills in my throat. Glancing around to make sure no one's watching, I lean over toward the table, subtly adjusting my push-up bra.

"Hey, guys." He looks relieved, his whole body relaxing once he's in our presence. Up close, his shirt looks damp with sweat, and, on anyone else, this would be disgusting. Instead, on Matt, I find it inexplicably sexy, and I force my eyes away.

"You were *wonderful*," Dee says, and my brain races to find a compliment. I mean, what am I supposed to say? *That song makes me feel like I already know you completely, like we existed together in a former life. Like you get me, without even knowing me. Like maybe I need to get you alone to find out how many other ways you can make me feel.*

"It was good." I flash him the hint of a smile. The more I see girls fawning over him, the less I want to be one of them.

If he knows I'm holding back, he doesn't let on. His smile is polite, as transient as my own. "Thanks."

"That new one," Dee says, grasping his arm, "was great."

"Thanks." Matt's eyes linger on me for a moment so brief that I wonder if I imagined it. I take a sip of my drink, just for something to do. The water feels colder in my mouth than it did before, further proving that I've heated up since I got here. "I should get going before anyone sees us together."

Dee nods and steps back from him. As if on cue, a girl walks up to Matt, touching him lightly on the small of his back. She's pretty—long, dark hair and hardly any makeup. She drawls in a sweet voice, "Hi . . . sorry to bother you. Could you take a picture with me and my friends?"

I don't like any girl who bites her lip in an attempt to look cute and innocent.

"Sure," Matt replies.

Before I'm forced to witness this, I announce, "I need some fresh air."

And by "fresh air" I, of course, mean "a cigarette." I wind my way through the maze of bodies until I find the front door. There are a few other people milling around outside, pooled into groups, talking and smoking. I head across the street to a sketchy little bodega, where I stand in line between a pimply guy holding an extra-large soda and a bag of Cheetos and a woman buying five lottery tickets. My hands sweat a little as I hand over my fake Tennessee license that says I'm twenty-one, but the cashier doesn't even blink. I walk away triumphant, cigarettes and lighter in hand.

When I cross the street, I move one block down from the bar, where I can hear myself think. I lean my back against a building wall and flick the lighter, hard metal spinning beneath my thumb. The cigarette ignites, and I watch it smolder for a moment. I press one high heel against the wall behind me, holding the smoke in my lungs and then releasing it. Time slows down as I savor each inhale, the way the heat blooms inside my chest. It feels disgusting and guilt-ridden and wonderful.

"You're a smoker?" a voice near me asks.

I turn to see Matt walking toward me, holding a cell phone in his hand. He's wearing a baseball cap now, pulled low to obscure his famous face.

"Nope." The smoke curls out of my mouth like steam rising from a cup of tea.

He steps closer, mere centimeters away. I freeze, my whole body paralyzed by his unexpected nearness. Leaning toward me, he closes his lips over the cigarette between my fingers. I expect him to take a drag—that long, forbidden inhale of a professional singer. Instead, he tugs the cigarette from my hand with *his teeth* and lets it drop to the ground. He stamps it with his shoe and bravado, his arms out like a matador who has conquered the bull.

My jaw slackens. I snap it shut, but it falls open again. "What. Did you. Just. *Do*."

Matt's close to me again, his pointer finger pushing the brim of his ball cap up so I can see his face. His self-satisfied grin makes his cheeks look dimply and smackable. I consider it, too, my right hand stiffening. But it didn't go great the last time I hit someone, thus the cast on my left arm.

"Cigarettes are terrible for you," he says. His eyes are as gray as smoke. That is how badly I want another cigarette: Matt's body is a mirage, a giant cigarette with smoky eyes.

I'm speechless. He's already heading back toward the club door with this jaunty, hands-in-pockets walk. He violated my personal space and at least five social boundaries, yet he walks away with a pep in his step. I grasp around my purse for something to throw at him, but all I have is the crumpled-up receipt from the bodega and a few coins. They'll have to do.

It's not even the heavier coins—only pennies and a dime

or two—but at least one of them hits the side of his leg. The others drop to the sidewalk, landing like metallic hail.

Matt feigns a gasp as he turns around. He gathers his shirt as if he's overexposed, and huffs loudly. "I am *not* for sale, lady."

Everyone outside looks at me like I'm deranged. Matt Finch is obnoxious and over the line and smug as hell. Before I can yell back, he shoots me a grin and trots back into the club.

Shit. I want that stupid song to be about me.

I stay outside for the length of another slowly smoked cigarette, both to spite him and regain my composure. A guy wanders over to hit on me, and I entertain the possibility for a while before getting bored with him. I figured Dee would come out and scold me about smoking eventually, but she hasn't even sent me a passive-aggressive text message. It's been over forty-five minutes. Maybe she's mad that I left her.

As I slip back into the bar, it's clear that the crowd has nearly doubled, with thumping music to replace Matt's acoustic session. There are even people on the dance floor, channeling that fifth beer into swaying hips and flailing arms.

I scan the crowds, but I can't spot Dee. Without her telltale blond hair, she's much harder to pick out of a crowd. I dial her number, holding my casted hand over my ear to hear better, but all I hear is ringing and then voice mail. I'm beginning to wonder if she left without me because she's always pissy about my smoking. As I look down to dial Mack, Matt finds me.

"Hey." He touches my elbow lightly. "Have you seen Dee?"

"No!" I throw my arms up in exasperation. "I'm, like, starting to get worried here."

Matt's mouth goes ajar, eyes wide, like he didn't even hear me. I follow his line of vision to the dance floor, where some frat boy with too much product in his hair is attempting to grind all over a thin brunette. A thin brunette wearing my clothes.

"Shit," I mumble, pushing toward her quickly, and Matt's right behind me. I know she's drunk even before I get close enough to smell the liquor radiating off her breath.

"Okay." I take her by the arm, pulling her away from the guy. "Come on."

"What the hell?" the guy says, stepping back as Dee slings her arm over my shoulder. She grins delightedly, her brunette wig stuck to her cheek. I smooth it away with my casted hand and glare at the guy.

"Shoo," I tell him. "You're done here."

"Bitch," he grumbles before storming off. His beefy stature and heavy footsteps make him look like a Neanderthal. Drunk Dee's taste in guys could use some work.

I make eye contact with Matt. "Text Mack. We need the car here now."

"On it."

"I feel so weird and happy," Dee muses, closing her eyes. "My tummy feels warm."

"You're drunk," I tell her. "Peach is going to murder me."

"I only had one drink. And it wasn't al-co-hol," she says,

punctuating the syllables. "I told him I don't drink, and he got me a very weird iced tea. It did *not* taste good, but I didn't want to be rude, so I drank it quickly to get it over with."

At this, Matt smacks his free hand over his mouth, trying not to laugh. I kick him in the shin, nearly losing my balance, between my high heels and half of Dee's weight leaning on me.

"It was a Long Island iced tea," I tell her. "It has five kinds of liquors in it. Dee, why would you let a random guy buy you a drink?"

"*Wait.* It had liquor in it?" The smile slides off her face, and she looks at me with glazed-over eyes. "Peach is going to murder you."

"Yep," I agree, moving us both toward the exit. Her knees buckle, and she laughs as Matt and I catch her. The quick movement attracts attention, people glancing over their shoulders at the little drunk girl about to make a spectacle.

"Okay," Matt says under his breath. "Do we need a quick exit or discreet exit? I don't think we can have both at this point."

"Quick."

"All right." He turns to Dee. "Sorry, little lady."

With that, he crouches down and scoops her over his shoulder.

"Whoaaaa," she says, laughing as Matt plows through the crowd. Great. Matt Finch is carrying his alleged girlfriend, who is in disguise and visibly intoxicated. If we get out of here without being noticed or photographed, it'll be nothing short of a miracle.

"Thank youuuuu, South Carolina, and good night!" Dee exclaims, waving at the people around us. The drunken masses cheer and wave back, and I pray to everything holy that no one has a camera phone on her face.

"Put your head down," I demand. She complies, giggling into Matt's back.

"Keep walking," I tell Matt as soon as we're outside. A block away from the club's entrance, Matt sets Dee on the sidewalk. Immediately, she starts dancing to whatever music she's hearing in her mind. I let her go, spinning with her arms out.

"This is bad." I place my hands against the top of my hair. "This is so bad."

"Eh." Matt shrugs. "She'll feel like hell in the morning, but she'll be fine."

We both watch as Dee sways delightedly, limbs rubbery with tipsiness.

I lower my voice, leaning toward Matt. My panic even supersedes my desire to make out with him up against this building wall. "What if someone realized it was her and got a picture or a video? It would be my fault. I shouldn't have left her by herself inside."

"Hey." He turns to me. "It's *my* fault. I invited you, got your names on the list, and persuaded Peach to let you come."

"She's *my* best friend." I say this more to myself than to him. "I'm supposed to be there. What if we hadn't come back in time? That creep gave her alcohol after she explicitly said she doesn't drink."

"I know, but it's all right now." He gestures at Dee. She's stopped dancing and is staring straight up at the night sky, her faux brunette locks tumbling down her back. Matt studies her, and I can guess what he's thinking: *Is she really so naive, to drink something that a stranger handed her at a bar?* The answer is yes. Although it won't be after tonight.

"Dee assumes that everyone has good intentions," I tell him, even though he didn't ask.

"That's Mack." Matt motions toward the approaching black sedan. The car pulls to a stop in front of us, and the passenger-side window rolls down.

"Mack!" Dee shrieks delightedly, throwing her arms open as if hugging the entire car.

Mack looks from Dee to me and shakes his head. "Peach is going to murder you."

"I *know*," I shoot back.

"Come on, come on." Matt guides her into the open car door. I climb in behind her, and Matt jumps in the front seat.

"You," Dee says, leaning over onto me, "are my best friend."

I nod, patting her head. "Yep."

"This night was so fun." She sighs and lays her head on my lap. "I wish we could trade lives."

"Now you're talking crazy."

"You get to have all the fun. You get to do whatever you want and get in trouble, and I have to be perfect all the time. I'm not perfect."

"I think you're pretty close," Matt says quickly, saving me from responding to such a ridiculous comment. Dee laughs but stops short, the sound falling off unnaturally.

"Jimmy doesn't think so," she says, a quiver in her voice. In mere seconds, she's transitioned from cheerful-drunk to weepy-drunk. I lean my head back on the headrest and mouth *SHIT* to no one in particular. Dee continues babbling. "I loved him, but he didn't want to be with me."

"Let's not talk about it right now."

"Okay," she says sullenly.

There are a few minutes of silence as Mack steers us into the hotel's parking garage. I have the key to the service elevator in my purse, so we can enter unnoticed. Dee struggles against my attempts to help her out of the car and into Matt's waiting arms.

"I can do it myself." Her voice is indignant, but she leans heavily against him.

"We know you can." I rub my fingertips against my forehead, massaging the stress headache that's forming quickly. Dee's tipsiness is an honest mistake, but Peach will lay into us both if she finds out.

Dee digs around in her purse and muses out loud, "Maybe I should call Jimmy. . . ."

"*No*," Matt and I say in unison.

"Give me that," Matt commands.

Jutting out her lower lip, Dee drops her phone into Matt's open hand. "You are the meanest fake boyfriend *ever.*"

When the elevator opens onto the top floor, Matt steps

out with us even though his room is a floor below. Dee rests
her whole body against him while I search for my room key.

"Can you get her inside without me in case Peach is still
awake?" Matt asks.

"Look at me," I demand, snapping at Dee. Her eyes aren't
focusing as clearly as usual. "Can you try your very best to
act sober for the next minute?"

"Yes." She nods solemnly, as if agreeing to a formal contract. She stands up straight and smooths her hair. As if to
prove she's good on her word, Dee walks to the door, arms
out like she's on a tightrope. She turns to us and bows, ever
the entertainer.

"I think you're good," Matt tells me. "I've gotta head back
to the club to get my stuff."

"Right." I follow Dee toward the door, but I turn back.
Matt's still standing by the elevator, waiting to make sure
we get in okay. "Um. Thank you. For getting her out to have
some fun. And for helping get her home safe."

"You're welcome." He doesn't say anything more, and
the words hang there, feeling oddly formal.

"Reagan," Dee says in a stage whisper. "Come *on*."

"I'm coming," I say, hurrying toward her. Tonight was a
series of questionable-at-best choices, but I still feel my mouth
forming a small smile. I open the door for Dee and can't resist
a glance back at Matt. He has the same smile on his face as he
waves good night.

CHAPTER SEVEN

Charleston to Little Rock

"Oh God, make it stop," Dee moans from a fetal position on her bus couch.

We left Charleston at 5 a.m. with Dee nursing her first hangover. We told Peach it was a migraine, which excused the three aspirins and the vat of coffee I administered to her. She's been sleeping it off for almost three hours. I've been awake the whole time, watching the valleys fill with morning fog so low that it could be snatched out of the air.

Matt hopped onto our bus right before the caravan left the hotel. He handed Dee the phone he'd confiscated the night before, and she groaned in response. Our eyes met, and he smiled wanly before ducking off the bus. It was a weird moment, and I wasn't sure why it happened—like, neither of us knew what to say.

In the three hours since then, my mind has replayed last

night again and again, rewinding over Matt's new song and his sly grin after murdering my cigarette and the quiet smile we shared at the end of the night. If I stood totally still, I bet my body would just slide toward him, carrying me like a moving sidewalk. It feels like I have to plant my feet firmly to resist the pull.

I've always gotten a thrill from being places I'm not supposed to be. As soon as I was old enough to read, I gravitated right to the EMPLOYEES ONLY door in the back of the grocery store. Even now, I frequent over-twenty-one clubs and sneak into the janitor's closet to make out with whoever interests me at that moment. Matt Finch, my best friend's faux boyfriend and reputation-saver, might as well have caution tape around him—of *course* he's where I want to be.

"Okay," Dee says, finally sitting up. "I think I could eat something."

"Start small." I toss her a granola bar from my purse. "And keep up with the water."

Dee chews deliberately, as if concentration alone can keep her from nausea.

"Why do people drink?" she whispers to me. "Seriously."

"Well, most people are better at it than you are."

She sighs. "You know, if someone got a picture of me last night, I might be back to square one with the media."

After all she's been through, I expect Dee to panic over the prospect of more bad press. But, earlier this week, her publicity team convinced a website to post the original, unedited photo. The innocent version didn't make huge headlines the way the "nude" photo did, but real Lilah Montgomery fans knew the truth, and Dee has felt better about it since.

Dee chimes in again before I can try to placate her. "Actually, I'm glad it happened. The whole experience sparked a new idea for a song."

My face must have registered alarm because she quickly explains, "I'm not saying I'd replicate the evening just for song ideas, but it's the silver lining. Made me think of how often we make decisions that we know will hurt us later, just because they feel good at that moment."

I know nothing about that.

Dee reaches for her guitar, her eyes already distant. I love this part, watching Dee summon a song out of thin air. It's always the same. She hunches over her guitar, barely touching her fingers against the strings. Then she closes her eyes, trying to feel for the right chords. When she finds them, she strums a little louder, making sure they sound right in full tone. Next come the humming, wordless notes that will soon be accompanied by lyrics. She'll pause, scribbling a possible first line into her notebook, and then try again, using the words this time. This can go on for hours or even days, editing and fine-tuning each piece.

By the time we pull into the next rest stop, she's still getting started—no humming yet.

"Hey." She looks up at me. "Can you run over to Matt's bus for me?"

I look up at her from my copy of *Rolling Stone*. After last night, I don't know how to be around him. There's a growing attraction that needs to be snuffed out, and being alone with him in an enclosed space is not the way to do that.

Dee gives me her best pretty-please face. "We're trying to write that song together, and he has the notebook I was using yesterday. I'd get it myself, but . . ."

But gas-station-goers will see her and cause a riot. I know this.

"All right." I put my magazine facedown to save the page. "He'll know what you mean?"

"Yeah. The notebook. He'll know."

I step out into the summer sun and make my way to Matt's bus, but not before fluffing my hair a bit. His driver is taking a smoke break, so I bang on the bus door. I can't see through the tinted windows, but it takes only a moment for the door to snap open. Then I'm looking head-on at Matt, who's wearing nothing but blue jeans.

His phone is pressed to his ear. "Corinne? Let me call you back in a minute."

"Sorry to interrupt," I say, almost cringing with awkwardness. *Thanks a lot, Dee.*

"No problem. Come on in." His hair is wet, and he pushes it back from his forehead. "Close it behind you."

I step onto the bus and push the handle to shut the door. It's just the two of us on an empty bus, and one of us has his shirt off. Matt crouches in front of a suitcase, back muscles shifting as he riffles through a pile of neatly folded shirts, and I still haven't found words. He's clearly fresh out of the shower, and the whole bus smells clean—but not like "mountain rain" body wash or mall cologne. Soap-clean, simple and familiar.

"What's up?" Matt says, glancing at me. His voice is almost dismissive, like he's trying to brush me off.

"Dee wants the notebook back if you're done with it." I try not to linger on the plaid boxers peeking out above his jeans. He selects a blue T-shirt and shakes it out.

"Sure." He stands up, pulling the shirt over his head, and I notice a large tattoo on his left side. It's script—several lines of it—in black ink, which I didn't expect. Matt Finch doesn't strike me as the tattoo type.

He hands me the notebook, and I can't help but ask. Not only am I curious, but I'm also trying to get his attention. I can't seem to stop myself. "Tattoo, huh? Can I see it?"

Maybe this is a brazen thing to ask, but hey—he's the one who had his shirt off in the first place.

He tugs his shirt up and turns to the side. I lean closer, peering at the carefully inked letters. Clearing his throat, he says, "It's from the second verse of—"

"'Forever Young.' Bob Dylan," I finish. Matt's tattoo is lyrics from a song I love, written by a singer I love. And I do not use the word "love" lightly or often. He nods. "You're a fan?"

"Yeah," he says. "My mom always sang his songs to us when we were little."

The seven lines of text on his skin are followed by a date, from February of this year. "What's the date?"

Matt pulls his shirt down and answers without meeting

my eyes. "The day my mom died. My brothers and sister all got a block of the lyrics tattooed. Between us, we have the whole song. My dad got a lyric from a different Dylan song."

Though I'm not the crying type, my throat constricts. Suddenly, I forget about trying to attract his attention. I forget about trying at all. His mom died just a few months back. That's it. That's the sadness I feel emanating off his skin like sonar. His lopsided grin can't shield it—not from someone like me, someone who knows.

"Which one?" I ask, almost whispering. "Do you mind if I ask? Which song your dad got?"

I'm close enough to see his Adam's apple move as he swallows. "The last line from 'You're Gonna Make Me Lonesome When You Go.'"

My dad listened to that song on repeat—that and a few other painful songs, in the months after my mom left. But I don't have a negative association with that song. I love it in a way that feels sewn into the fabric of who I am.

"That's really beautiful." My voice is quiet. There it is: my accidental, Dee-like attempt at earnestness.

Matt gives a sad smile, his cheeks barely creasing into dimples. "Thanks."

"And I'm sorry you lost your mom. It's the worst." I say this because I think it might be nice to hear someone sympathizing with your pain. No one ever told me they were sorry about my mom or suggested that they understood how hard it was to have her leave. It's too awkward for people to broach, so they say nothing. At least, not to your face.

"Yeah, it is," he says after a moment, staring down at his feet. Then he looks back up. "Wait. Did you lose your mom, too?"

"Yeah. Literally." I shove my hands in my pockets. I don't normally volunteer this information—in fact, sometimes I lie about it. But I want Matt to know that I understand this part of him, at least a little bit. "She ran off when I was in third grade. Haven't seen her since."

"Oh my God." He looks horror-struck. "I'm sorry—I shouldn't have pried."

"No big deal."

Now his eyes clutch mine. We stay like that, staring at each other with a weird kind of intensity, until my throat beckons words on my behalf.

"So, um," I stutter. "I'll see—"

"See you in Arkansas, yeah," Matt says quickly, breaking the gaze.

I flee, still clasping the notebook in my hand. Dear God, how I wish that the notebook were a giant pack of cigarettes. Walking back to the bus, I practice what my therapist calls "self-talk." She meant it to be used when I'm on the brink of a bad decision, and pacing beside the highway, I'm certainly on the brink.

The self-talk concept is simple enough: no matter the noise around you—in my case, usually laughter and thumping music at parties or bars—find a quiet place in your mind and address yourself directly. For example: *Reagan, do you really think it's a good idea to shimmy your bra off so you can put it on the guy who passed out drunk on the couch?* Next, mentally answer your own question. *Sort of, yeah. Have you thought about the consequences? Yes. This guy will wake up on someone else's couch, wearing a bra. I'm doing it.*

Needless to say, it doesn't always work. But it's worth a shot. I close my eyes, internalizing my thoughts away from the rush of cars on the highway and the chatter of roadies on their smoke break. *Reagan, do you actually like this guy or do you just want him because you can't have him? I don't know. Maybe both. Have you thought about the consequences? Dee could feel betrayed, the press could find out that the whole thing was a sham, her reputation and integrity could be skewered yet again.*

By the time I reenter our bus, my resolve is solid: nothing can happen with Matt, ever. It's the one indelible line I have, the only one I'd never cross: Dee's trust.

Still, after I hand Dee the notebook and settle into my couch, my mind trails back to Matt's bare chest. Even his abs don't interest me as much as the inked sentences across his ribs, and I feel a strange jealousy. Matt got to know his mom, and he loved her enough to get a tattoo commemorating that love. I technically have two mothers—the biological mother who left me and the stepmother my dad married—but neither of them feels like a mom. It seems as if there's only a tiny lexical difference between "mom," "mother," and "stepmother," but that difference matters. That difference can leave a moon-crater-sized dent in your childhood.

The press often calls Dee's small-town-girl rise to fame a Cinderella story, but I'm the one saddled with an evil step-mother. Don't get me wrong. The other women my dad dated were no better—mostly bottle blonds bathed in cheap perfume.

With neatly combed, mousy hair and her local librarian job, Brenda isn't like any of those other women. She's the only one who never stayed the night, never bustled out awkwardly in the morning, shirt on inside out. My dad was fun before Brenda. It took us some time after he got sober, but we were figuring it out. The more I spent time with my dad, ordering pizza and watching movies, the less angry I felt. But then he ruined everything and proposed to Brenda. He didn't even ask me first, nor did he seem to notice my resistance.

They got married the summer before I started high school, and the past three years have wedged us farther and farther apart. Brenda moved in, of course, and the more she hovers, the harder I thrash. When I'm actually in the house, I hole up in my makeshift dark room—my bathroom, where I change out the regular lightbulbs for red ones. Brenda is not, and never will be, my mother, and I don't hesitate to remind her of that. So . . . not exactly a tattoo-worthy relationship.

In the camera bag I brought on tour, I stashed a picture, stuffed up against the padded side. It's the only picture I have of my parents, taken when I was five—one of my first attempts at photography. The focus is imperfect, the angle is tilted, but it's still one of my favorites. I snapped it right as they looked at each other, smiling like two people who were in love.

Dee's still far away in songwriting land, so I sneak a look at the picture, tilting it toward me from within the bag. People always say I look like my dad, with the dark hair and faintly olive complexion that comes with Native American ancestry. But my mother's eyes are my same color green, her bony arms and legs mimicked by mine.

My mother left almost a decade ago, and my mind has since blacked out many of the places where she used to be. Maybe it's a hardwired coping mechanism, my brain keeping me from remembering the best and worst of her.

There's only one memory that stands out with sparkling clarity—from when we lived in Chicago. She took me to downtown in a subzero windchill to see the department store windows decorated for Christmas. I remember the bitter cold on my face, my puffy jacket zipped to my throat, my hands balled up in wool mittens. She was thrilled, skipping through the snowy streets, and I felt so special that she let me go with her.

With equal clarity, I remember arriving home to a mix of relief and fury on my dad's face. I huddled upstairs as he told my mother: *You can't just leave with Reagan and not tell me! I've been panicked for hours, not knowing where you two were or if you were okay!*

My mother, with her swinging, waist-length hair and skinny limbs, was like a wild horse. The more fenced-in she felt, the more she bucked. Six months after having me, she took off on a road trip, leaving only an *I'll be back next week* note on the coffee table. I only know this because of my dad's drinking problem. One night, two years after we moved to Tennessee, he'd come home from the bar bumbling poetics about how fast I was growing up. *You were so teeny when you were born,* he said. *I could hold you in the crook of one arm.* I'd mumbled *uh-huh* as I poured him another glass of water. He kept musing, mostly to himself—*When your mom ran away after six months, I was scared as hell because you were so tiny, and I didn't know what to do. But we stuck it out, me and you, kid, and I fed you formula bottles and rocked you every time you cried. We're gonna be okay, pal.*

Before long, he fell asleep sitting up in the recliner, and, though I braced myself by hugging a pillow, the tears never came. Crying doesn't change things, and it certainly can't change a person's nature. My mother was built to run, unfit to be settled. Throughout the course of my childhood, she took off for weeks at a time until, finally, she never came back.

Of course I wondered what I did wrong, but that's not why I resent my mother. I resent her because my dad loved her, and she destroyed him by leaving.

If I lost my dad the way Matt lost his mom, I don't know how I'd cope. My dad's not perfect, but he does love me. Even in the years he was drinking, he held down a job, put food on the table, got me birthday presents and everything I needed for school.

I give my secret picture one last glance, at my dad's smiling face. I may not have a mom, but, for maybe the first time ever, I feel lucky all the same.

CHAPTER EIGHT

Wichita

I woke up in Wichita with dread in my stomach, as thick and slimy as motor oil. This morning, Dee has her usual routine: early-morning radio shows, sound check, preshow press, concert. But I have my own appointment today, to get my cast off. I *hate* the doctor's office, with all the invasive questions and probing. I hate it so much that I consider, as I have so many times in recent weeks, wrenching the cast off with a pocketknife and a few tugs.

"Ugh, I feel so bad I can't go with you," Dee says, tapping her finger on my cast.

"Dee, seriously." I roll my eyes. "Not a big deal."

Peach ducks into the room. "Ready?"

Dee nods, climbing off the bed. She glances back at me. "You sure you're okay going by yourself? Maybe Peach could go with you. . . ."

"Nope," I insist. "I'm fine."

Peach chimes in. "Reagan, one of the drivers is scheduled to meet you in the lobby at nine. He has the address of the doctor's office that I booked, and your dad faxed the consent form, so you should be all set."

"Sounds good," I say, but Dee is still making a pouty face. "I'm fine. I am."

"Okay, okay." She smiles on her way out the door. "See you at the stadium!"

When I move into the suite area for coffee, there's a small, square package wrapped in sparkly paper. A card shows my name in Dee's handwriting. I open the card and read her message—*Happy cast-off day! Cheers to focusing on the positive.* Below that, in place of closing, there's a hand-drawn infinity symbol and a simple "D."

I slide my thumb under the wrapping paper. When it falls away, the box shows a picture of one of the nicest camera lenses that money can buy. She shouldn't have. I love her for it, but she shouldn't have. Of course she left it here instead of giving it to me in person. She knew I'd try to refuse it. Now that it's in my greedy, snap-happy hands, there's no way I'll let it go.

I fumble for my camera bag, eager to try the new lens. I brought three cameras: a point-and-shoot, a Diana for film, and my DSLR—a Canon Rebel. The Rebel is my inner photographer's spirit animal. I bought it with the employee discount from my on-and-off job at the local Supermart. I man the photo-processing station, but sometimes I quit or simply don't show up. They also occasionally fire me for not showing up . . . or for showing up but failing to be "customer service–oriented." I'm perfectly nice to the nonidiots. I teach the grandparents how to work their digital cameras; I show the harried moms how to edit slightly blurry pictures of their kids. A lot of the time I actually like it, so I always come back. And I'm so good at working with other people's photos that they always take me back.

An hour later, I've completely forgone showering. I meant to get ready, but I couldn't stop playing with the new lens. I snapped photos of the hotel bed and curtains, just to admire the quality of texture it can pick up. I can't wait to do this again with both hands bare, to lift the camera with my left arm unbound by plaster. That's the thought I'll cling to when nervousness becomes nausea in the doctor's office.

I need to be in the lobby in less than five minutes, so I glance in the mirror. Not too bad. My hair still looks decent, and a few quick swipes of eyeliner and mascara are enough to make me look human. I exchange my pajama shirt for a low-cut tank top and tiny shorts—the kind of outfit that says, "Look at my body, not my unwashed face." On my way out, I grab a pair of tall wedges and wrangle them on once I'm in the elevator. In the reflection of the mirrored doors, I stare at my forearm wrapped in blue plaster one last time.

The doors open to the lobby, and I see the chauffeur standing next to the concierge desk. Beside him stands Matt

Finch. I walk up to them, heels smacking against the marble floors, and the driver says, "Good morning, Miss O'Neill. I'll go get the car."

He leaves me alone with Matt, who I look up and down at. "What's up?"

"I'm coming with you."

"No, you're not."

"I am." The dimples form, and I hate him for being so cute. "Dee called me."

I hate her, too. "I'm a big girl."

"Actually, you're very little." His grin widens. If he keeps this up, I'm going to give the cast one last hurrah against his arm.

"I'm fine by myself."

"I believe you. But I don't want to let my *girlfriend*, Dee, down, so you're stuck with me."

Without moving my eyes from him, I say, "Fine. Whatever."

I can't resist another eye roll as I follow him to the sedan. We both slide into the backseat, and I use my good arm to buckle my seat belt.

"So," Matt says once the car pulls onto the main road, "since I'm going with you, I should probably know how you broke your arm."

"I fell in my high heels." This is my stock answer and exactly as much as I'm willing to reveal. I don't like to think about it, much less talk about it with someone who's barely more than a stranger. Matt Finch doesn't get a backstage pass to my life—only Dee does.

We're quiet on the way to the doctor's office, which turns out to be located in a building so generic that it's creepy. This office complex looks like somewhere I'd imagine a call center—not medical care. I'd prefer a doctor's office that looks established, like a hospital.

Matt opens the door for me, as if trying to prove his presence is helpful, which it is not.

"Okay, really," he says, trailing behind me down the hallway. I can tell he's grinning impishly without even looking at him. In the limited time I've known him, Matt Finch has never looked more delighted than when he is intentionally pushing my buttons. "You tripped in high heels?"

"Sure."

"That's what I'm supposed to say if someone asks me how you broke it?"

"Why would anyone ask you instead of me?"

"I don't know, Reagan—I'm not a psychic. But it could happen, and I'll feel like a jackass for not knowing the history of my friend's injury."

Apparently we're friends now. "Make something up."

There's a glint in his eyes, like he sees an opportunity reflected back at him, but I don't have time to worry about that. I'm too overcome by the stale smell of medical supplies— latex gloves and plastic-wrapped syringes and other forms of evil that lurk here.

We walk up to the office window, and I sign my name on a clipboard. The window opens to reveal a nurse, who hands me another clipboard of paperwork. She glances at me, then at Matt, and her face turns as pink as her scrubs. "Omigawd."

My eyes flick to Matt, who has turned on his polite-charmer smile.

"You're Matt Finch," she says. I focus on filling out the paperwork, ignoring the overeager look in her eyes. "Hi."

"Hi there." There's a pause as he glances at her name tag. "Kelly."

I look up from the form to roll my eyes at Matt. Smarmy celebrity.

"My friends and I love your music." She bats her mascara-thickened eyelashes at him, which is borderline tragic because she's at least in her midtwenties—too old for this behavior. Also, she really needs to dye her roots. "You're so talented."

"Thank you," Matt says. Kelly giggles at nothing until her idiocy catches the attention of an older nurse, who glances up from a chart and frowns.

"How do you know each other?" Kelly asks both of us. She's obviously trying to feel out whether I'm his girlfriend. I want to reach into the window and yank her dye job. Instead, I shoot her a look that I hope says: *Stop slobbering all over him and get this damn cast off my arm.*

Matt shifts uncomfortably. Like Dee, he won't outright lie about their "relationship." Instead, as usual, he gives a vague response. "We have a mutual friend."

His presence is grating on my nerves, so I lie for him.

"He's dating my best friend. She couldn't come with me, so I get him instead. Yay."

The younger nurse stifles a gasp. "Lilah Montgomery? I totally read that in *Stargazer*."

"Kelly," the older nurse says, finally intervening. "I need you in room seven. Zach, take over for her, please."

Kelly looks crestfallen as she retreats, and Matt glares at me for referencing Dee. From the back, a tall guy emerges in black scrubs. He looks too young to be a doctor, with almost-messy hair and half a day's worth of stubble on his face. *Now we're talking.* He sits in the chair that Kelly abandoned. "Sorry about her. She won't say anything—doctor-patient confidentiality."

"It's not a big deal." I hand over the paperwork, which he looks over while I examine him. Dark hair, blue eyes. *Hello, doctor.*

"Okay." He shoots me a sexy smile. "Come on back. That door's right there, and I'll meet you in room four."

I wish room four was a hotel room. Matt walks with me, but the polite smile is gone from his face. Quietly, he says, "Don't worry. I won't leave you."

"Lucky me." I push the door open, and all of my attitude dissolves inside me. The room is smaller than I expected—stiflingly small, in fact, with an industrial-clean smell that makes my stomach turn.

Fortunately, Zach enters right behind us, and I focus on him instead of the terrifying equipment in the room. He gestures for me to sit down on the padded table. I attempt to do so in a sexy way, but, with tissue paper crumpling beneath me, I can't quite pull it off. Matt settles into a chair on my right. After a moment, I tell Zach, "You're too young to be a doctor."

He smiles as he sits down on a stool in front of me. "I'm not a doctor. I'm a nurse."

"You look too young to be a nurse."

He gives me another grin, and the cast almost melts off my arm. "I'm twenty-three."

"Do you know what you're doing?" I raise my eyebrow a bit as I ask this, meaning it to be suggestive.

"I sure do." Smiling at him, I decide that I'd really like to know more about his bedside manner. "Let me just grab an Ace wrap, and we'll get this thing off of you."

"Get a room," Matt says when the door closed behind Zach.

I glare at him. "We'd have this one if *you* weren't here."

I meant this to piss him off, but instead he tips his head back and laughs. He shakes his head, grinning as if I'm some sort of cute pet that has performed a trick.

Zach returns and sits back down in front of me. I'm feeling vindicated in my wardrobe choices—short shorts, sexy heels. He selects a tool from the tray, and my appearance is suddenly the farthest thing from my mind. The tool in his hand looks like a handheld power tool gone horribly wrong.

"I'm sorry." I hold up my free hand to stop him. "*That* looks like a miniature buzz saw."

Nurse Zach considers this. "It kind of is."

"Oh no," I tell him, retracting my arm. Zach's sexiness is depleting by the second. "I'd rather chew this thing off my arm."

"I won't hurt you," he says, taking my arm back gently. "Trust me."

If it were as easy as simply obeying this command—*trust me*—my therapist could have saved us both a lot of time. I exhale, mouth in an O shape. I wish I could smoke in this room.

"It's just loud," Zach assures me. "And you don't have to look."

"Fine. Whatever. I'm fine," I lie. Saying it doesn't make it true.

The saw begins to whir, and he directs it toward my arm. Instinctively, my other hand grabs for something to steady myself. Before I even realize what I'm doing, I'm clutching Matt's hand. I hear him scoot his chair closer to me, but I can't take my eyes off the saw.

"Look at me," Matt commands, and I pull my eyes away from the rotating blade. I feel it touch the top of the cast, vibrating down my arm.

I settle my eyes on Matt. His eyes are unblinking, the color of worn blue jeans. I focus on them—the way his irises look bluer because he's wearing a heather-gray T-shirt—until I feel the pressure of the cast release. The buzzing stops, and I glance back in time to see Zach snipping the gauze off with scissors. It falls away from my arm, and I feel the air against my bare skin. Even room temperature feels cool to an arm covered by insulation for almost two months. My arm looks smaller, and I stretch my fingers. Gingerly, I bend my wrist up and down like a hinge.

"How does it feel?" Zach asks.

"Good. Kind of . . . stiff."

"That's normal," he says. He runs his hand down my arm, flipping it over to examine the other side. "Lost some muscle mass, which is also normal, but it looks good. The doctor will be in to check it out shortly. He'll walk you through a few exercises that'll help you regain mobility. You'll just have to go easy on it at first."

"Thanks." I remove my other hand from Matt's, embarrassed that I've been holding it this whole time. With my right hand, I touch my left wrist for the first time in two months. I'm relieved, but not at the sight of my arm or even the freedom of movement I've missed in these long weeks. No, I feel relief that healing is a real thing after all—that every day, I'm a little less broken than the day before.

Last April, I spent an evening at Dee's recording studio in downtown Nashville, taking pictures as she recut one of her songs for the album. She was on a short break before the tour began and, though she couldn't be in school with me those few weeks, I was glad to have her close. I felt good. Centered. My community service was done, I was halfway through therapy, and I hadn't gotten in any trouble since the arrest that earned me those activities in the first place.

On my way back home that evening, I stopped at Blake's apartment to grab a jacket I'd left there the night before. I hurried up the walkway to the two-story, faded stucco build-ing, past the overgrown shrubs. Someone held the door for me as I walked in—I don't know why I remember that. The door to apartment 2C was propped open, as always, since the building is too cheap for anyone to bother robbing it.

Blake's roommate was sitting in the living room with a few other guys, a cloud of pot smoke hovering over them. There were cans of beer strewn about, while the TV played a show that could only be interesting while under the influ-ence of drugs.

"In his room?" I asked.

His roommate's head lolled in my direction, giving me that glazed-over look. "I dunno."

I turned the doorknob into Blake's room, and the first thing I saw was skin. Lots of bare skin, tangled in his striped sheets. And a discarded bra on the edge of the bed, in a soft, girlie-girl pink color I would never wear. For a moment, I couldn't move. They both froze, too, at the sound of the door opening. My mouth couldn't find words, but my right hand somehow found a desk lamp. I didn't actually decide to hurl the lamp across the room, but my arm retracted on its own. The lamp was weightless against my fury, and then it was airborne. I heard the lightbulb break as it hit the wall, a few feet from Blake's head.

That was when the expletives started, firing toward Blake—bullets out of my machine-gun mouth—and everything became blurry. I remember the girl looking unapologetic and annoyed as she wrapped herself in a sheet. I remember the rage and embarrassment pulsing in my ears so loudly that I couldn't even hear the TV as I stormed out. I'm sure his roommate and friends were gawking, but anger blackened my periphery like blinders. I remember pulling the apartment door shut with enough force to rattle the entire doorframe. Then, for good measure, I turned around and kicked the door, leaving a scuff mark from the sole of my shoe.

I nearly ran toward my car, pausing only to dig for the keys in my purse. My hands were trembling, unsteadied by the toxic mix of anger and adrenaline coursing through my veins. By the time I grasped my keys, the building door was reopening from behind me. Blake chased after me, yelling my name. Despite my instinct to run, I whirled around to face him. He tried to tell me that it wasn't what it looked like.

"Really?" I screamed, my voice so shrill and uneven. "Really?"

Up close, he reeked of booze, which took me aback. Blake smokes pot because he hates the way that alcohol makes him feel—too out of control, he says. Call that a harbinger, call it a self-fulfilling prophecy, call it whatever you want. I should have known what might happen.

I don't remember exactly what I screamed at him. I think I was making up new profanity that the world had never heard before. In my mind, I can almost see myself from a distance, arguing with him outside the apartment complex. I can float above the memory and stare down at it like an

outsider—watching the girl in high heels, red-faced, screaming. The words we exchanged were so ugly, so emphatic. I
told him to go to hell; he told me I was overreacting like a
little bitch. When he said that, I pushed him away from me,
unable to keep my anger inside my skin.

Then he smacked me across the face so hard that my
whole body flew sideways. I felt the heel of his hand connect
with my cheekbone, and the noise pounded in my ear. Before
I even realized what had happened, I hit the sidewalk with a
horrific, time-slows-around-you thud. My wrist broke the
fall, cracking beneath me, and my knee bled through my
jeans. Pain pulsed through every part of me—that sort of
white-hot ache that halts your breathing.

Blake sank to his knees beside me, immediately remorseful. "Oh God, oh God, Reagan, I'm so sorry—shit, I don't
even know what happened."

I didn't cry. I *don't* cry. Instead, I called Dee.

At the emergency room, I lied. I told them I had fallen in
my high heels and that my parents were out of town. It was
like I couldn't yet say out loud what had happened. While I
was getting the X-ray of my wrist, Dee called my dad and
Brenda. Deep down, I knew she would. They were all waiting when I walked back into the lobby, carrying a prescrip-
tion for painkillers and a sadness in my chest that I couldn't
even begin to process.

"Geez, kiddo," my dad said, frowning. "We gotta get you
some flat shoes."

By the next morning, the bruise on the left side of my face was undeniable, and the police brought a sobered-up Blake into custody for parole violation. I didn't want to press charges; my dad threatened to kill him. It was lovely.

Here's the worst part: before I parked outside his apartment that night, nothing—not Brenda's disapproving looks, not the gossip of my classmates, not my arrest—made me realize how badly I was treating myself. Blake disrespected me doubly, in a matter of minutes, and I couldn't believe how far it had gone. As I lay there on the ridged concrete, my mind pressed the zoom-out button, so far out that I saw the whole picture. Once I did, I wanted to laugh at the ludicrousness of it and shake myself by the shoulders, screaming: *What the hell are you doing?*

The fog lifted from the scenes of my life, so clear that I couldn't believe I'd never seen it before: I'm better than all this. I'm better than all the losers I'd been dating for the cheap thrills. My therapist said my "high-risk choices" stemmed from a "distorted sense of self-worth." But I know I'm smart, and I work hard when I care about the work, and I actually have goals that matter to me. Sure, I regularly make shit decisions, but they're just choices, and I can make different ones. And finally, I *wanted* to.

So I've spent the past two months atoning, keeping to myself as I carried my own brokenness beneath the heavy plaster of a blue cast. This whole time, I've been trying to figure that girl out—the one who got too drunk at parties just for attention, the one who dated a loser pothead because it seemed cool. My wrist bone was the fault line between that girl and me, and, the moment it cracked, I separated myself from her. Sure, we share a wardrobe, a preference for heavy eye makeup and classic rock. That girl was me, but, especially now that the cast is off, I'm not her—not anymore.

CHAPTER NINE

Los Angeles

Scanning the scene from the inside of the limo, I feel almost light-headed—a surreal, dizzy feeling makes my legs shake. Luckily, I'm a pro at walking in high heels. It's the dress and the paparazzi that are throwing me off.

We're in LA and have been since yesterday. I've seen shockingly little of California so far: the airport as we hurried through it, the boutique where Dee and I were fitted for our dresses, and our hotel room. And now: the inside of a limo parked on the edge of a red carpet.

All around, stars are emerging from limos and town cars in formalwear, flanked by handlers who shuttle them from one reporter to the next. Backdrops and banners include the Dixie Music Awards logo, ensuring that celebrity photographs will advertise the show. Event workers signal limos to pull in, corralling people across the red carpet to prevent bottlenecks. Waist-high gates keep the media fenced out, and all the reporters are screaming first names, asking for interviews. Behind them, fans cheer in the stands, so loud that we can hear them from inside the limo.

Matt is waiting in the limo behind us, with another publicity manager from the record label. He'll be taking on the red carpet solo, occasionally meeting up with Dee for pictures of them together. It's all part of the label's attempt to market Matt to the country music set.

"Ready?" Dee asks, forming her Lilah smile. It's like she mentally turns a dial in her cheeks and voilà—zero to full-watt.

In a pale pink gown drenched in gold beading, Dee glows. Her hair is swept back, each blond hue picking up the blush and metallic gown.

"Yeah." But then I hesitate. "No, wait."

My dainty evening purse isn't big enough for my new lens, so I take a photo of Dee now. She stays seated with her legs curved primly to the side, her gown spilling over the car seat and floor. Her hand rests on the door handle: a starlet ready to emerge. But her smile slides back into Dee again— happy, if anxious. No photographer on the red carpet will get a picture like mine. Even through a lens, you can't imitate the connection between real friends. I turn to Lissa, who is sitting across from us in the limo. "Can you take a picture of both of us?"

"Uh-huh," she says flatly, glancing up from her phone.

I lean over toward Dee, and we both put on our trying-to-look-pretty smiles. Lissa presses the button dispassionately, proclaiming the picture "cute" in a dull voice before handing the camera back to me.

Dee claps as I pack the camera up and slide it under the seat. "It's like prom."

We attended a dress fitting at an exclusive LA boutique last night. It was after hours, with the curtains pulled over the windows, and the designer himself had crouched on the ground to examine the hem on Dee's bajillion-dollar loaner dress. You know—*just* like prom.

Laughing at her, I say, "Something like that."

Mack opens the door, and before Dee even has both legs out of the car, the entire mass of people roars in excitement. She smiles graciously, giving a quick wave to the crowd. After the photographers have a few moments to take shots of her getting out of the car, Lissa climbs out, ready for action.

With a deep breath, I place my glittery heels on the carpet. I feel a flash of self-consciousness as I stand to my full height. Previously, I'd planned to wear a castoff dress of Dee's—a black satin number that was a bit too small for her. Instead, at Dee's fitting last night, the stylist team insisted on putting me in a green chiffon dress. It's a bolder color than I'm used to, a deep emerald with a silver belt at the waistband. The sweetheart neckline shows off my shoulders and chest, and the tight fit pinches my waist into nothing. It's elegant and subtle, which is new for me.

Lissa ushers Dee to the first group of reporters and pho-tographers. I stand off to the side with Lissa, admiring the cameras they're using to snap pictures of Dee. She places her hand on her hip, turning toward several angles to allow them different shots.

We continue down the row, with Dee answering a ques-tion or two as we go. They're mostly straightforward: "Who are you wearing?" "What song are you performing tonight?" "How's the tour going?" A few questions are leading—ones about Matt or, more abstractly, Jimmy. Dee shuts them down with grace.

Most reporters haven't realized that Dee doles out face time based on respectfulness. If a reporter is especially nice to her, with thoughtful questions, she always remembers.

"That's Missy up there," Dee tells Lissa. Missy Jameson is a young entertainment-channel reporter who's always been kind to Dee. "I'm going to stop for her."

"Fine, but be quick," Lissa says. "You're expected inside shortly."

"I'm Missy Jameson, live with Lilah Montgomery." She speaks clearly into the camera lens while still managing to keep her mouth in the form of a bright smile. "Who, I might say, is looking just gorgeous."

"So are you!" Dee says, gesturing at Missy's tasteful black gown.

"Oh, stop," Missy replies, but she looks nearly giddy at the compliment. "So tell me. You're in the midst of your summer tour, which sold out every concert. How's it going so far?"

She tilts the microphone to Dee. "You know, it's the best experience of my professional life. Getting to headline with my songs, to plan the stage and the sets and meet fans every night. It's perfect."

"Matt Finch is now opening for you, an addition to the tour that came a few shows late in the game. Can you explain what led to his participation in the tour?"

"Sure." Dee wouldn't have explained this for another reporter, and she knows she's giving Missy a scoop here. "Matt and I share the same record label, and we've been friends for a while. He became available for the summer, and I begged him to come on tour. He's an incredible talent and an all-around nice guy. We're lucky to have him."

Missy beams, surely aware that she's logged her sound clip. "Are you here with a date?"

"Yes." Dee gestures in my direction, motioning for me to come into the camera's shot. "My best friend, Reagan."

I keep my stilettos planted firmly on the carpet, avoiding her gaze by toying with the bracelet on my wrist.

"Reagan is the friend mentioned in your song 'Open Road Summer'?"

"That's right," Dee says. I can feel her eyes burning into me.

Missy waves me in. Her teeth sparkle like five-carat diamonds—a gaudy tiara of a smile—but her eyes say, *This is live television. Obey me or else.*

I roll my eyes at Dee but stand in line with the camera anyway. Dee links her arm through mine, and I try not to think of the people watching from our hometown. And by "watching" I mean "judging." I know what they're thinking—that I don't belong here, Reagan O'Neill with her police record and trashy ex-boyfriend.

"Hi, Reagan. What's it like being best friends with one of music's rising stars?"

I look over at Dee, who is smiling at me encouragingly. Why she trusts me to say something appropriate is beyond me, but I decide to do her proud. "She's the best friend I could ask for, but it actually has nothing to do with her being a rising star."

"I paid her to say that," Dee quips, and I want to laugh, but I stop myself. I don't want to have a sort of laugh-face-double-chin on national TV. It's hard to believe that Dee has to think about that kind of thing all the time.

There's loud sigh from behind us, and we both glance back. Lissa's lips are pursed as she pointedly glances at her watch.

"I'd better get going," Dee says. "Nice talking to you, Missy!"

As we turn away, I can hear Missy speaking to the camera again. "That was a few questions with Lilah Montgomery. She's performing tonight. One of her . . ."

We're out of earshot, passing more reporters who scream her name. She stops one more time to pose, gamely spinning as requested.

Once inside, Dee is whisked off to do some sort of back-stage prep for her performance. I find my name on a seat in the third row and I slump down, happy to relax my posture in this fussy dress. Lissa will be sitting in the very back with the other publicity people. Glancing around at the seats near mine, I recognize a few names of country music stars. So far, there are only a few celebrities in the room. Most are milling around, talking with their dates and to one another.

"Hey," Matt says, plopping down next to me. Whoever organized the event put Dee on the aisle, then Matt, then me. This arrangement allows the camera to get easy angles of the two of them sitting next to each other and honestly, it pisses me off. I'd much rather sit next to Dee. Matt glances over, taking in my dress. "Wow. Look at you."

I dodge this. "How was the red carpet?"

"Loud. Did Dee do okay?"

"Perfect, as usual. Most reporters were pretty tactful, so it was good."

"Not with me." He shakes his head. "Some jerk asked if I was sleeping with Dee. Not dating. Sleeping with."

My stomach clenches in anger. "What did you say to him?"

"Nothing. I walked away. What else could I do?"

"Say that you're sleeping with that reporter's daughter. Or wife."

He laughs. "I'm sure that would have gone over great."

In front of us, there's a young guy in a well-fitting tuxedo and white cowboy hat approaching. He walks slowly, sauntering like a true cowboy.

"Matt Finch," he says, widening his arms. "Long time, my friend."

I busy myself with examining my nails while Matt hugs him and clasps him on the back, guy-style. "Chet Andrews. How the heck are you, man?"

"Things are great," he says, nodding. In a quieter voice he adds, "You guys doin' okay?"

"Yeah, we're good," Matt replies. "Better. Tyler's wife just had their first baby, so that's been huge for all of us."

"I heard that!" Chet says. "Congratulations, Uncle Matt. Glad to hear some good news for y'all. Is this your date?"

I look up from picking at my nails like an elegant lady.

"Actually, she's Dee's date." Dee must know Chet or Matt would have called her Lilah. "Her best friend, Reagan."

Three years since Dee's first album dropped, and I'm getting more than a little sick of being introduced as "best friend Reagan." I don't begrudge her the fame—*obviously*. I just don't want it to define me. But I take a note from my gracious best friend and offer him my hand. "Nice to meet you."

Chet lets out a low whistle as he shakes my hand. "Prettiest girl in the room, and this guy wasn't even gonna introduce me? Some friend!"

Matt laughs, clapping him on the arm. "You comin' to the after-party?"

"Better believe it," he says. "I'll catch up with you there."

They hug again, and Matt says, "It's so good to see you, man."

After Chet has gone, I ask, "Old friend?"

"Yeah. We met when we were really young. Chet's a good guy."

As the night continues, I notice that the whole country music scene seems surprisingly close-knit. When Dee gets up to perform, the crowd goes crazy. Tonight, she sings "Middle of Nowhere, Tennessee," the version with her full band. The back screen projects a field of wildflowers, and I'm wishing I had my camera. At the last chorus, Dee's band cuts out, and she sings with just her acoustic guitar. Everyone joins in, the mingling of some of the world's most famous voices.

"Old country home, you know it's where I belong," the crowd sings. *"It's the only place for me—middle of nowhere, Tennessee."*

After the last note hits, the stage goes black. The audience is on its feet, cheering like Dee is its collective five-year-old daughter who has just performed at her first dance recital. The lights come back up, and Dee waves to everyone. A light pops up on either side of the stage, counting down three minutes of commercial break.

From in front of us, a guy wearing a turquoise bolo tie turns around and says to Matt, "That little girl is goin' places."

Matt shakes his head solemnly. "Don't I know it."

There's a reason why reporters aren't allowed into award-show after-parties: the parties are wild. Country royalty, and other various celebs, make repeat visits to the bar while the dance floor nearly shakes from overuse. I'm washing my hands in the restroom and, here, in the quiet by myself, it feels bizarre—that outside the door is a crowd of people I usually see only on TV.

When I emerge from the restroom, I wander toward the last place I saw Dee and Matt. They'd been mingling with industry professionals in the lounge room, but they don't seem to be here now. I head to the main room, where our reserved table sits near the edge of the dance floor.

I'm only a few steps in when I spot Matt on the dance floor, swinging around some leggy brunette in a thigh-grazing black dress. I survey her appearance, which is so *obvious*—long hair in full curls, skintight dress, and stacked heels. This look is amateur, the one I'd resort to if I was feeling lazy. I thought Matt had better taste than that.

I can't find Dee, and the awkwardness of standing around alone overpowers me, so I turn toward the bar. The glasses of champagne are huddled together on trays at the end of the bar, waiting to be grabbed up by tuxedoed servers. I lift a glass to my lips, but I pause at the sight of my own reflection. The back wall of the bar is a mirror, peeking out between the hundreds of liquor bottles on display. So I raise my champagne glass just barely—a toast to myself and to the broken girls past, present, and future. To all of us who can't outrun our messes. Or stop making them.

The champagne is sweet, fizz tickling my tongue, and it tastes like abandon. Like recklessness. Old Reagan would drain it and grab for another, but New Reagan decides to savor it. One, and only one. A few more sips and my whole body loosens like corset strings, tension unlacing and giving way to a deep sigh.

When I return to the main room, Matt's mingling with Dee and the grown-ups again, so I head straight for our table. It's near the dance floor, a perfect view for people-watching. But when I get close to the table, I see it's already occupied by one person—a guy in a cowboy hat. He stands up when I get to the edge of the table.

"Well, hello again." It's Chet Andrews, Matt's friend from before. He tips his hat at me.

I look him up and down, debating whether the hat-tip thing is cheesy or cute. He gives a lopsided smile from beneath the hat. Cute. "Hey."

"What happened to your compadres?" he asks, pulling out a chair for me. I sit down and glance back up at him. He almost reminds me of Jimmy, a sweet, small-town boy with a little bit of swagger. "I was gonna sit here and wait for them, but they're takin' forever. I was gettin' lonely."

"They're *hobnobbing*," I tell him, recalling the exact word that Lissa used earlier. He sits down next to me, settling back into his seat. "That's a country thing, right?"

Chet's grin widens. "Mind if I hang here with you for a while?"

I quickly assess the situation. If Matt is to be believed, Chet is a nice guy, but I'm not really into nice. Nice, in my experience, equals boring. New Reagan will give it a shot, though. "Sure."

I hope Matt comes back in time to see my proximity to

Chet. And I hope he likes it as much as I liked seeing him on the dance floor with that random, overdone girl.

"Champagne?" Chet asks, reaching toward an open bottle at the center of the table.

I wrinkle my nose, already disappointed by my answer. "I shouldn't."

"Not a drinker?" He pours himself a glass.

"On probation, actually," I tell him, smiling as I relish the shock value. "For drinking."

"Get outta town." He's grinning again. "Nice girl like you?"

I laugh because he's obviously shocked behind his easygoing smile. "Yeah. Sure."

"So, Miss Reagan." Chet leans back in his chair, his eyes never leaving me. For being in a room full of people, he's good at remaining undistracted. It feels nice to have someone's full attention. "What's your story? All I know is that you're best friends with Dee."

"I am." I nod, tracing my finger against the tablecloth. Blinking flirtatiously, I glance up at him. I'd rather be in control of this conversation. "You always wear that hat?"

"Not always. Why?"

"I feel like I can't see you." I duck down, moving my face a bit closer to his, almost under the brim of his hat.

"Okay." Chet grins. "Fair enough."

He removes the hat, revealing sandy-blond hair in an unexpectedly short cut. He ruffles it with his hand, giving it a cute-messy look. In an act of overfamiliarity, I reach up and smooth down a piece on the side. This isn't something I'd normally do, but I'm hoping that Matt comes back any moment now.

"See, now it's like talking to a real person," I say. "Instead of some guy on the cover of a country album."

"You're a piece of work, aren't you?" He shakes his head. "Are you Dee's age?"

I nod. "Going into senior year."

"Planning on college next year?"

"Definitely."

"For?"

"Photojournalism."

"Now we're getting somewhere." He stretches his arm over the back of my chair, a matching gesture of familiarity that doesn't feel out of place. In fact, I adjust in my chair so we're sitting a bit closer. "How'd you get into photography?"

"I took a class my freshman year."

He nods, and I take the pause as an opportunity to turn the questions on him.

"So," I say, leaning in. "Is Chet Andrews your real name?"

"Oh boy." Tipping back his head, he lets out a surprised laugh. "What a question."

My smile widens, encouraging him.

"Okay," he says, tilting his head toward me conspiratorially. "Get this."

I look right back into his eyes, our faces close.

"My given name is Andrew Chetterson."

With that, I laugh genuinely. "Really?"

He nods, almost proud. "The label wanted to flip it. More marketable or something."

"I like it," I tell him with a smile. It's a real smile—not the one I use for most endeavors of flirtation. Chet is more than just nice. He's a happy surprise, a pleasant distraction amid Matt's groupie-wrangling.

I've got him locked in—I know I do. But, without warning, Chet pulls his arm away from the back of my chair.

"I'm not going to make a move on you," he announces.

What the *hell*. I know when a guy is interested, and, up until now, Chet has been interested. I try to recover quickly, raising my eyebrows. "Playing it cool, huh?"

"Not exactly." Chet smiles. "Look, Matt's my buddy, and I'm not gonna mess with someone he's interested in."

"He's not." I can hear my own voice, and it sounds defensive—almost overwrought.

Chet nods to a spot across the room. "Then why does he keep looking over here to check up on us?"

Glancing in that direction, I see Matt and Dee chatting with an older gentleman in a crisp tuxedo. Dee speaks animatedly, hands moving, while Matt seems fidgety and distracted. Sure enough, he turns to glance at our table. I look away.

"I don't know what you mean," I say. "He's dating my best friend."

"Now, we both know that's not true."

I cross my arms on the table. "Yes, it is."

"Oh, c'mon. I know 'em both. He talks about her like she's his sister. I'm nobody's fool."

"Well . . ." I scramble to prepare a cover-up lie for Matt and Dee, but Chet puts up his hand to stop me.

"I'm not askin'." He smiles kindly. "So you don't have to tell me a thing."

I clamp my mouth shut.

"All right," he says, setting down his empty champagne flute. "I've now had a few drinks, and the urge to dance cannot be stopped. Can I interest you in a spin around the dance floor?"

"Depends," I retort, arching an eyebrow. "Are you going to boot-scoot or whatever?"

He takes my hand, leading me forward. "You'll have to find out."

Chet isn't kidding. He literally spins me around the dance floor, with the confidence of a cowboy who's done his fair share of line dances. Near us, I notice when Dee and Matt join in the dancing, and I know the whole room is watching the two of them. They give their audience a show, looking believably enamored of each other. It's not especially fun for me to witness.

The fast song winds down, transitioning into a ballad, and I feel a presence beside us.

"Can we cut in?" Matt asks.

Chet winks at me, like he knew this would happen, and he slides over to Dee. They're cute together, both blond and down-home charming. But my mind flashes to Jimmy's face, and I wonder if Dee will ever look right next to anyone else.

Without a word, Matt wraps his arm around my waist. I place my arm around his neck, our free hands meeting at our sides. Close up, I can smell bourbon on him. Great. A cute boy and whiskey. It's like a two-for-one deal on my worst vices.

"So. Having fun with Chet?"

Maybe he's jealous after all. I smile. "I *was.*"

"Must be hard, fending off all the guys."

"Oh, like you're one to talk." I roll my eyes. "All those pretty girls who wear basically nothing to your shows. They run up afterward like: *Oh, Matt Finch. You're so dreamy.* And you're like: *Ladies. One at a time.*"

As I imitate Matt, I use a deeper, pompous voice.

Matt's jaw drops. "That is *not* how I am. Those people are fans. They buy my music. I'm *polite* to them."

"Sure you are." I wink at him, the way he always does at me.

His mouth stays open, his eyes boggling, like he can't believe I think this—which I don't, really. I only said it to get under his skin. He's under mine, and I enjoy returning the favor.

Matt scoffs, trying to recover. "Look, Chet's a nice guy and a decent dancer, but can he do this?"

Before I can ask him what *this* is, he dips me low, my knees bending automatically. He doesn't even give me time to react before pulling me back in, directing our arms so that I'm pressed against him, even closer than before.

"Trying to make Chet jealous?"

"What? No." Matt grins, completely unembarrassed.

"Why would I be? I mean, we both know you're going home with me."

"I'm going home with Dee."

"Details." I can feel his breathing, his chest rising and falling against mine. I'm struck by how different this feels from the last guy I was pressed up against. Blake is tall, with amber eyes and a sinewy form. His body moves with a slow grace, almost feline. Of course, his constant state of bodily relaxation is a direct result of marijuana. Compared with him, Matt feels solid. He might not be as tall—it's hard to tell since everyone is taller than me—but his chest is broader, his limbs sturdier. There's a density to him, so much that his body feels reliable, like he could lift me up or simply stay planted beside me.

We continue swaying, Matt holding me closer than he should. His cheeky grin falls away and so does any doubt that he thinks about me the way I think of him. Even though nothing can happen, it feels nice to have an excuse to be chest to chest, his hand clasping mine. I look straight into his eyes, imagining things that I shouldn't be imagining. I'm glad I didn't have any more champagne, because champagne makes me stupid. The champagne would want to undo his bow tie, unbutton his shirt enough to expose his bare throat, and that is just for starters. Soon, his nose is nearly touching mine, and we're getting too close, too careless. People are watching him—Lilah Montgomery's supposed boyfriend—moving slowly to the music with her best friend locked inside of his arms.

Using the willpower that is still so new to me, I take a step back, putting space between us. It feels like pulling two magnets apart.

"Good call," Matt whispers, as if my distance has broken some sort of spell. "Sorry."

I nod, unable to speak. Now, backed away from him, I can see his face better. We stay this way for the remainder of the song, at a modest distance and looking at each other head-on. The unbroken eye contact should feel awkward, without a word exchanged between us, but it doesn't. We're saying a lot within the silence: *We can't* and *I know* and *But I want to* and *Me too*. The effort of restraint burns in my chest—a physical ache from holding back.

"Okay," Matt says when the last chords of the song play. But he doesn't move his arms.

"Okay," I repeat.

We're breathing in and out at the same fast pace, and I'm such a goner. When his hands drop from my body, it feels like withdrawal, like I could develop the shakes. But it's worse than my usual addictions. I'd throw my emergency pack of cigarettes into the Pacific Ocean if it would make everyone in this room disappear. It was way too easy, forgetting Dee's career and how precariously Matt Finch has glued her tabloid reputation back together. I may want him, but Dee needs him—or, at least, her media presence does.

And as someone who's prone to addiction—genetically, behaviorally—I know there's only way to handle Matt Finch. Quit him, cold turkey.

CHAPTER TEN

Los Angeles

We're up preposterously early for a magazine photo shoot, the three of us crammed into the backseat of a town car. Matt and I have both been quiet this morning, each silently choosing to ignore last night. Dee's nodding off between us, and it's a relief that we're separated. If I had sat right next to him, if my leg slid against his as we make a sharp turn, then the car would be pulsing with even more awkwardness than it already is.

The car pulls into the parking lot of a high school, where their photo shoot is taking place. Palm trees are staked across an impossibly green lawn—the exact way that you imagine a high school looking when you've seen too many movies.

"Holy crap," I mumble, sitting up to peer out the window. "The ocean is, like, two streets away from this school."

Matt nods. "It'd be hard to show up for class with the waves two blocks away."

I snort. "It's hard anywhere."

A handler appears, poised to shuffle Dee and Matt toward wardrobe and makeup. Peach and Lissa are in another car, but they haven't arrived yet. As usual, my mind flits from lack of supervision to the possibility of escape. I can't stay here, with Matt and my wandering mind, and sightseeing sounds like the deep breath I need. I'm even wearing flats for once, thanks to stiletto blisters from last night, so I can stroll the streets of California with ease. At the prospect of scenic alone-time, I congratulate myself on having the foresight to bring my camera bag, stuffed full with my DSLR and new lens.

"Hey," I say to Dee, nudging her arm.

She glances over at me, blinking heavily. If she doesn't get a nap in somewhere, no makeup artist in the world would be able to cover her dark circles.

"I'm gonna go see the beach, okay?"

"Sure. You wanna take the driver?"

"Nah," I said. "I'll walk, and I won't be gone long. I want to scope out the camera equipment they use for your shoot. Maybe steal some of it."

Dee laughs, but then stops herself, like she's debating whether I'm actually joking.

Matt wrinkles his nose at me. "I'm jealous."

"Me too," Dee says wistfully. "Have fun."

The handler—a stylist's assistant, a photographer's intern, whatever she is—shifts impatiently, and Dee turns to go inside. Denying my urge to make eye contact with Matt, I move toward my freedom. The nearest street is lush, brimming with neatly trimmed trees, pops of red hibiscus, and spiky palm leaves. Rodeo Drive didn't do it, a Hollywood red carpet event couldn't do it, but this—the lushness, the quiet morning, the nearness of the ocean—*this* feels like a trip to California.

The air smells salty and fresh as I wind my way down the streets. As I pass by each sight, I snap pictures of the Spanish-style homes, the railings painted bright aqua, the leather-skinned man walking a hairless dog. Following no direction but my own wanderlust, I eventually come across a long pier. It extends into the ocean, waves slopping against its sturdy legs.

I walk the length of the pier, lifting my camera to the horizon. The ocean water hits the horizon line right beneath a bed of clouds, and I take a picture, even though I wish I could be here for sunset instead. It'd be the perfect vacation photo—a postcard image: *Greetings from Manhattan Beach, California!* On the back, I'd write: *Dear Old Me, Wish you were here. It'd be a lot more fun if we were doing things your way. Love, New Reagan, who is still trying.*

After a while, I wander to a nearby café for a coffee and some sort of health-nut bran muffin. I pace the length of the pier before finding a spot on an empty bench. Soon, the promenade begins to fill with joggers in nylon shorts and older men in straw hats. I savor my solo California morning the way I'm savoring my coffee: slowly, taking in each moment. When I'm done, I take my time going up the streets back to the high school.

I'm not ready to face reality yet—the reality of at least half the summer left, trying to keep myself from Matt. Thinking about him is an unnecessary complication and the last thing I need.

At the set, production is in full force. A tall security guy in a black T-shirt decides that my tour VIP pass suffices as proof that I belong here, and I roam the halls looking for Dee. Even in a school as beautiful as this one, the smell of K–12 education curls under my nose—the stale scent of lockers and tile cleaner and years of desk drool from back-row naps. I hear Peach's voice, and I follow the sound.

She's in a large classroom, with all the desks pushed to the back to make room for lighting and assistants. They have Dee in an argyle sweater and pleated skirt, posing in front of a blackboard. Rows of white chalk read: *I will not write songs during class. I will not write songs during class.* The photo shoot is for the September back-to-school issue, and Dee will, of course, be on the cover—probably next to an all-caps title: *QUEEN OF THE SCHOOL SCENE.*

"I'm not sure about this," she tells me as the on-site beauty team sweeps in to reapply her makeup. "It seems snotty, posing like high school royalty."

"I mean, it's cutesy," I admit. It's worse than cutesy; in fact, it's trite and cheesy. And so not who she was in school.

But everything has been set up already—no use in stressing her out now. "It's not that bad."

"I guess." She rolls her eyes, her false lashes nearly reaching her eyebrows. This display of attitude makes it even clearer: she needs some sleep. "Did you have a good time at the beach?"

"Yeah, I went to—" I begin, but she cuts me off with a sigh.

"Never mind. Don't tell me," she says, her eyes pleading. "I'm so jealous and tired that I could cry off all my makeup."

I give her a pitying smile, and she sighs again. "Will you go check on Matt? I haven't seen him all morning."

As she says this, I watch the makeup artist's eyes flicker with interest. Even the people closest to celebrities seem desperate to know the juicy details. I nod, taking off for the other side of the school. The empty hallways are dim, echoing only the soft padding of my ballet flats.

The magazine is shooting Matt for their "Hottie of the Month" column. He mimed barfing when he told me, claiming that the record label's publicity department insisted. Having Dee and Matt in the same magazine will do wonders for magazine sales and for the rumor mill. That's what Lissa would call "win-win" and what I would call "whoring out my friends." Still, I'm curious to see Matt being photographed like the celebrity he is. It's easy to forget, day to day, that he's well-known enough to be in a column called "Hottie of the Month."

Stomach fluttering, I press open the door to the boys' locker room, entering as quietly as I can. A team of people are manning the lighting equipment—stretched black umbrellas on metal rods and a few freestanding spotlights—and it all points toward Matt. He looks almost unrecognizable, wearing a football jersey and posing with one leg up on a weight-lifting bench. I bite down on my lip, trying not to laugh. It's so un-Matt-like, the whole jock-guy stereotype.

Moving closer, I have to admire the scene, despite its discord with Matt's actual personality and interests. His hair has been styled with a significant amount of hair product, making him look tougher than his usual "sweet-hearted musician who's skipped a few haircuts" vibe. I like it.

"A few more and then we go outside," says the photographer, who is gauntly thin with a mass of wiry curls. She holds the huge-lensed camera with a slack wrist, like she's so used to it being a part of her hand that she forgets it's there. My hands would shake if I held a camera that powerful and expensive. I wonder what other publications she works for, which countries she's traveled to. She must have a hell of a career, to be that relaxed with a five-thousand-dollar camera.

Matt nods complacently at her and then catches my eye. I waggle my fingers, teasing him even with my wave. In return, he rolls his eyes at me, which only makes him hotter. What can I say? My favorite indulgences these days are boys with bad attitudes and shoe sales.

"Can we lose the shirt, love?" the photographer asks.

Matt's face falls, and all semblance of confidence with it. This strikes me as odd. I've seen Matt shirtless, and there's certainly nothing to hide.

"I, uh—" he stammers. "I don't think so."

"Let's not be prudish," she quips hurriedly, fiddling with her beautiful camera. Matt lifts his hand as if to place it on his hip, but instead he rests it against his side. Then it hits me—his tattoo, the lines of black script on his left side. He'd have to expose the inked memorial, which would beg questions about the loss of his mom. Matt can take care of himself, but protectiveness surges inside me all the same. Lissa's not in the room, so I take matters into my own hands.

"He can't," I say authoritatively, stepping forward.

The photographer looks me up and down, almost amused. "And you are . . . ?"

I ignore her, flattening my voice into a Lissa impression. "Shirtless or otherwise nude photos are prohibited per Mr. Finch's contractual obligations with Muddy Water Records."

Her eyes shoot to Matt, who lies seamlessly. "Exactly."

"Very well," the photographer says, looking exasperated. "Change into the formalwear and we'll move outside for the shots with both of you."

As the crew packs up, Matt comes toward me. Without heels on, I'm jarringly shorter, and it feels like he's looking directly down at me. His smoky-mountain eyes find mine, and I glance away.

"Thanks for that," he says quietly. "I owe you one."

My memory flashes to us dancing last night, and I douse the image out like the fire it is. I step back because even our proximity now could be suspicious, undermining the rumor of him and Dee together. And also, honestly, because he smells like Ivory soap, and I'm too tired to pretend I don't like it. "No big deal."

"Yes, it was."

"Matt!" a voice calls, bailing me out. "You ready?"

When he's out of sight, I exhale, putting my hands on my hips as I pace like a crazy person. *Get it together, O'Neill. You're better than this.*

I take a few minutes to collect myself before wandering outside. Dee's already out there, in a deep-blue homecoming gown that will certainly sell out the day the magazine is released.

In one glance, I recognize Dee's empty-stomach crankiness, and it's a three-alarm situation. With slouched shoulders and mouth twitching into a frown, Dee is letting her trademark perkiness falter. I dig around in my purse until my hand finds a small package of airplane peanuts from our flight here. An assistant flutters about the bleachers, testing the lighting arrangement while Dee stands with her arms crossed.

"Here." I hand her the package.

She lets out an enormous sigh and dumps half a handful of peanuts into her palm. With her mouth full, she says, "Thanks. I was about ready to eat my own arm off."

"That dress is couture," the stylist calls nervously before I can answer. The poor woman's eyes display sheer horror, like she's watching peanut salt fall onto the dress in slow motion.

"Oh no," Dee says sarcastically. "Well, good thing I didn't eat it."

I snort with restrained laughter. Grumpy Dee, rare as she is, sasses everyone in her path.. She holds a peanut out in front of her and makes a production of moving her mouth toward it.

"I've been here for hours, and they haven't offered me anything but water," she grumbles.

"Well, starlets are supposed to be used to starvation, I guess."

The makeup artist appears, and she doesn't even bother to hide her annoyance. "I need to touch up your lipstick now and make sure there's nothing in your teeth."

"That's what Photoshop is for," I snap, and the girl returns the glare before examining Dee's teeth as if she's competing in a dog show.

From below us, Matt emerges in a fitted khaki suit, complete with a trendy tie that brings out the color of Dee's dress. It's too sophisticated for homecoming, but he looks great. At least, he looks great until a prop assistant ducks in, sliding a sash over his chest. It reads: KING. She positions a plastic crown on his head. I can't help it. I cover my mouth with my hand, but the laughter will not be squelched.

He climbs up the bleachers while Dee receives her sash and crown.

"Are they kidding with this?" He gestures at his new accessories.

Dee shrugs, dusting peanut salt off her hands. The stylist looks like she's watching a horror movie.

"Let's just get it over with," Dee says, "so we can go home."

Home is our tour bus, which is waiting for us in Tucson, along with the band's buses and two semis full of stage equipment. Beside me, Matt flashes his best fake celebrity smile.

"Charming," I tell him.

"Hey," he says, mouth still stretched into an uncomfortable-looking smile. "Anything that'll get me out of here."

While Peach and I look on from down below, the photographers pose Matt and Dee. They stand at the edge of the bleachers in their regalia, pretending to wave at adoring fans.

"Can we get a kiss?" the photographer yells.

"No!" they yell back in unison, smiles still plastered on their faces.

Still, they clasp hands in solidarity, sharing a different secret than the rest of the world suspects. I know instantly that this'll be the shot—the one they use in the magazine. In this moment, Dee and Matt's connection is real. The look between them—the locked eyes and knowing expressions—is nothing more than a good friendship and mutual admiration between artists. I know better than anyone. But their display of affection is convincing, and I have to glance away. It's the same reason my dad can't have dinner with any friends who might order a beer. It's too damn hard to watch someone else get what you want.

And that's when my mind repeats Matt's sentiment exactly: get me out of here.

CHAPTER ELEVEN

Shreveport to Jackson

We make our way through the Southwest, Arizona to the Texas shows. After Austin, Dee's lack of sleep catches up with her in the form of a nasty cold. She has tonight and tomorrow, the Fourth of July, to recover. Lilah Montgomery has never canceled a show, and the fear of disappointing her fans is visceral to Dee. Faithful to the doctor's orders, she's on medication, vitamins, and vocal rest, communicating only on a whiteboard that Peach got her.

Peach is riding on the band's bus again, to avoid getting sick, but I won't leave Dee. Dee attends business meetings as a competent professional, but she reverts to a kindergartner once she has a cold. A *mean* kindergartner. But she's taken care of me during countless hangovers—with her special brand of love, served with a side of judgment—so I won't bail on her. Oh, and because there is absolutely no way I'm riding with Matt Finch.

After the trip to LA, I did something so completely pathetic that I can barely think about it without hating myself. I don't even know what compelled me. Well . . . actually, I do. Morbid curiosity, my competitive instinct, passive-aggressive jealousy: take your pick.

I searched for pictures of Matt's old girlfriends online.

Apparently I'm one of those girls who stalks a crush she doesn't have the nerve to act on. I cleared the search history immediately, in an effort to pretend it didn't happen. But now I know that the girl he dated while in the Finch Four was a long-haired brunette. I can't deny that she's beautiful— but it's such an uninteresting beautiful. Medium height, slender, with no features that particularly stand out. Beautiful but forgettable. Besides, based on the fact that she sold their breakup story to the tabloids, I assume she has the personality of a trash bag.

There were also a few photos from events he'd attended with a girl named Corinne. She's petite and curvy, a sort of guitar-shaped body. With freckles and a friendly smile, she's cute, but not in a threatening, Hollywood way. She's more like best-friend-in-a-rom-com cute.

Basically what I'm saying is that I think I could give either of those girls a run for their money. Or at least I could if Matt was really a consideration for me. Which he's not. In light of my girlfriend-stalking attempt, I've faced fact: getting too close to Matt makes me pitiful. No, thank you. Old Reagan sneers at New Reagan's descent into loserdom.

Across from me, Dee buckles into a hacking cough. It hurts my spine just to hear it. I get up from my couch and pull another bottle of water from the fridge.

Setting it next to her on the couch, I say, "Drink this. The doctor said tons of fluids."

She ignores me, scribbling on her whiteboard. When she holds it up, it reads in sloppy loops of handwriting: *At this stop, go ride with Matt.*

"No." I sit back down, settling my computer onto my lap. If I'm looking at my photo-editing software, then I can't look at her whiteboard.

"Reagan, I feel bad enough," she says, her voice croaking. "If you get sick, I'll feel worse."

"Stop talking. You'll make your throat worse."

Dee glares at me, which is impossible to take seriously. Her angry face looks as threatening as a kid's whose mom won't buy her a bouncy ball at the grocery store.

"I'm not going to leave you by yourself on this bus, not while you're coughing like a ninety-year-old who smokes six packs a day."

The bus pulls into the gas station, and Dee stands up as if she's planning to storm off the bus and tattle on me to someone.

"Dee, stay here. If you get out, it'll cause mayhem." There are already people taking interest in the line of buses. Having Dee's face on the side of them is not exactly subtle.

She plops back down with an exaggerated harrumph, but the bus doors open anyway. Matt climbs on, looking perfectly chipper. Easy enough, since he's not riding with the attitudinal equivalent of Oscar the Grouch.

"Hey, sickie," he chirps at Dee. "How ya feelin'?"

She wrinkles her nose at him and crosses her arms, clearly irritated.

"Don't take that charming expression personally," I tell him. "She's unbearably bratty when she's sick."

As if to prove my point, Dee flicks me off. Matt bursts out laughing at this complete diversion from her usual behavior. In retaliation, she scrawls on her whiteboard, then holds it up to both of us.

Stop laughing, it reads. *I'm on a lot of meds.*

It's true. Her pupils are dilated, and she looks a bit crazy. Then she rubs off the writing with her palm and scribbles something quickly.

She points the board toward Matt, but I can still see the message, which reads: *Take her with you. She's getting on my nerves.* There's an arrow pointing to me.

Traitor. "You'll just pawn me off on anyone, won't you?"

She rolls her eyes and squeaks out, "She's going to get sick. Make her go."

"What did I tell you about not talking?" I demand. Looking at Matt, I say, "She needs someone to keep an eye on her."

"Are you sure she can't stay?" Matt asks. "I was kind of hoping I could hang here with you guys. I'm lonely."

Dee considers this, returning to her whiteboard. *Want to write together?*

"Well," Matt says, laughing, "I *was* planning to screw around. But, sure, we can work."

By the time the bus pulls away from the gas station, Matt is sitting cross-legged on the floor between the couches. Dee's on her couch, guitar in her hands, and she's plucking out the chords they've already settled on. Matt hums along as they look back over their notebook.

"Oh, hey," he says, gesturing for her guitar. "Idea for the bridge."

Instead of strumming, Matt's fingers move over the strings in broken chords. The notes waft out of the guitar like weightless dandelion seeds. Dee nods enthusiastically, then holds up her whiteboard to him, and when he nods, she scribbles something else. Beside me, my phone alarm goes off.

"Medicine time," I announce, getting up.

Dee jumps to her feet and croaks, "I can get it myself. I'm sick, not helpless."

"Stop. Talking." I glare at her. "Peach left everything out on your bunk."

She hurries to the back, but not before rolling her eyes at me.

Matt's still playing, and I follow the sounds of one note touching the next. He's right. It's a good idea for the bridge of the song. "I like that."

"Yeah," he says. "But I'm worried it's too similar to this."

Matt switches to playing one of his own songs, which has

a simple title like "With You" or "For You" or something. The images of his ex-girlfriends pop into my mind, and I can't help but wonder.

"So," I say, "who'd you write it for?"

The chords stops. He looks up at me. "That's not fair."

"What's not?"

"You get to ask personal questions based on my songs."

"You don't have to tell me if you're embarrassed."

"I'm not embarrassed." He begins strumming again. "I just wanted to point out that you have an unfair advantage."

"So who was she?"

He smiles. "Amy."

"And?"

"And we dated for a long time," he says, looking down at the strings as they bend beneath his fingertips. This has to be the boringly beautiful brunette from the photos. "Then she got really into the fame."

"How could you tell?"

"She didn't want to stay in and hang out anymore. Always wanted to go out, be seen."

"So you ended it?"

"No." He shakes his head softly, in time with the chords. "She did. When I went back to high school for my senior year. She had no interest in dating a regular guy."

"I wouldn't say you're regular."

Matt looks up again, smiling as if he can sense the sass coming his way. "Oh no?"

"I mean, you are legally an adult, and yet you feel like it's okay to consume strawberry milk with a pound of Twizzlers. That's irregular to me."

"What I like about you is that you're sweet."

I decide to throw him a curveball by actually being nice. "I think it's cool that you went back to high school."

"Yeah?"

I nod. "I mean, I understand why Dee took her GED earlier this year and got it over with. But you can't go back later in life and be in high school again, you know? It's a big experience to miss out on, even if it sucks."

Matt looks thoughtful for a moment. "It must especially suck to be there without Dee."

He doesn't know the half of it. I've been trying my hardest not to think about spending this next year with the people in our grade. I always get invited to their parties—half because I'm a notoriously rowdy partier and half because I'm Lilah Montgomery's best friend—but I have no interest in going. I'll have to pick up a hobby for my weekends. Maybe knitting or watching documentaries. "It really, really does."

I don't like the subject being turned on me, shining a light on my vulnerabilities. "So. "Any Way You'll Let Me." That's for Amy too?"

"No." Matt smiles. "That one's for Corinne."

"A groupie? One-night stand?" I ask this even though I'm almost sure it's the cute girl from the photos. He looked relaxed with her, smiling genuinely.

"The opposite." He switches chords, softly playing the song in question. "My best friend in the world."

"Did you date?"

"I wanted to." He says this so straightforwardly that my stomach gurgles with acidic jealousy. "I've known her almost my whole life—literally the girl next door."

"You're not her type?"

"Guess not," he says. "Besides, she's been dating the same guy since sophomore year of high school, followed him to college in Ohio and everything."

"Huh." I begin applying the lyrics to my new information.

I want you because you make me laugh.
I want you because you get me.
But if it can't be the way I want it to be,
I'll love you any way you'll let me.

"Do you still love her?"

"Man," Matt says, meeting my eyes. "What is it with you and the questions today?"

"I'm trying to get to know you."

"You can't get to know me by asking my brothers' names or whether I'm a dog or cat person? You have to ask me if I love a girl I wrote a song for?"

"Yes, I do." Besides, I know his brothers' names, and he's clearly a dog person.

"Fine." He plays louder, as if trying to cover his answer.

"She's my closest friend—of course I love her. But not like that, not anymore. She's happy, and that's what I want."

"Does she know you're not really dating Dee?"

"Of course. At first she thought it was a bad idea, but she likes Dee."

"Who doesn't." For a moment, I feel another rush of gratitude for Matt, whose presence changed our entire summer. "It's a good thing you're doing for her."

"For Dee?"

"Yeah." My eyes find his, and I hope he knows how much it means to me. He pulled my best friend out of media quicksand, and he did it with grace and a sense of humor. "It was pretty bad before you got here."

Matt smiles at me, with no trace of his patented mischievousness. "It's not hard. I mean . . . travel, play music, hang out with two cool girls all summer. It's not exactly a sacrifice."

Dee finally emerges from the back, picking up her whiteboard before she settles herself into the corner of the couch. She holds up what she's scribbled to Matt: *Pretty sure you mean cool AND beautiful.*

Dee's hair is piled into a sloppy mound on top of her head. She's wearing a ratty sweatshirt, and her nose is chapped and red from continual tissue use.

Still, there's not a trace of sarcasm as Matt agrees with her. "That's exactly what I mean."

For the next few hours to Jackson, Matt keeps coaxing Dee out of her foul mood with music and laughter. The exploration of guitar chords, Matt's low voice, and Dee's hoarse giggling make a summer soundtrack I'll replay even when the tour is over—in the moments when I feel like being truly happy is an impossible puzzle, one I'm not meant to figure out. If you have a best friend you can laugh with and a few good songs, you're more than halfway there.

CHAPTER TWELVE

Jackson

By the next day, Dee is on the mend. She's still on vocal rest, downing cup after cup of hot tea with honey, but her eyes are less bleary. So far today, we've been primarily watching trashy television from the comfort of our hotel sofas. Dee's tucked under a blanket on one couch, perusing the comments on her website. I'm propped up on a pile of pillows on the other couch, reading a thick guide to college-application guidelines and standards.

The Fourth of July is a scheduled free day for the whole crew—a provision Dee made sure of when her label planned the tour. Everyone over age twenty-one on tour, including Peach, took off early for a restaurant on the river. I overheard that there would be a patio and lots of day drinking, and I'm more than a little jealous.

"Helloooo," a voice called at our door, followed by Matt's signature, rhythmic knock.

"I'll get him," I tell Dee, who settles further under her blanket.

Pulling the door open, I open my mouth to say hello, but Matt cuts me off.

"I'm so bored," he announces loudly, walking into the room. I release the handle, and the door heaves itself shut. "*So* bored. You guys have to entertain me."

"Then I hope you like reality television."

He settles down next to Dee, and she smiles over at him.

"How ya feeling, little lady?" he asks. Picking up my college guide, I stretch back out on the other couch.

"Better," she whispers. "Probably still contagious, though."

Taking the hint, he moves from the couch, and I expect him to sit down in the overstuffed armchair. Instead, he plops down at the end of my couch, lifting up my legs so there's space for him to sit. Before I can react, my legs are resting on his lap. This is totally not okay. This is how I might sit with Dee, not with a guy I am trying not to think about when I close my eyes at night. Pulling my knees up, I prop my book up against my lap.

Beside us, Dee grabs a handful of tissues and stands up.

"Going somewhere?" I ask, eyeing her.

Her cheeks flush, and it's not the fever. "Into the bathroom to blow my nose."

I struggle to keep from laughing. "Um. Why . . . ?"

"I'm not going to blow my nose in front of Matt! It's so disgusting!" Her voice is nasal, and she sounds completely congested. I've been sitting by her all morning and, I have to admit, her productive nose-blowing is not the cutest sound in the world.

Matt laughs uproariously as Dee shuffles to the bathroom. "Are you kidding me, Montgomery?"

She shuts the bathroom door and yells hoarsely, "Don't listen!"

Now Matt and I are both laughing. Shaking my head, I say, "Such a lady."

"She's cute," he says. It's an offhand comment and, moreover, it's a universally accepted fact: my best friend, Lilah Montgomery, is cute. But still, hearing him say it makes me flinch. He looks over at me and asks, "Whatcha reading?"

I peer at him over the book. Slowly, I slide it up so he can read the title: *Mastering the College Application: A Guide to Top Colleges, Strategies, and Requirements.*

"That's a good one," he notes, eyes flicking over the title.

Tilting my head, I study him with a new curiosity. "Are you thinking about college?"

"Um," he says, glancing away. "Yes. No. I don't know."

I blink. "That was an informative answer."

He sighs, as if I've caught him in some sort of compromising position. "Yes, I've been thinking about it for a while. Is that surprising?"

"Kind of. I mean, most people have to go to college before pursuing a career. You have a career, so . . ."

"I know." He runs his hand along the edge of the sofa. I close the book, now invested in our conversation. "But if I don't do it now, I don't think I ever will. I'm already a year behind people my age."

"I think you're a decade *beyond* people your age."

"But I'm not sure I want to do this forever."

Matt Finch curveball. He throws 'em low and outside. "Really? It seems like you love it."

"I do," he says. "But I want a family someday. Being a musician means touring, erratic schedules . . ."

"You can do that with a family. Lots of musicians do."

"Maybe I will. I just . . ." he trails off, looking out the window behind me. "I want options, you know? All my buddies from high school seem like they're having so much fun at college, and I guess I don't want to miss out."

"I think you should do it. At least talk to the label. Maybe you could go to school and keep working on stuff. Keep recording and touring over the summer."

His mouth pulls into a smile. "I didn't have you pegged as such a higher-education enthusiast."

Dee, emerging from our bathroom, chimes in, "Oh, she is. Reagan's grades are, like, amazing. Minus the disciplinary record."

She sounds much less congested, but I wish she would shut up.

"Dee," I say, giving her a warning look. Dee always talks about my grades like they're some big accomplishment. Schoolwork never came easily to Dee, but she always put the work in. To me, high school is like anything else: simple once you learn to play the game. Early on, I figured out how to study to the test. I get most of my homework done in study hall since I have nothing better to do, and I *never* take honors classes, even though I test into them. Yes, I skip class sometimes, but only classes that I know I can pass easily. And yeah, I go out on the weekends, but I save Sundays for sleeping off my hangover and doing homework.

"*Really.*" Matt's looking at me like I'm a creature on Animal Planet, newly discovered and exotic. "Academic achievement?"

"I have to pay for college, and I'm not exactly athletic, am I?"

Dee shakes her head, settling back onto the couch. "She's being modest."

I shrug. "Better grades, better options."

"So what's your number one?" Matt's still watching my face closely, as if nerdy glasses are going to manifest on my face.

"Number-one what?"

"Option. School choice."

"Oh." I wrap my arms around my legs. "Probably NYU."

"New York University?" His disbelief almost offends me. "Do you have backups?"

"Well, depending on whether I major in photography or photojournalism, maybe Boston University or Purdue. I'm also considering Vanderbilt and *maybe* Belmont."

"Wow," he says. "Those must be some really good grades."

I prefer to keep my academic record to myself, as to not tarnish my hard-earned image. The truth is that I have my sights on finishing in the top ten of my class. Now that I've quit drinking and Blake, I should have plenty of time to take down at least Daniel Estrada and Molly-Anne Mitchell. Those nerds are both so wrapped up in cocurriculars that they won't even see me coming. Reagan O'Neill, the girl featured in so many bathroom stall scribblings: in the top ten of her class. It'll be the ultimate "screw you" to the teachers who doubted me. It'll show my runaway mother that I made something of myself, if she ever decides to come looking for me. It's also my way of shoving it in Brenda's face that I don't need strict rules to succeed.

"So, what is there to do in this town?" Matt asks, bouncing his knees like a hyperactive child. "It's the Fourth of July; something good has to be going on."

"Let's see." Dee types something on her keyboard. "Hm. In the next town over, there's some sort of festival. Sounds like Founder's Fest. . . ."

"Oh, yes!" I say, sitting up excitedly. I love Founder's Fest in our hometown, with its cheap carnival food and sketchy rides. "We have to go."

Matt nods. "Um, *hell* yeah."

"Oh, yay, that'll be so fun for you guys!" Dee says happily, but the rasp in her voice is persistent. I got so excited that I forgot—of course she can't go.

"Maybe some sunshine would be good for you . . . ," I venture.

She shakes her head. "Even if I felt better, I don't feel like putting on some sort of disguise. If I don't wear one, we'll spend the whole day signing autographs. And if I go, we'll have to bring security, and Mack's off for the day. . . ."

"You're right. We'll hang here."

"No, no," she insists, waving her hands. "You guys should still go. I need some quiet time anyway."

I glance at Matt, whose eyes are unwavering on mine. It becomes a game of chicken, both refusing to back down.

Matt shrugs. "I'm game if you're game."

This is our own little poker table, hedging bets. And if he's calling, I'm raising. "Oh, I'm game."

And so, somehow, I find myself standing next to Matt Finch outside the hotel, staring at a shiny red convertible. We could have called a cab to take us—the festival is only a few miles away, but Matt insisted on renting a car. The front desk of the hotel booked it for us and had it delivered within an hour.

"Well, well," I say, surveying the convertible as Matt swings the keys around his finger. "Aren't you just a fancy celebrity."

He grins, hopping over into the driver's seat instead of opening the door. "I miss driving, that's all."

I do, too. I climb in the car and buckle up, and Matt revs the engine. Show-off.

"Besides," he says as he slides the car into drive, "it's part of the experience."

He's right. My hair whips around me, and I tilt my head back to watch so that all I can see is the limitless blue sky and the way we're outrunning every cloud. I wish Dee were here because this reminds me of her song "Open Road Summer." It's an open road, all right, and we're getting more of it than we ever bargained for. I pull my camera out of my bag, turning to Matt. His hair and shirt are fluttering against the wind, and his sunglasses reflect the white dashes on the road that we're passing now and now and now.

Right before we pull into a gravel parking lot, the festival crests into full view. The Ferris wheel stands tallest, spinning like the queen of a twinkling kingdom. I can already smell the food—the dense, sticky scent of summer.

Matt wastes no time. Pulling his baseball cap low to avoid recognition, he pulls me toward the first of many rides. In the Gravity Scrambler, my stomach rises to my throat until my whole being feels jumbled. I clutch my purse the whole time, protecting my camera. When we exit the ride, I struggle to walk in a straight line, and Matt almost topples over, laughing riotously. On the swings, I hold my arms out and close my eyes, pretending like I'm flying. When I glance over at Matt, he's doing the same thing. He even insists that we ride one of the kiddie rides, so we spend a few minutes sitting on plastic elephants, which move in slow circles.

The sun is setting as we climb onto the Ferris wheel. It's

relaxing compared with the rest of the rides, easing us up toward its apex. A Lemon Shake-Up perspires in my hand, occasionally dripping water onto my bare leg. The taste is achingly sweet, and my mouth moves to the straw like a hummingbird to nectar.

"So, is the tour what you hoped it would be?" I ask. I'm not proud of it, but I purse my lips around the drink's straw, trying to look cute in case Matt notices.

"Yes," he says, nodding, but he doesn't elaborate. "Is it for you?"

I nod, too. "Yeah. I can't believe it's July already."

What I mean is: I'm in complete denial that I have to face reality at the end of next month. Our car stops at the top, and we stare down at the festival below us. I can hear the low pulse of a local band playing cover songs, the rustle of water in the lake nearby, and the carrying laughter of kids our age—eating cotton candy and flirting with summer loves. The sun has melted down to the horizon line, leaving trails of orange and pink in its wake. In the distance, our hotel's roof peeks over the tree line.

"These rides are the best," I say stupidly. I can't think of anything else. Matt jumbles me worse than any carnival ride, and I struggle to maintain a facade of only mild interest in him. "They're so much scarier than roller coasters."

"Absolutely," Matt agrees, taking a long drink of his lemonade. "They were set up earlier today by someone who was probably drunk at the time."

We both pause to peer over the car's edge, looking for the carny who's operating the ride. He's smoking some sort of cigar and scratching his belly.

"Sexy," I say, and Matt laughs. Hunger gurgles inside me, and I place my hand over my stomach.

"You okay?" Matt asks. "The rides getting to you?"

"No. I just need food in my stomach after this lemonade."

"Now you're talking."

As we disembark from the Ferris wheel and stand in line for funnel cakes, Matt regales me with his best psycho-groupie stories.

"She'd come to, like, every show that was within ten hours of where she lived," he says. "I was polite and everything— took pictures once or twice like I would with any fan who waited around. And then she shows up with a tattoo of my first name on her foot."

"No *way*," I whisper. The vendor hands me a greasy paper plate, piled with fried dough and powdered sugar. I resist the urge to lift it right to my mouth and eat it like a sandwich.

"Yes way," Matt says. "I was only fourteen. Seeing 'Matt' tattooed on someone was more than a little overwhelming."

He pays the funnel cake guy, and I let him, no argument. I'm not sure why. The first bite is hot, but not too hot, sweet and melty in my mouth.

"Well," I say, following Matt to a nearby bench. The wood feels smooth, almost waxy, like it has been sat upon so many times that its ridges have worn down. "Maybe she'll meet another guy named Matt. Maybe it'll be a conversation starter when they meet, and they'll wind up together. Because of you."

He glances up at me from his food. "You believe in stuff like that?"

"Ha. *No*," I say. His eyes travel to a place on my cheek.

"You have . . . ," he says, reaching toward me. My impulse is to swat him away, defensive, but my arms stay at my sides. "Powdered sugar. Right here."

With that, he brushes his thumb over a spot on my cheek. It catches me off guard, and I take a moment to react. Not that it's a graceful reaction. "Uh. Thanks."

"No problem. Wouldn't want anyone thinking that you were sweet or anything," he says, and then, in a display of barefaced arrogance, he *winks* at me.

I narrow my eyes at him. "It's cute that you think you know me."

He gives me that smug laugh, leaning his arm behind the bench. Somewhere in the distance, a familiar melody catches my ear—familiar enough to momentarily forget how annoying Matt is being.

"Hey, hey," I whisper. "Do you hear that?"

Matt pauses, ducking his head until his eyes light up. "Let's record it for her."

Trashing our empty plates, we race toward a big white tent and the sounds of a full-band cover of "Middle of Nowhere, Tennessee." The dance floor is packed with fair-goers— middle-aged couples reliving the summers they met, groups of girls my age with deep tans, a man with a white mustache and a broad cowboy hat, holding his granddaughter as they spin and spin. I sing along, completely caught up in the heavy summer air, the plucky country bass, the way small towns feel familiar even when they're brand-new to you. Matt points his phone at me, and I make a smooch face and wave to Dee. After he sends the video, he holds up her response to me: *OMG I LOVE IT!*

The band picks up in a twangy cover of Tom Petty's "American Girl." The sugar and adrenaline rush through my veins, and I can't play it cool. "Oh my God, I *love* this song."

Matt turns to me and holds out his hand. I take it, and we join the Southern folks on the dance floor, shimmying to the classic-rock-gone-country. I put my arms up, eyes shut in a moment of total freedom. Matt dances in this un-self-conscious way, complete with air guitar and lip-synching.

The band is winding down when a girl zeroes in on us— or, more specifically, Matt. She's compact and curvy, topped with round curls that must have taken some serious hot rollers. Her hair dye is probably called Goldenrod or Honeysuckle, but it's actually the color of Aging Butter or Dry Cornbread.

"Oh my Lawd," she drawls, eyeing Matt head to toe. "Aren't you Matt Finch?"

"Nope!" Matt says quickly, grabbing my arm. We hurry off the dance floor, still giggling. I feel tipsy, despite having nothing but fried food and sugar in my stomach. When we get closer to the food trucks, Matt slows down his stride. "We should probably go before someone sees us."

I nod, biting my lip. We should have been more careful. One phone picture of Matt and me, and his "relationship" with Dee is blown. She'd career through tabloid hell all over again. This has been careless, this whole night, but I want to stay here with him.

"I'm not ready to go back to the hotel," Matt decides. "Let's walk somewhere."

I feel a smile spread across my face. "Okay."

We follow other groups of people until we find the docks. Boats fan out on either side of the lake, flanking the long pier. Each boat is crammed full of people, laughing and drinking and waiting for the fireworks to start. Something about the scene makes me vaguely homesick, for the familiar dirt road to my house. If I were a sappier person, this might look like the perfect summer night—the smell of fresh-cut grass, the boats rocking on the water, the boy by my side.

"Okay," Matt says, surveying the expanse of the lake. "Let's just follow the lakeside around until we find a spot where no one else can see us."

As I walk next to Matt, I feel a flutter beneath my rib cage that hasn't been there in months. I'm *nervous*. Worse than that. I actually find myself wondering if he'll reach over and grab my hand. Such a simple gesture—one I normally don't even think about. I've done much more scandalous things with guys who I know and like less than Matt. And yet, I haven't cared about, or even noticed, those little things with other guys. The anticipation is actually kind of great, in its own achy, heart-pounding way.

Somewhere in the distance, a radio is blasting Springsteen. We're near another pier, and there's enough light to see that we're right at the edge of the lake. I can hear laughing from the boats and in the distance, the whirring of the festival's rides. I'm not sure if I'm sweating from the muggy air or Matt's closeness.

When I glance at him, a sly smile creeps onto his face. "Have you ever been skinny-dipping?"

"I live in Tennessee. Of course I have."

"Let's do it."

"No way."

"Why not?"

I shake my head firmly. No, no, no. Danger—flashing-red-light, tempting danger.

"Oh, c'mon."

"You're fake-dating my best friend."

"The keyword being 'fake.'"

He's hard to resist, and I'm rapidly losing my resolve. It's the best day I've had in a long time—the most carefree I've felt since April.

"Okay," he says, bargaining. "Then at least swim with your dress on."

With that, he tosses off his hat. At first I assume that he's bluffing, but he tugs his T-shirt over his head. I have to admit: this is a persuasive move.

"You're serious."

"Yep," he says, going for his belt buckle. "Avert your eyes if you want. I wouldn't want to offend your delicate sensibilities."

There are no delicate sensibilities to be found, but for some reason, I cover my eyes as the metal of his belt buckle hits the ground. I feel almost guilty, like I'm doing something behind Dee's back. But I still peek through my fingers in time to see him wading into the water, boxers only.

"Water feels great," he calls to me. "You're missing out."

I uncover my face, and I can see his grin in the moonlight. He waves me in, but I stay still, weighing the possible regrets. The scale tips quickly in my mind, and the play-it-safe side hits the ground with a plunk. Before I can overthink, I kick off my heels, make a run for the water, and squeal as it hits me. It's exactly the rush I remember, wild and rebellious but somehow oddly innocent. The water closes around me, and my dress becomes heavy with its weight.

I tread water, nearing Matt slowly—up to my bare shoulders and grinning like an idiot. I tug at my strapless dress, willing it to stay up against the water's movement.

Matt's smile slides off his face, replaced with a thoughtful expression.

"What?" I ask, smoothing my arms against the water's surface.

"I don't think I've seen you smile like that before."

"Like what?"

"Like, smiling all the way. Grinning, even."

I shrug. "I'm a hard sell."

"I know. Gotta make people earn it."

"Something like that."

We're both moving slowly in the water, circling each other with a perfectly appropriate amount of space between our bodies. Somewhere in the distance, the first firework pops in the sky. Red sparkles drip down the night sky as the sizzling noise fades. I can just barely make out Matt's face, which seems paused in serious contemplation.

"What?" I ask.

He looks startled out of his thoughts. "What do you mean *what?*"

"I mean, just then," I say, "that look on your face. What were you thinking about?"

"I was thinking . . . that if I were going to kiss you, now would be a good time. Fireworks and all. Typical songwriter, always looking for poetic parallels."

It takes me a moment to react to his unabashed honesty. Every interaction up until now has been an undertone, a flirtation that I could be making into more than it is. I struggle to remain in control of the situation. I roll my eyes, even though my heart is racing fast enough to cause ripples in the water. "Pick a groupie, Finch."

He shakes his head, still grinning. "Nope."

My foot moves forward in the water, but I don't place it down. I won't let myself make a step toward him, into him, melting together in that desperate, hungry way that only happens when you're kissing someone you shouldn't be kissing. Self-talk takes over: *I know it would be so fun now, but what will it be tomorrow, Reagan?* Awkwardness as we pass on our way to the tour buses. Uncomfortable silences that Dee will start to notice. Disappointment in myself for falling into the same old routine.

Faced with my silence, he elaborates. "I think you like me more than you let on."

"I think you like me because you can't have me," I counter. Maybe he thought he'd throw me off with honesty, but he won't. I've never stood down in the face of candor.

"Well, only one way to find out."

I almost smile back, but I'm deep in thought, busy concocting a way to catch him off guard, to match his straightforwardness. So I say, flat out, "Look, I'm not Dee. I'm not some good girl. Believe me, you don't want my mess."

"Oh, but I do."

I shake my head, the tips of my hair swaying in the water by my shoulders. I'm not risking Dee's reputation over a fleeting attraction, especially when one of two things will happen: I'll get bored with him and back out or, worse, he'll hurt me. Guys like Matt—guys who have girls falling at their feet—they float to each destination like unchartered boats, no set course. I can't sink if I never climb aboard.

"Try me," he says, still keeping two feet between us. "I'm no saint, either."

"I know that." I catch myself smiling because I *do* know that. Even this—swimming in a lake in a city we've never been to on the Fourth of July—is not what I'd expect from Matt Finch. Besides, he'd run like hell if he knew what a mess Old Reagan made of everything. But maybe that's the way to end this temptation, to shock him away from his sly smiles and innuendos. "I met my last boyfriend during court-mandated community service."

"For what?"

"Underage drinking. But I got charged as an adult because I was in my car."

"Whoa." Matt doesn't even bother to hide his surprise and disappointment. I don't blame him. Some criminal offenses are sort of funny or even impressive. A DUI is not, to anyone, ever. Least of all me. For all my delinquent behavior, I would never, ever drive drunk.

"It's not what you think," I explain quickly. "I'd had a few drinks, and I went to my car to get my lighter. I couldn't find it, and it was freezing, so I turned the car on."

"A cop caught you drunk, underage, in your car with the door closed and engine on?"

"Exactly. Fortunately, the judge believed me that I had no intention to drive anywhere—I really didn't. But I still got community service and probation." And therapy. But he doesn't need to know that.

I can hear him exhale after holding his breath, relieved that I'm not a drunk driver.

"So the boyfriend," he says. "What was he busted for?"

"Ex-boyfriend," I correct him. "And possession. Marijuana."

Matt's expression falls again. "Ah. So you're a pothead?"

I wrinkle my nose. "God, no. That stuff smells like dirty gym shirts."

"Well, that's not so bad, then," he says. Another firework explodes in the sky, the lake reflecting its greenish glow. Matt raises an eyebrow challengingly. "What else ya got?"

"Ha," I say with a snort. "You don't even want to get me started on my family."

A purple firework illuminates Matt's expression and then fades away. He's quiet, and I can make out the sound of crickets around us. There's a peal of laughter in the distance, the echoing sounds of a few beers and freedom.

"Well, no one's family is perfect, I guess," he says finally. As a white firework crackles in the night sky, I see his sweet, sad expression and know he's thinking of his mom. The cocky, joke-cracking, celebrity Matt Finch falls away, and he's just this guy I know—a little broken and a little lost.

We're in waist-deep water, and I take a step toward him. I'm near enough that I consider crossing my own line. I'm near enough to consider draping my once-broken arm around his neck.

"No way," he says, stepping back. "Don't pity kiss me."

"*What?*" I scoff, laughing as if he's misread the situation. "You wish."

No—*I* wish. Thankfully my flush of embarrassment is hidden by the darkness.

"However," Matt says, recovering his playful tone, "you could pity-dance with me."

In reply, I groan. "*Ugh*, what a line. Does that work with the groupies?"

"You tell me." He grins, and we're too close now. But I

won't let myself. The real Matt—the one who is struggling through grief, the one I can't take my eyes off of—has retreated. Without him, a situation that felt romantic a minute ago now feels cheesy and cheap.

"Groupie? In your dreams."

"Indeed," he says, winking.

In the water, I place my hand on my hip and, just to throw him off, I say, "Enough with the winking. Not gonna happen."

Matt laughs, delighted with himself. "Okay, okay. I'm sorry. Friends?"

He extends his hand and, hesitantly, I shake it. "Friends."

But he doesn't release my hand; he grabs it tighter. Before I can tell what's happening, he's dunked himself underwater, pulling me with him.

"Matt!" I shriek, but it was too late. My entire head is submerged in the water for an instant before he pulls me up again. I should be mad, but Matt's hair is dripping down his face and he's laughing so hard. I can't help it. Tilting my head back, I laugh, too—a real, uninhibited laugh, beneath the fireworks' grand finale.

But it isn't the pinnacle. It isn't at the lake or even during the ride back to the hotel in the convertible, air rushing though our soaked clothes. Not as we walk into the lobby across the marble floors. And no, not as we ride the elevator together in silence.

When it rises to Matt's floor with a cheerful beep, he turns back to me, stepping intentionally further into my personal space. My heart feels stuck in a gap between my ribs, thrashing like a caged bird.

Leaning in, he says, "Today was a good day. I . . . I needed one. Thanks."

It draws me in again, this tiny confession that he's not nearly as untroubled as he pretends to be. He gives me a quick kiss on the cheek, and there—at the feel of his hand on my waist, at his cheek against mine—I see flecks of blue and green like floaters in my eyes, zapping electricity in the air between us. As I watch him go, every blooming firework in the world explodes.

CHAPTER THIRTEEN

Mobile

In Alabama, Dee's dressing room is painted navy, and there's a lounge area filled with plush furniture. She's ready early tonight, in full hair and makeup, to meet with two radio-contest winners. This happens pretty often before the shows, and Dee usually chats with them backstage. But since the dressing room is actually three full rooms, Dee has kicked out her hair and makeup team so the winners can hang out in her personal space.

The winners are two girls who look twelve or thirteen, both cowering delightedly in Dee's presence. One looks like she's on the verge of tears, while the other almost faints when Matt hugs her. I confess a certain soft spot for how sweet he is with his young fans. Amused, I stay curled on a love seat as Matt and Dee greet them.

"So," Dee says, settling back into a more casual posture, "what grade are you guys in?"

"Seventh," they answer in unison.

Even Dee's perpetual smile can't get them to relax in her presence. "And how's school going?"

One says "good" and the other says "okay." They're both sitting up incredibly straight, like everything their mothers ever taught them should be used in the presence of Lilah Montgomery.

"Really?" Dee cocks her head. "Huh. I kind of hated junior high. The girls were mean, and Reagan was my only friend."

They glance over at me, and I give a wave.

One of the girls says hesitantly, "Well, like, there is this one girl who is really super mean to me, and I don't know why."

"There's *always* one of those girls," Dee says with a knowing nod.

The girl opens her mouth to say more, but instead she casts a sidelong glance at Matt. I get it. They don't want to talk about these things in front of a boy. Maybe they don't want to talk in front of me, either.

I sit up and nudge Matt. "Let's go get some Cokes."

He lags his head in my direction, with that impish grin. "Are you asking me on a date?"

This is a careless joke to make in front of young fans, but Dee laughs. "Easy, you two."

Shooting him a glare, I decide not to bicker in front of these impressionable girls. I stand from my chair and gesture at him to come along. Matt follows me into the adjoining room's kitchenette, and once we're out of the way, I turn to him.

"I wanted to give them some privacy."

"Or . . ." He gives me a suggestive look. "You wanted to give *us* some privacy."

"Nope." I've been on my best behavior since last week, resolutely dodging both physical and conversational contact. Matt has been on his worst behavior, lobbing subtext-filled comments my way for no other reason than to amuse himself. It's exhausting.

I pull the refrigerator door open, perusing the selection provided by the venue. He leans against the wall across from the refrigerator, watching my every move. There's a long pause, and he says, hesitantly, "Hey . . . you know I'm just messing with you, right? When I say stuff like that?"

"I know," I say, grabbing a bottle of Coke. I glance back at him. "You want one?"

"Nah." He runs his hands through his hair, and I can tell he's dropped the flirty routine. These glimpses of him are rare and dangerous. I'm impervious to celebrity Matt Finch, but I'm a hopeless sucker for the sweet boy who got a tattoo for his mom. The boy who can barely talk about that tattoo without his voice breaking.

But looking down at me, his eyes filled with earnestness and the smirk gone from his face, he sounds almost defensive. "I'm a good guy, you know."

"And modest." Twisting the cap off my Coke, I rest my

back against the nearest counter in an attempt to look casual.

"I really am." He tilts his head a bit, examining me in his quiet way. "I just like ruffling your feathers."

"Don't flatter yourself. You ruffle nothing."

We stand across from each other, head-to-head, and I cross my arms. This is partly a reflex—defensiveness—and partly because the stance draws attention to my cleavage. What? He can ruffle my feathers, but I can't ruffle his?

"I'm debuting a new song tonight. I think you'll like it."

"New song?" My eyes trace over him, and I feel almost betrayed that he hadn't mentioned that writing was going well. I'm not sure why I feel I should be privy to this information, but I want to be. "That's two now since you came on tour. Writer's block cured?"

"It's been more than two songs. So, yes."

"Good for you." I don't mean this to sound disingenuous. I mean it: good for him. But, my voice's default tone is sarcastic, so I sound like I'm being a smart-ass.

"Hey," he says, defensive again, "songwriting is hard."

"I know." Great, now I feel bad. "I've watched Dee work through it."

"She's crazy talented," he says. The jokey Matt is definitely taking a break from hitting on me, and we're just friends who are hanging out. I can feel the shift in the mood, the change from bantering to really talking. "It's incredible, the way she takes the pain from her breakup and makes it something beautiful . . . and so personal."

My mind goes immediately to "Human," the song I listened to before I even met him.

"You do it, too." Oh God. I did not mean to say this out loud.

"Oh yeah?" He arches his eyebrow. I can't have him knowing that I feel his music like a vibration through my body. I can't have him knowing that it feels like heartstrings are a real thing inside me and that he plucks them.

"Yeah. I mean, I guess." I take a long drink of my Coke, stalling because I don't know what to say.

He shudders. "I don't know how you can drink that stuff."

I swallow my huge gulp down. "Excuse me?"

"Coke is so . . . thick and syrupy and bubbly. Ick."

"You're messing with me, right?" I ask, eyeing him carefully. "Because I'm pretty sure they don't let you go anywhere south of the Mason-Dixon Line unless you love Coke."

"I swear," he says, laughing at my genuine concern. "I can't stand it."

"Ugh." Turning away from Matt, I reach for the cap I left on the counter. "I like you so much less than I thought I did."

"Is that so?" He places his hands against the counter, one on either side of me. I spin around between his arms, squaring off against him. But he ducks closer to me, his mouth close to mine. Somehow, I know he's not doing this to mess with me, not to entertain himself on a tour that's becoming otherwise monotonous. No, this is all us—two live wires crossing each other, dangerously close to touching, just to make a spark.

"We can't," I whisper.

He doesn't move for a moment. When he speaks, his voice is low. "Because people are in the next room or because you like me *so* much less than you thought?"

"Both," I say, ducking underneath his arm before it can go any further. If I don't put some space between us, it's only a matter of time before we torch the whole place to the ground.

Against my better judgment, I glance back at him. He's still leaning his arms against the counter, the space where I was now empty. When he looks over at me, his hair falls across his forehead, and I want to smooth it back for him. At least I want to until he smirks at me like he knows exactly what I'm thinking.

"Stop that," I hiss, pointing at him. He shakes his head, grin plastered on his smug face. I walk out of the room, trying to disguise how flustered I am. Before walking back into the lounge, I pause to make sure I'm not interrupting.

"So is Matt Finch your boyfriend?" I hear one of the girls ask.

I can tell Dee is smiling as she diverts the question. "You know, boys don't matter nearly as much as friends. Your friends stay with you through all the boys you date, no matter what, and that's more important."

This is my entrance line, I suppose, and I walk in as if on cue. Smiling, I ask, "Are you telling them how I'm more important than Matt?"

She laughs. "Pretty much."

"It's true," I tell the girls. "I'm significantly better than him."

Matt gives a dramatic scoff as he enters the room behind me. I plop back down in the love seat, resting my drink next to me. After a few minutes, Dee winds down the conversation. The girls hug her, still clutching their signed VIP passes, and once they're on the other side of the door, their squeals are uncontained. For the rest of their lives, this will be the night they met Lilah Montgomery. The night Lilah Montgomery gave them advice.

There's a sharp rap at the door, and Dee yells to come in. It's Peach, beckoning Matt for his set. As he walks out the door, I blatantly check out his ass. Whatever. I can't help it. Annoying as he can be, the guy was born for a pair of Levi's. It's like he can feel me doing this, and he swivels around before the door shuts, in time to catch me red-handed and grin about it.

Dee grins, too, shooting her foot out to play-kick me in the leg.

"What?" I ask.

"I think my fake boyfriend has a crush on you."

"He does *not*."

She grins even wider, as if my denial only proves her point. "Then what was that all about? Plus, I've totally seen him checking you out. I oughta be offended, since I'm faux-dating him and all."

"That doesn't mean he likes me. That means this bra was worth its price tag."

Dee's eyes are on still on me. I sift through excuses to leave the room, to flee from her line of questioning. She may as well point a lamp in my face, interrogation-style. "Then why did I totally just see *you* checking *him* out?"

Shooting her my sliest smile, I say, "Because his jeans are also worth their price tag."

"Uh-huh," she says, unconvinced. "You know, it really is okay if you want to date him. In fact, I kind of wish you would. Anything to release some of the sexual tension."

It's hard to embarrass me, but Dee's coming close. I swear, I'm almost blushing. I blame Matt for being so damn obvious at every turn. "God, Dee."

"Seriously." She shoots me a look that's intended to portray seriousness. "Ever since Jackson, you two have been so intense."

Making a face at her, I say, "*No*, we haven't. It's nothing. He likes to mess with me. And I like to mess with him. It's just a game. You don't have to worry."

"Why would I worry?"

"Because everyone in America thinks you're dating him. And they're talking about that instead of . . . you-know-what."

The photo scandal that started it all. Jimmy. I shouldn't have brought it up. Dee's legal team made major websites pull it down because she's a minor, but the Internet is forever. Dee isn't bothered by the mention of it. "I know you'd be discreet. Besides, Lissa will probably have Matt and me 'break up' as soon as the tour's over, so I doubt she'd care."

"Well, that's nice of you, I guess." Also: incorrect. Lissa would care. Lissa would snap my neck like the deranged robot she is. "But I'm not interested."

Dee frowns, looking almost offended. "Why not, though? I mean, what's not to like? He's smart, he's funny, he's cute. . . ."

"I know." *Believe me*, I know. "But think, Dee—*really think* about the guys I've dated and how I've treated them."

She's quiet, her mind surely racing from Vance Kelly, my first real boyfriend, who I unceremoniously dumped before high school began, to Ethan Wilder, who I cheated on for weeks before setting him loose. Only recently have I developed any regret for how I treated Ethan. In fact, I apologized to him on the last day of school before leaving on tour. I pulled him aside, almost chickening out. But then I looked down at the cast on my wrist, which compelled me to swallow the little pride I had left. He was receptive to the apology—sweet, even—but it didn't make me feel better. I'll always wish I could take back how I treated him.

"Yeah," Dee admits. "I see your point. I guess I thought . . ."

She trails off, but I know what she was going to say: she thought it might be different because *I'm* different. In the past three months, I've started thinking about how my actions affect other people. I used to only think about the people I love—Dee, my dad, Dee's family—and sometimes not even them. These days, I can't seem to help second-guessing my choices, considering them from everyone else's viewpoints.

"I know," I say, sighing. "But after what happened . . ."

Dee rests her hand on my leg, blue eyes studying me. "Not all guys are like Blake. You have to know that, don't you?"

"Of course I know that." Why the hell does everyone think I'm so obtuse? I may be severely handicapped in "making good life choices," but I'm not a moron.

Dee's expression softens into a look I know. She's circumscribing my pain, trying to figure out what is hurting me. "I want you to be happy."

"I am happy. Really. Most of the time." In a rare moment of transparency, I confess the full, therapy-case truth. "But I have fresh wounds, Dee. Literally. I can't run back into battle while I'm still bleeding."

Dee has scars of her own. Or, at least, one scar. Sometimes I imagine there's a tiny hole in her heart, in the shape of a horseshoe, where only Jimmy could ever fit. She must understand why I'm keeping my distance from Matt, why it feels like my own heart is stuck together with a few pieces of flimsy masking tape. It wouldn't take much to break it all over again—a mere flick, a tap, and I'd crumble all over again. I'd be back on the ground, reevaluating my entire life.

I slept at Dee's house for a week after Blake hit me. I felt like I wanted to cry, but the tears never came. Instead, I felt hardened. Before, I thought I had it all figured out. I could do well in school while partying, like I thought you were supposed to in high school. Getting knocked out of that life— literally—revealed that I have pathetically few things that I care about: one parent, one friend, one hobby. So I clung to them, to Dee, to my dad, to my photography. I'll have to fill in the rest of the gaps when I get home in August. But, as for now, I need to hold fast.

Dee smiles, brushing her fingertip over her necklace. "You know what? I think it's the bravest thing in the world . . . to run straight at love, even knowing how badly you could get hurt."

"Whoa," I say, holding up my hand. "Who said *love*?"

With a laugh, Dee says, "I'm a songwriter. I always say *love*."

It's part of Dee's charm, that every spark is *love* to her, every first kiss, every tingle of anticipation. Each moment has big possibilities for Dee.

"A part of me wants to," I admit finally. "But I can't."

And there it is: I can't. I can't put Dee's career on the line, I can't lower my walls, I can't whatever-metaphor-you-want-to-use-for-being-completely-screwed-up.

"All right," she says, standing up. "I understand. I'll let it go."

"Thank you." I stand up, too.

"You wanna go catch the rest of Matt's set with me?"

"That's your idea of letting it go?"

She links her arm through mine, tugging me forward. "I always watch his set. You know that. You watch it, too. Stop being so sensitive."

A laugh erupts in my chest. Me, sensitive. That's a first. We wind around the dark backstage area. Some of the crew members move aside for Dee, and we find a place in the wings. Dee leans against the wall, watching Matt. I like seeing him like this, fronting the band and moving all over the stage. It's the one time when I can keep my eyes on him without being obvious. He's so confident up there, never once second-guessing himself, and he loves every moment. It's contagious.

There are a few girls in the front with shirts cut so low that they make my neckline look modest. Like, honestly—if Matt so much as glanced down, he could probably see all the way to their belly buttons. Some girls have no self-respect, and even though they can't see me, I make a face of disgust. Case in point: if Matt and I were together, I'd have to put those girls in their places. And I really can't afford another misdemeanor.

"All right," Matt says over the cheers. "This next one is brand-new. World premiere. You Alabamians are the first people to hear this song, other than my bus driver and the band. It's called 'Give.' "

The song is up-tempo, with a sort of sultry, bluesy feel that's new for Matt. At least, I've never heard any of his music take this direction. I listen as he starts to sing.

Girl, you're as hot as your temper,
And you won't let me through.
But I think you would be good for me.
I know I'd be good for you.
Oh, but then that night at the lake,

You said we'd be a mistake.
But you're wrong there, honey.
I'm a chance you wanna take.

Heat floods over my cheeks, hotter than the summer sun on my face. It was bad enough when Dee brought it up. Now I feel like I'm naked in front of the entire class—only it's not a class. It's an auditorium of thousands. Sure, they don't know the song's about me, but they know a piece of my life now. A piece that should be mine.

Do you want me to beg you?
Do you want me to say please?
Then this song is the rest of my pride, girl.
This song is me down on my knees.
Just give in, give in to me, girl.
I'll give you everything I've got.
I won't give up, give up on you, girl,
Till you're giving me a shot.

Dee leans over, whispering, "Are we going to act like this one's not about you?"

"Shut *up*," I hiss, but I can feel her smiling beside me.

So go on, pretend you can fight it,
Walk away like I'm not in your head.
Brush me off like I never cross your mind
At night as you lay down in bed.

I cross my arms, shifting uncomfortably in my heels. He had to do it. He had to put me in a song. It feels so cheap, like every girl who'd gone before me and gotten her own song as a parting gift. Matt keeps singing while I fume. Really? *Really?* This is the new song he said I'd like? There's too much steam coming out of my ears for me to even hear the final verse. By the time I snap back into reality, he's repeating the chorus again, singing a sort of ad-libbed fade-out.

Till you're giving me a shot.
C'mon, girl, give me a shot,
One shot.
I'll give you everything I've got. . . .

The crowd loves it, clapping and hooting in approval, and he thanks them as the band starts playing his final song.

"Well," Dee says tentatively. "That was . . . something."

I make a snorting noise—a bull about to charge.

"I've gotta go get set for my entrance." She nudges my arm. Her expression looks confused—hesitant—like she can't read me. "See you after?"

"Yeah, yeah," I say, waving her off. I'm too preoccupied with my anger to remember to wish her good luck. Instead, I stand completely still, seething as he finishes his last song. Matt exits to the other side of the stage while the crowd erupts in cheers.

Here I've held myself back, so careful this whole summer. I made a decision to keep my distance to protect both of us, and I've actually made good on that decision. But he insists on stamping across the line I drew between us. My restraint was for his own good, and for mine, and for Dee's. I listened to his whole song, but now? Now Matt Finch is going to listen to a *tirade* from me—for being presumptuous, for being pushy and careless.

My wedge heels echo against the floor as I storm toward Matt's dressing room, guns blazing. A security guard near his door glances between my VIP pass and the angry look on my face, and he doesn't bother to stop me. I'd like to see him try.

Without knocking, I twist the door handle and push it open. Matt is standing near the couch, frozen in surprise at me barging in. His hands are still on his shirt, halfway through unbuttoning it. Using my once broken arm, I slam the door behind me.

"Who the *hell* do you think you are?" I demand, settling myself into a fighter's stance.

"Whoa," Matt says, holding his hands up in innocence. "Okay. I sense I've done something wrong."

"Don't try to be cute."

"Reagan. Seriously. What did I do?" He looks at me like I've lost my mind, and he steps forward, placing his hand gently on my arm.

"You think you can just *use* me as songwriting material?" I pull my arm from his grasp.

His face is caught between surprise and confusion. "What? No."

"You'll stand onstage and undermine your 'relationship'"

with Dee, and for *what?* Because you get some small thrill from hitting on me?"

"Reagan," he says, his voice serious. "C'mon. That's not why I did it."

"Then why?

He gives me an exaggerated shrug. "I have no idea! I feel something; I put it in a song. It's what I do, but there's no agenda."

I can't believe that he doesn't realize how messed up it is to drag our—our *whatever this is*—into a public forum, in front of a crowd.

"God," he mutters. "Most girls love it when I write them a song."

"Well, I'm *not* most girls," I snap at him.

"No shit!" His voice rises into a frustrated laugh. "That's why I want you to stop being like this and just go out with me!"

" '*Go out with me*'?" I repeat angrily, gesturing to the closed door. "Where is 'out' to you? We can't go out in public, since you're supposed to be with Dee. We can go to your bus or your hotel room. That's it."

"If you insist," he says, trying to make light of the situation. Bad move, Finch.

"I'm serious. We're on a tour bus for another month, and then what?" I ask. I can feel myself getting more worked up, the blood whooshing through my veins. "I'm an easy lay for the summer, and we go our separate ways?"

"Whoa," he says, stepping back as if I've gone too far. "That's not fair."

"And you know what else? I don't even like this version of Matt Finch!" I shake my open hands in his direction, as if that explains my point.

"What is *that* supposed to mean?"

"I don't like the arrogant celebrity who winks at me and writes these cute little songs as a cheap way of flirting with me." I'm raving like a lunatic, voice raised and hands flailing. "You know who I *do* like? My friend Matt, who is so good to Dee and who has a lot more going on beneath all the charm. I don't want the showmanship, Matt. I don't want it. My life is screwed up already, and I want . . . realness."

I didn't know how true it was until I said it aloud. I'm a taped-together girl, but I can carry my own baggage. What I can't do is pretend I'm weightless, unburdened. Dee never hides her heartache from me, and that makes it okay to feel whatever I feel alongside her—no censoring, no embarrassment. I can't surround myself with people who are hiding their pain beneath swagger and a grin.

"Okay," he says, quiet now. His eyes are searching my face, processing all this. "I don't know what to say."

My chest is rising and falling, my breath ragged in the quiet room. "Say one real thing to me. Or don't say anything. And don't write songs about me, either."

He takes a deep breath in, preparing to hand my outburst right back to me. "Okay. *Fine.* You want honesty? I'm nineteen years old, and I've already seen a successful career come and go. I have no idea what I'm supposed to do with myself. The band broke up, I wrote some songs for an ultimately half-assed solo record, I finished high school and found out my mom had cancer. How's that?"

The room throbs with silence. My speechlessness only spurs him on. He throws his arms out in exasperation. "She died eight months after her diagnosis, and I devoted *every waking second* of that time to making her feel joy instead of fear or sadness. I took her to chemo, I made her laugh, I sang for her. I gave her everything I had, and then she was gone, and I was empty, okay? For the past couple of months, I've just been living with my dad and hanging out with my baby nephew and watching a lot of bad TV. My brothers and sister have their own lives, and I have no *idea* what I'm doing. So *excuse me* for trying to put on a brave face instead of bringing everyone down with a sob story."

I open my mouth, but he's revving up again. He steps toward me, voice loud and determined. "And one more thing. You can call them *cute little songs*, but that doesn't mean they're not honest. Those *cute little songs* are my way of dealing with everything you won't let me say to you. I have to be around you every single day, but I can't do anything about it. If I didn't channel it into *somewhere*, I'd be going crazy, alone on my tour bus thinking about you. And another thing . . ."

Before he can finish and before I can stop myself, I throw my arms around his neck and press my mouth against his. He reacts like he knew I'd do this, his hands already at my

waist. Light-headedness is winning me over, and only clinging to his neck keeps me upright. I shouldn't be, I shouldn't
be, I have to. He moves us until my back presses against the
cinder block wall, and I slide both my hands beneath his collar, just to grab him closer. I can feel each muscle in his back
as he tightens his hold on me. Every feeling coursing through
me is a bad country-song cliché, but I can't help it. My
thoughts are all sparks and honey and how a kiss like this
can make you believe that you've actually invented kissing
right here and now, the first two people to discover the feeling of your lips against each other's.

We're both breathing hard when he pulls away from me.
He keeps his face close to mine, and I know I shouldn't, but I
let him kiss me again. This time is slower, his hand against the
back of my neck. As one final defense mechanism, I attempt
to talk myself out of him one last time: *Reagan, is this really a
good idea?* But, with his lips against mine, I can't answer my
own question or ask a new one or even think straight. The
only response is simple and true: *Reagan, you are in trouble.*

There's a tornado siren going off in my head, and I press
my hands against his chest—in part to feel close to him
and in part to push him away. I'm not sure which feeling
prevails.

He must sense my inner conflict because he asks, "What?"

I shake my head, his lips still almost touching mine.
"This is still a terrible idea."

Matt grins, raising his eyebrows in complete confidence.
His hands are warm on either side of my face, lingering so I

have to look him in his storm-cloud eyes. "This is gonna be so good. You'll see."

He speaks so slow and sure that it almost sounds like a promise—not that I'd believe it. But I want to, fool that I am. I want to climb into his arms and just stay there until my life makes sense. Matt pushes my hair behind my ear, leaning toward me again, and I don't care if it makes sense. This is my gut feeling, which I usually defy just for the thrill of it. I never knew the rush that comes with following your gut feeling exactly. So, closing my eyes, I stake the rest of the summer—the rest of everything I have—on the hope that he's right.

CHAPTER FOURTEEN

Knoxville to NYC

"Well, well." I hold up the open magazine like I'm reading a story to a group of children. My audience is only Matt and Dee, but I'm making a show of it all the same as we hurtle toward New York City. "Look at this beautiful couple."

The glossy page shows a spread of celebrity fashion from the Dixie Music Awards two weeks ago. It feels like a lifetime ago—a bizarre, previous life, in which I had never kissed Matt Finch. On the left side of the magazine, a big picture of Matt and Dee takes up the whole page. Matt's hand is wrapped loosely around her waist, and they're poised, gorgeous, and beaming. It feels weird, looking at them the way the rest of the world sees them: as a couple. I should be jealous, but the impulse doesn't come. They're different guys to me—celebrity Matt and the Matt I kissed three nights ago. And every night since.

"Ugh," Dee says, making a face at me from the couch across from mine. We're rolling toward New York for a talk-show appearance, followed by a few East Coast tour stops. "It's weird to see that picture now that you guys are . . . whatever."

Matt laughs, apparently pleased at the idea that he and I are *whatever*. From his spot on the floor below me, he's leaning against my leg and tuning the strings of his guitar.

"Let's see what we have here," I say, glancing over the magazine's write-up of the awards show. "They say that you are 'enchanting' and 'a natural-born performer.'"

"Well," Dee says. "That's sweet."

"And *you*," I say, glancing down at Matt, "are a 'charming addition to the country music scene, complete with the boy-ish earnestness from his Finch Four days.'"

"Damn it," he says, hanging his head. "That's the second reporter to call me 'boyish.'"

"Boyish is nice," Dee offers.

He tips his head toward her. "I'm nineteen. I'm not boyish."

"It's your hair," I tell him without glancing up from the magazine, and Dee laughs.

"My hair?" he asks, incredulous. "What's wrong with my hair?"

"Nothing. But you had it that way when you were younger, right? During the Finch Four years?"

He frowns. "Yeah, I guess. I don't know."

"Yeah," Dee says. "You did. Same haircut. Kind of almost shaggy."

"*Shaggy?*"

"Yeah." I gesture near his ear. "It sort of starts to curl right here. The look is a little . . ."

Dee and I both study his face for a moment.

". . . boyish," Dee decides.

We both giggle, and Matt's eyes widen as if we've betrayed him. "Girls are mean! I'm bailing out of this bus at the next rest stop."

"Unlikely," I tell him. He smiles, wrapping an arm around my leg. As soon as we kissed a few days ago, the barrier between us fell. Since then, Matt has had no hesitation being close to me. Any moment when we're not in public, his arms go to my waist, my shoulder, my legs, anywhere. Though I'd never admit it out loud, I like this familiarity and how it feels like we've known each other for longer than we have.

Our eyes meet, and I smile at him. Smiling isn't often involuntary for me, and the easy movement of my lips feels almost foreign.

Dee's attention returns to her laptop, typing out responses to a reporter's written interview questions. "Um. Uh-oh."

"What?" Matt and I say it at the exact same time.

"Lissa just e-mailed me. She wants to do a conference call in five minutes . . . to talk about this picture."

She turns the laptop toward us. The picture is of two smiling, college-aged girls, both of their faces a bit shiny from heat and the camera's flash. They're cute, dressed casually, in some kind of bar. And that's when I see it. Behind them, on the left side, Matt Finch is talking to a brunette girl, who has her hand on his arm. The girl is Dee, in her wig, from the night she accidentally got drunk.

"This is not good," Matt says.

"Lissa says in her e-mail that this photo is not bad— apparently the tabloid wanted confirmation that it's me, but the story they're running is about how cute it is, that I wanted to see your show so badly that I went in disguise."

"But . . . if there are other pictures . . . ," I trail off. She nods, unaffected. "Why are you not freaking out about this?"

She shrugs. "I mean, I hope there are no unflattering pictures. But that night already happened. I can't undo it."

I'm impressed but skeptical. We're pulling off the exit ramp now, and I had planned to ride the rest of the way on Matt's bus. Instead, I lock eyes with Matt as the bus pulls to a stop.

"Give us a second, will you?"

"Of course." He ducks off the bus without another word.

"I'm going to keep riding with you," I announce to Dee.

"Reagan." Dee looks up from her computer. "I'm *fine*. I'll do the conference call with Terry and Lissa, and we'll figure something out. I knew it might happen after that night."

"But . . ."

"Really," she says. "I've got this."

"You'll text me if you need anything?" I don't want to be

that friend who abandons Dee to hang out with a guy. I *won't* be that friend.

"Reagan, get off this bus right now," she says, whipping a pillow at me. "It's summer. At least one of us should be kissing a cute boy."

"Okay, fine. See you in New York. Tell Lissa I send my love."

On my way to Matt's bus, I still feel conflicted. I came on tour to spend the summer with Dee, and I don't want to run off with a guy every chance I get. Or maybe I'm just shaken by the fact that I *do* want to be with Matt every chance I get. I already feel myself getting hooked.

Heading toward his bus feels like the reverse Walk of Shame—only I'm not leaving someone's bedroom. I'm heading straight toward it. Matt's driver is pacing by the bus, finishing up a cigarette. He gives me a friendly nod, and I want to snatch the cigarette and smoke it as my own. Instead, my nose catches the trailing curls of smoke, and I inhale deeply.

I step onto the bus, and I'm barely off the last stair when Matt grabs me around the waist with one arm, using the other to push the lever that shuts the bus door. When his hands reach me, it's like jumper cables touching either side of a battery, jolting every nerve ending to life. He's kissing me before the door even latches, and I wrap my arms around his neck, pulling him down closer to my height. I could do this all the way to New York, but he pulls away seconds later.

"Sorry, had to get that out of the way," he says, exhaling. He leans back, pretending to crack his knuckles as if he has

performed some sort of laborious task. "This secret relationship is really starting to get to me."

I arch an eyebrow at him. "It hasn't even been four days."

"I know. Exhausting."

"Isn't it a little fun sneaking around?"

"*No.*" He touches his fingertips against the ends of my
hair, then slides his hand around the back of my neck. "I'd
rather everyone know we're dating."

"Hmm." I narrow my eyes at him. "Are we really dating,
though? Doesn't that involve going on dates?"

He narrows his eyes right back at me. "You enjoy toying
with me, don't you?"

I shrug. And just to mess with him further, I wriggle out
of his arms and step past him. Behind me, he pulls the door
latch back open so his driver won't be locked out.

I've been on Matt's bus before, but not since a few days
after he joined the tour. Then, there was more clutter in the
front area—a half-unpacked suitcase, a stack of DVDs, an
electric guitar. Now the front two couches look barely lived
in, which makes sense, I guess. It's a big bus for only one person, and he probably stays in the back.

As I start toward the private area where his bed is, Matt
says, "Um, sure. Make yourself at home. . . ."

I glance over my shoulder at him without saying anything.
I don't have to. My I'll-do-whatever-I-want look is finely
honed and impossible to misinterpret.

"Hey," Matt says from behind me as his driver boards. I
keep moving to the back of the bus, but I hear the driver

start the engine as he says, "New York–bound! ETA, three hours."

Matt's bed is pristinely made, which is hilarious to me, and his guitar is resting on one side of the bed, as if waiting to be cuddled at night. The bed itself isn't freestanding like the one on Dee's bus. An L-shaped leather seating area covers the whole right side of the bus and half of the back. Matt's bed, on the left side, looks like it pulls out of the side of the built-in sofas. I set my purse on the floor and start clearing a spot for myself on the sofa, perpendicular from his bed. I pick up a sweatshirt and a paperback, stacking them tidily. I place the pile on the floor next to two heavy-looking free weights.

Matt settles onto his bed, directly across from me. I stretch my legs out, mostly to keep myself from crawling onto the bed with him. In the space between us, there are a few photos stuck on the wall. The first one that catches my attention is a casual snapshot of Matt and a pretty, older woman. They're sitting on a bench, outside somewhere, and Matt's arm is wrapped around her as she leans against his shoulder. Other than her petite frame and pale pink cardigan, she looks a lot like him—same light brown hair, same gray-blue eyes. His mom. I feel a gut punch of sadness for him.

Next to that photo there's one of Matt and his siblings. The oldest, Tyler Finch, is holding an infant, still wrapped tightly in a striped hospital blanket, and they all look exhausted and thrilled. The third photo is of Matt and the cute girl whose photo I saw online—the one he called his best friend, Corinne. They clearly took the picture themselves, squeezing close to fit both of them in the frame. Matt looks really happy, and she has a lot of freckles across her cheeks and the bridge of her nose. She looks . . . wholesome. And friendly. Like a Muppet.

As if he can sense the hate rays that I'm shooting at his friend, Matt kicks his foot against mine.

"So," he says, "you wear high heels a lot. What's that about?"

"They make my ass look good."

I can't get over the dimples that spring to his cheeks when I make him grin like that. "You always wear them?"

I nod. There's something about wearing heeled shoes that makes me feel more powerful. More in charge. As I strut the hallways of school, that distinctive clack turns heads, announcing my arrivals and departures. Matt's still looking at me, as if it's my turn to say something. "I prefer to be closer to eye level with people."

"Aha." It's like something in his mind has clicked, like he finally understands me. I'm sure he doesn't. "Leveling the playing field."

"Something like that."

"But if you're always wearing the heels, then you're always expecting a fight."

I tap the nearest photo with my finger, in an effort to change the subject. "Who's this?"

"My nephew, Noah." Matt's face is so proud that you'd

think he contributed to the child's birth. "Born April twenty-first of this year."

Glancing back at the picture, I study Noah's tiny red face. I don't especially like babies. I don't coo over the gurgling noises they make, and I don't want to hold them, because there's too much to think about—supporting their wobbly little heads and praying that they don't spit up on you. This is possibly the only thing I have in common with my stepmother. When a baby starts screaming in public, most women jut out their lower lips and say, "Aww, somebody's sad." Brenda squeezes her eyes shut, as if imagining a Zen place where the world is quiet and babyless. And I am right there with her.

Still, I say, "He's cute."

Matt looks amused by my obvious impassiveness. "He *is* cute, but in that picture he looks like any other newborn baby. Here."

He leans forward, touching the screen of his phone. When he turns it to me, there's a close-up picture of a baby with fat cheeks and a big, gummy smile. I have to admit, the baby's sheer delight is enough to make me smile back. "Must be hard to be on tour when he's so brand-new."

"Way harder than I thought," Matt says, leaning back on the bed. "My brother and sister-in-law send a lot of pictures, but it's the *worst* when my other brother, Joe, sends one. He's definitely one-upping me in the uncle department."

"Is your family coming to any of these shows?"

"Yeah. The Nashville show and maybe a few others. My dad will be at the Chicago one, maybe Joe and his wife, too, and Corinne. Carrie's spending the summer in the UK, so probably not."

"Does your dad live in Chicago?"

He nods. "We grew up there. Tyler and Joe married girls they met while we lived in Nashville, so they stayed. Carrie has a place in New York but stays with my dad a lot, in Chicago."

"I was born in Chicago. Lived there till I was eight."

"Really?" He seems puzzled, as if he is trying to place me in his world—conjuring a mental image of me in a Cubs shirt, eating Chicago-style pizza while standing in front of the Hancock building. "I knew you didn't have that born-and-bred Tennessee vibe going."

Of course not. I don't have the Southern drawl, and I sure as hell don't have the manners. "Where did you guys live when you were doing the Finch Four?"

"In Chicago, when we could. But we had an apartment in LA and one in Nashville. I lived in the Nashville one until . . ." He stops himself midsentence, like he almost forgot that I already know. "I lived in the Nashville one for a few months until I moved home to help my mom."

His eyes glaze over for a moment, like a memory is overpowering him. I imagine him making the long, sad drive home, where he would spend the next few months saying good-bye slowly. The thought of it makes me want to slide onto the bed next to him, to gather him up in my arms.

Nurturing is not in my nature, but his sadness is so raw, like burns on his skin.

"Okay," he says. "My turn."

"Your turn?"

"My turn to ask you a question."

"Is this a game? I thought it was a conversation."

"Well, with you, I feel like it's both."

Fair enough.

"How'd you meet Dee?"

The image of eight-year-old Dee pops into my mind—wild-haired and smiling shyly with full cheeks. "I don't know. I mean, I don't remember the exact moment or day. We were in the same class in third grade. I was new, and she took me in."

He smiles. "Huh. She tells it the opposite way."

"How?" I run my left hand over the sweatshirt I placed on the floor. It's soft and worn-in, and I bet it would smell like soap, like him. I want to slip it on, to curl up inside and let the oversize sleeves swallow me up.

"She says you took her in. That you were the cool new girl, and no one else in the class really talked to her before you."

For some reason, I'm startled at the reminder that Matt was friends with Dee long before he met me. "What else did you know before you met me?"

He's amused by my curiosity—that I'm uncomfortable with not knowing. "That Dee loves you and relies on you for a lot. That's all, really. What did you know about me?"

My mind moves back to that day on the bus before I met

Matt, listening to "Human", and I almost say: *I knew that you understood pain in a way most people our age don't. I knew that Dee trusted you, that I wanted to trust you, too. I did not know that you were bracingly sexy and funny and unpredictable.*

I clear my throat. "That you were cute when I was in eighth grade."

He grins, running a hand through his hair, and I see my opportunity to get a dig in.

"Stop messing with your hair. It already looks nice. Boyish-nice."

"Oh, you think you're funny?" Before I can anticipate his movement, he grabs me by the legs, pulling me onto the bed with him. Something about the suddenness makes me laugh, and he takes the opportunity to brush his fingers against my sides, tickling me.

"Stop," I squeal, swatting at him but laughing nonetheless. Tickling is the worst, my reactions jerking out of my control.

He releases me, and we both land on his comforter. I rest my head against one of his pillows as he stares directly at me. The back window is tinted just enough to filter the setting sun's light. That's the best for photography—filtered light, where the view is aglow but soft. In it, you can be illuminated without being overexposed.

It's not the first time he's run his hand through my hair, almost absentmindedly. Normally I'd pull away from being petted like a house cat, but it isn't like that. His fingers weave through my hair the way he touches his guitar strings, as if I'm something cherished, something he's connected to. Instead, I stare back at him, at his salt lake eyes and the strong lines of his face. In coming on tour, I had hoped to find escape—enough distance to figure out how to start over. I still don't know the whens and hows of repairing my own life. But I know that Matt Finch makes me want to feel everything. Instead of numbing myself in any variety of ways, I want each sensation; I want to feel the way they pool together—his touch and smell, the sound of his voice. I want the tipsiness, the giddy ache that comes as he slides his thumb across my lower lip, as his eyes fixate on my mouth.

He leans over, drawing me into the kind of deep kiss that pulls the air out of my lungs. For the past few years, everything I've done has been so fast—a flurry of late nights and red plastic cups and frantic undressing, too quick to stop and think. I was driving my life way over the speed limit, swerving the wheel just to make myself feel more alive. It took me half a summer to get here, with a buildup that simmers still. Now, with Matt's hand tangled in my hair, I can't believe I never knew how good it feels to slow down.

CHAPTER FIFTEEN

NYC

"You're exactly what I was looking for," I coo, peering into the shoe box that houses my only New York purchase thus far: a pair of sky-high, black suede booties. I extract one from the box and slide it onto my foot, admiring the way it rises to just below my ankle. I thought I had invented these shoes in my head, but there they were—as real as I had pictured them, in a storefront near the TV studio building where Dee's filming a talk-show appearance this afternoon. I pull the other shoe on and place both feet squarely on the ground. "Except you're even better than I imagined."

Matt eyes me from his spot on Dee's dressing room love seat. "You're crazy."

"Excuse me," I snap. "Can't you see I'm in the middle of a conversation?"

From the makeup chair, Dee laughs. "Don't worry, Matt.

I get jealous, too. Reagan cares about her shoes more than she cares about her own best friend."

"That's *ridiculous*," I say, looking up at her. Then I glance back down at my beautiful new shoes. "It's a tie."

Dee laughs again, which is clearly exasperating to the makeup artist. He stands, smileless, with some sort of wand in his hand. When Dee stops laughing, he swipes gloss on her lips. She's wearing a polka-dot miniskirt from J.Crew, a collared shirt, and her trusty denim jacket—perfectly summer-casual and perfectly her.

The makeup artist pronounces Dee's face complete and packs up his supplies. As soon as he's out the door, I slide onto the love seat next to Matt. We've been in New York for two days, shuttling to and from press events and sightseeing in between. It feels frantic to me, but Dee says it's nothing compared with "Street Week"—the release of her album last May. Peach is in the city, too, but she's taking a day off to visit the 9/11 Memorial and the Statue of Liberty with the band.

The door jerks open to Lissa's hawk face. "We need to have a conversation."

Matt sighs loudly. Lissa's been on his case all morning about appearing on the talk show with Dee. Matt and Dee have protested, but the fight has been passive-aggressive and tense. "I'm really not going out there. You *know* Zoe will ask about our 'relationship,' and we won't lie."

Lissa shakes her head. "It's not that. I've just been alerted to some . . . unflattering press."

Matt's mouth snaps shut, and Dee's complexion turns

chalky. She moves next to me on the couch, already wide-eyed.

Lissa continues. "I think it's wise if we talk strategy before the show. It seems this spread will be released tomorrow in a tabloid that went to print earlier today."

With that, Lissa turns her tablet toward us.

LILAH MONTGOMERY: PREGNANT? The full-page picture is from yesterday—Dee emerging from the Disney Store, where she'd bought presents for her brothers. The curve of her stomach is slight—easily caused by our huge lunch at the Russian Tea Room, followed by frozen hot chocolates at Serendipity. Hell, it could have been caused by a deep breath. I reach over, and her hand is clammy, gripping mine hard.

Worse still, the sidebar speculates three possible fathers of this supposed baby. Number One? Matt Finch, accompanied by another photo from yesterday. Number Two is "Mystery Man" with a photo of Dee hugging a good-looking guy in the audience of a show. It's her cousin Dan, who attended the Knoxville show three nights ago—her *cousin*.

Bachelor Number Three is Jimmy. It's hard to tell where the photo was taken, but he's standing next to a blond girl, and he looks pissed. I'd be pissed, too, if I was caught standing next to Alexis Henderson, who is a cheerleader but also a goody-goody. I can't bear to look at Dee. The caption reads: *Jimmy Collier, Lilah's former boyfriend from June's photo scandal, is pictured here with a new blond. But perhaps reconciliation occurred between the high school lovebirds earlier this summer?*

Dee's mouth barely moves. "They're still following Jimmy?"

"Not consistently. It's likely that they sent a photog to Nashville specifically for an updated picture." Dee turns the tablet away. She's seen enough. "After you film the segment in a few minutes, we'll need to get on a conference call with Terry and at least one of your parents, all right? We'll figure this out as fast as possible."

Dee nods once, her expression unreadable.

Lissa sighs. "Obviously, I've been a proponent of allowing the public to believe that you two are in a relationship. At this point, I'm comfortable with anything you want to do with that."

This means: *Dee, if people think you're pregnant with Matt's baby or even sleeping with him . . . well, the parents who buy concert tickets for their tweens will not be happy.* The publicity stunt has taken a turn.

I feel Matt glance over at Dee. "I'm going to come on the show with you, okay?"

"Yes," Dee says. "Thank you."

Dee seems so numbed-over that even Lissa sounds concerned. "Lilah, are you all right?"

"Yes. Could you please give me a minute?"

"Of course. Matt, let's get you to hair and wardrobe quickly," Lissa says, standing. Matt follows, but not before ducking down to Dee on the couch. "We can handle this."

Dee nods mechanically, still grasping my hand like a falcon clutching its prey. When Lissa and Matt are gone, it's eerily quiet. She releases my hand and wanders across the room, toward the mirror.

"Honestly, Dee, it's the *stupidest* rumor. No one's going to believe—"

"Don't." Dee squeezes her eyes shut. I clamp my lips together. Her shoulders rise and fall, deep breaths to calm herself. It's not working. Her face is rose-colored, practically pulsing. Without warning, she swipes her arm across the makeup table, products clattering to the floor. A bottle of aerosol hair spray hits the floor with a metallic clang, then rolls under the table.

"It's so *unfair*!" Her voice is so shrill that my ears ring. She whirls around, pushing the director's chair onto the floor, where it lands with an echoing thud. I have never, ever seen Dee like this. It shakes me. My instinct is to move toward her, to reach out, but it's like trying to comfort a growing hurricane. "I do everything right. *Everything.*"

Without warning, she strips off her jacket, then unzips her skirt.

"What are you . . . ?"

"I'm changing into something skintight so people can tell I'm not pregnant." She balls her shirt up and throws it onto the floor. As she riffles through her rack of dresses, the metal hangers clash against each other. Dee examines a coral lace dress. She looks so vulnerable, standing there in a nude-colored bra and spandex underwear.

"Dee," I say, taking a hesitant step. "You don't have to go out there. You don't have to do the show."

"Of *course* I do, Reagan," she snaps. My eyes widen, startled by the tone she's using with me, but she either doesn't notice or doesn't care. "You have no idea—you have *no idea*—what the stakes are. What I look like, what I say, how I react, whether or not I go out there . . . it all matters. There are people whose jobs literally depend on me not screwing up."

I reach out, touching her arm, but she jerks away. "Dee, I know, I just—"

"You *don't* know!" she cries. The coral dress flies in her hand as she makes wide gestures. "No one does! I'm tired constantly; I'm not allowed to have an off day. Everything I do is scrutinized. No, you *don't* know. You get to go around doing whatever you want, making out with your new boyfriend, and I have to find out that Jimmy is dating someone by reading a magazine. That is not *normal*."

There it is: the real problem. She doesn't care about the pregnancy rumor. Of course she doesn't—it's ludicrous. The pain stems from Jimmy, like always. When it comes to songwriting, he's Dee's superpower. But when it comes to real life, Jimmy is Dee's Achilles' heel. He's the only one who can dismantle her professionalism, who can break her down. I watch as she tugs the coral dress on with a few angry movements.

"Dee, just because he was seen with Alexis Henderson doesn't mean—"

"Ugh. Alexis Henderson?" She yanks the stretchy fabric down, forcing the skirt to a more modest length. "*Seriously*, Jimmy? That's my follow-up act? Alexis Henderson?"

Dee has never said a bad word about Alexis Henderson before now. While all the other cheerleaders were going toe-to-toe with me at the keg, Alexis hung back. Dee admired that—thought it showed maturity and restraint. But, of course, it's easy to like any girl who's not a part of your world. The moment she slides into an ex-boyfriend's orbit, we all have the same instinct: destroy.

The dress is taut against Dee's flat stomach. Though it's a bit on the fancy side for a talk-show appearance, the dress will certainly squash pregnancy rumors. Without looking at me, Dee turns back to the mirror, stepping over the director's chair that she felled. She dabs her eyes with a tissue and stands up straight, examining herself. I can tell she's still breathing so fast, so angry, but I can't find words. Dee centers her necklace and fluffs her hair gently. Then she places her hand on the doorknob, pausing to take a deep breath, and she leaves me here.

I'm immobile for at least a minute after the door closes behind her. Dee has never lashed out at me like that, and I don't know what to do. Do I let Dee go out onstage, as volatile as she is? Do I chase her down; do I call Jimmy? Or Peach? Maybe she and the band are sightseeing somewhere nearby; maybe she could rush down here and try to fix it. I'm not equipped to deal with this.

As I duck into the hallway, my vision becomes a kaleido-scope. Before, I noticed the pictures that line the walls—each featuring the talk-show host, Zoe, with her arm around one celebrity or another. The pictures are vaguely square-shaped blurs to me now. Somehow, where the hallway's end becomes the soundstage, I find Matt. He's wearing a blazer, his hair tousled to look effortless, and a production assistant is pinning a microphone to his shirt. Dee is a few people away from him, standing near a camera and nodding at something the director is saying.

"This is so bad," I whisper. "She's totally rattled."

Matt sighs, his face grave. "I know. But she only has to get through three minutes, and then they'll call me onstage after the first commercial break."

With that, he moves toward Dee. Zoe starts the introduction, lauding the many talents of Lilah Montgomery, and the studio audience is already peering toward the place where she'll enter. Matt stands shoulder to shoulder with Dee, their backs to me. He grabs her hand, whispering something into her ear. Zoe calls Dee's name in an exuberant voice, and Matt drops her hand. Dee's stride is confident—steady, even—as she waves toward the cheering crowd.

My nerves won't let me watch this live, so I retreat to the dressing room to view the show on the flat-screen TV. Dee looks radiant, her hair complemented by the dress's peachy fabric. No one would ever guess she's hiding a reopened gash across her heart. If emotional wounds showed up on the body like physical wounds, Dee's dress would be blood-soaked.

I'm taking control. Someone has to. I text Jimmy: *Dee's publicist just warned us that a magazine is saying Dee's pregnant and you might be the father. There's a picture of you with Alexis Henderson, your supposed girlfriend.*

His response is almost immediate. *Is Dee okay? (Am NOT dating Alexis)*

I flip my phone in my hand, debating. *Not great. But she's tough.*

When Jimmy texts back *I hate that they do this to her,* I don't bother to reply. He knows I hate it, too.

On the TV, Matt walks onstage, waving. Dee's posture relaxes when he sits beside her, and she glances at him in this grateful way, like she's so relieved to not be alone on that stage. To the average viewer, it will look like admiration or even love. Matt turns on the charisma with Zoe, who seems girlishly smitten with him.

"So I have to ask the question," Zoe begins. "There's been chatter all summer that you two are dating, and you've responded with denials."

"And we'll continue to," Matt says. "She *is* one of my closest friends, though."

Dee looks genuinely flattered. "Same."

Zoe sees that she's hit a wall in this line of questioning. Instead, she asks about the omnipresence of Dee's necklace— the horseshoe charm. Dee looks unnerved by the question. It's an indirect question about Jimmy, and Zoe doesn't even realize it. Matt reaches his arm across the back of the couch. It may look like he's stretching, but I know he's reminding her that he's there.

Dee regains her composure and replies, voice steady, "I usually say that my necklace is a good-luck charm, but that's only partially true. It was given to me at a time in my life when things were simpler, and I wear it as a reminder that all I really need are my family, my friends, and my guitar. I don't want to lose that perspective."

Matt smiles in this proud way, which sets Zoe off again. "Are you *sure* you two aren't together?"

"Positive," Dee chirps.

"So you're both single?"

"*I* am." Dee elbows Matt.

"Uh-oh." Zoe is clearly thrilled. "Do I sense some gossip here, Matt?"

"Well, uh . . . ," Matt looks torn, but he's smiling. I wasn't expecting this. My heartbeat sounds like a horse race. It's bad for his career, to be seen as unavailable, but I want him to say it anyway.

"I'm . . . ," he begins, and I can't guess the next word. "Single"? "Dating someone"? "In a relationship"? "I don't know what I am."

"Smitten?" Dee suggests.

"Shut up," he says, laughing embarrassedly. "But yes."

"And I approve," Dee adds.

Zoe arches a perfectly stenciled eyebrow. "Is that all I'm going to get out about this secret relationship?"

Matt's tone stays friendly but firm. "It's new. I don't want to jinx it."

"Well, well," Zoe says. "Lucky mystery girl."

Despite the tabloid chaos and the fact that my best friend freaked out on me not ten minutes ago, a sheepish smile spreads across my face. That boy just does it to me.

There's still a remnant of a smile when they walk offstage, and I start planning what I'll say to Dee. She bursts through the door much sooner than I expect, with no Matt in sight. I sit up, awaiting some kind of direction, but Dee leans back against the door with an exhale that whooshes into the air. She's exerted the last of her energy by remaining poised on the talk show.

"I'm so sorry about before." She shakes her head, eyes closed.

I blink. "It's okay."

"No, it's not," she says, but I'm not sure if she means her behavior or the tabloid situation. The soft arc of each eyebrow turns to a flat line, and she slides her back down the door until she's crouched on the floor. I move from the couch to the floor beside her, leaning my back against the door. I expect her to cry, but she doesn't. I almost wish she would because her silence—her resignation—feels even sadder. It's like watching a boxer take his final punch—no fighting back, no tears. Just lying there, done.

She sighs, stretching her legs straight out. "I don't mean to complain, because I know I'm so lucky. But, I swear to God, Reagan, every once in a while it's so damn hard that I want to pack up and go home."

In desperation to fix this, I confess in a breathless slur, "I texted Jimmy. He's not dating Alexis Henderson."

"I should have known that," she says after a moment. "Alexis Henderson, ugh."

"He only wanted to know if you were okay."

Dee snorts. "Did you tell him I'm an emotional basket case?"

"I said things aren't great, but you're tough."

She stares down into her lap. "He already knew that."

Yes, I imagine he did.

"And anyway, it's not just Jimmy. It's everything." Dee sighs, eyes following an invisible path on the ceiling. "You know, I don't even recognize myself sometimes. I catch a glimpse of myself in the mirror—the clothes, the makeup, the hair—and I think: *Who is that?* It's all happened so fast that I'm always on to the next thing before I have a chance to process."

She pauses to take an uneven breath in, and I give her a discerning look. "Hey. You're still Dee under all that Lilah."

This gets a lip purse—not quite a smile.

"You want to know something embarrassing?" She presses her horseshoe charm between her thumb and pointer finger. "I really, genuinely thought Jimmy and I would get married after high school. Like my parents did."

"I know."

Dee shakes her head, unsurprised that I already knew. "It feels naive and pathetic now, and I think it's the reason I can't regain my balance. For so long, I had these images of how my life would look—marrying Jimmy under the oak tree on his grandpa's farm. Buying a house with some fenced-in acreage for pets. Having my brothers over to watch movies and eat junk food. Now my life is changing so quickly. I keep searching for new images of my future, and I can't see anything—it's like a line of blacked-out Polaroids."

She stares down at her lap. "Sometimes I think about flying home, showing up at his doorstep, saying I'll do whatever it takes. But this is my dream, and I get to live it. I'm not walking away."

In anyone else, I'd admire the determination to not *need* someone. But, even as their breakup approaches a full year, Dee and Jimmy belong beside each other in my mind. Secretly, I'm like a kid in denial about her parents' divorce. I still believe they're a set—a package deal.

"Sometimes I worry that no one other than Jimmy will ever really love me. I worry that anyone I meet for the rest of my life . . . their idea of me will be colored by all this Lilah stuff. Jimmy loved me before anyone else *saw* me, even when I was"—she whispers this, as though it's new information—"shy and awkward, with crazy hair. Those things are still a part of me, and I want someone who loves all of it. Do you think I'll find that?"

"Of *course* you will." The words leap from my mouth, mostly out of instinct to comfort her. But the thing is: I believe it. I believe she'll find someone who loves the real, cranky-when-she's-sick-or-hungry, laughs-like-a-twelve-year-old Dee, this girl whose presence in my life has made up for so many absences. I believe someone—maybe Jimmy, maybe someone else—will realize that Lilah Montgomery, the perfect girl on magazine covers, has nothing on Dee.

She shrugs, trying on a smile. "If not, I guess I'll just buy an apartment overlooking Nashville, and you and I can live there together like those two crazy ladies in that documentary, the ones with scarves on their heads and lots of cats."

"*Grey Gardens?*"

"Yes." Her smile widens. "I'll write crazy songs, and you'll take crazy photos, and we'll start a collection of antique teacups and eat macarons for every meal. And we'll dance a lot and not give a crap what anyone thinks about us."

She's laughing like this is an unreasonable idea. For someone who is such a dreamer, so imaginative in her songs and vision for her career, Dee is surprisingly bad at realizing she can do whatever she wants. "Sounds good to me. Let's do it."

The smile drops from her face. "I can't just, like, get an apartment."

"Of *course* you can."

"But I love being with my family."

"So you'll stay at your parents' house whenever you want. But you'll also have a place in the city. You can wake up there and walk to a favorite coffee place and all the antique shops. You'll have your brothers over to watch movies and eat junk. You've seriously never considered this? I think about it literally every day that I live with Brenda."

"I guess once or twice. But I'm not even eighteen yet. And I don't want to live alone."

"So I'll live with you."

"But then you'll go off to college." She presses her forehead into her hand. "And I'll hardly ever see you."

"Well, if I go to NYU, I'll get a studio apartment with the

money I get from selling a kidney, and you'll stay with me as often as you can. Or maybe I'll attend Vanderbilt or Belmont, and we'll go with the *Grey Gardens* plan in a Nashville apartment."

"It would be like a sleepover all the time." I can't tell if she's realistically considering it, but at least she's entertaining the idea. "My business manager did mention that I need to think about investing, and my parents said real estate might be a good idea. Is that weird and codependent? Would you really move in with me?"

"Are you kidding me? Of course I would." I hate to be a sap, but I've thought about this before. Girls will move across the country with a boyfriend they've known for less than a year, and people think that's normal because it's romantic love. But living with your best friend? Or, for Dee, staying close to her parents and brothers? I don't think that's weird or codependent. I think it's basic: if you find people you love, you want to be near them.

Dee still looks lost, though. Her thoughts have created the perfect storm—career, love, family, independence, the future—and she's flailing in the waves. "Sometimes I worry that my fans will think I'm obsessed with having a boyfriend. But I'm not. I just don't want to come home to an empty house. I want to have someone to go out to brunch with, someone to stay up talking to really late."

"Well, you have me."

She nudges her shoulder against mine. "You're not going

to go off to college and make all these cool photojournalism friends and forget about me?"

"Nah. What's that thing your mom always says? You can't make new old friends?"

"Yeah." Dee reaches her pinkie out, and I lock it with mine. "Wouldn't want to anyway."

A knock on the door jolts us both.

"It's me," Matt says. "I'm not going to interrupt best-friend time, but I need you to open the door. Delivery."

We scoot forward on the floor, enough room for a person to slide in. Instead, it's a white Styrofoam cooler, with Matt right behind it.

"Open it," he says to Dee.

She peers inside, hesitant, and then gasps like it's a trunk full of gold coins. "*How* did you get this?"

From inside, she pulls out a frosty pint of ice cream— Jeni's Ice Cream, the best ice cream in the world and Dee's one, true sugar weakness.

"I have my ways," Matt says, holding out two plastic spoons. "One for you, and one for you."

"Oh my God." Dee cracks open the pint's lid. "I could kiss you right now."

I'm really not sure if she's talking to Matt or the ice cream.

"Seriously," I say. "How'd you do it?"

"Paid a production assistant to sprint down the street to a specialty grocery store I saw earlier." He grins. "Or . . . *magic*."

"Howidoono?" Dee tries to ask, but there's a mound of

Brown Butter Almond Brittle ice cream on her tongue. "How did you know I needed this?"

He gives her an "oh please" look. "I have a sister and a girl best friend. This is not amateur hour. Anyway," he says, "I'll leave you to your ice cream. See you in Baltimore."

I tilt my head back, and he leans down to kiss me.

"Fank oo, Matt," Dee says through another mouthful of ice cream.

"Don't mention it." He disappears out the door, then pops his head back in.

"And you," he says, looking at me. "Don't make plans for the day off tomorrow, okay?"

"Okay . . ." I furrow my eyebrows, suspicious.

"Okay, bye."

I try to give Dee a "what was that about?" look, but she's really busy mining a piece of almond brittle out of her ice cream. She pries it loose, but with a little too much force, and a huge chunk of ice cream hits her chest and slides down the coral dress. Her face registers shock for a split second, and then she bursts out laughing—that nerdy, middle schooler, goose honk of a laugh. She scoops up the glob and flings it at me, hitting my T-shirt. This sets me off, giggling uncontrollably because, what else can we do? We sit there on the floor while ice cream melts on our laps, laughing until we're both crying. Laughter feels like our flotation device—it won't pull us out of the storm, but it might carry us through, if we can just hang on.

"I think I'm gonna go home for the day tomorrow," Dee announces once we recover. "Book a flight out of Baltimore as soon as we get in, even if it means I'm only in Nashville for twelve hours."

"You should. I bet Terry will let you, after what happened today."

She sighs, blowing a hair out of her face. "Matt's really something else, you know."

"Yeah." And he really is—the impromptu talk-show appearance, the ice cream, the automatic understanding that Dee and I needed time for just the two of us. He went into crisis mode so naturally, perhaps because he's been through crisis himself. I turn to face Dee. "Hey, did you, uh . . . did you know about Matt's mom?"

She nods slowly. "Not until after, though—he never told me while she was sick. He was in Nashville after his nephew was born, and we went out for coffee. I told him about the tour and that you were coming because I couldn't do it without you. I laughed about that and called myself pathetic. He said it wasn't pathetic, that his mom had died a few months back, but his best friend was still flying home at least one weekend a month to be with him."

"Corinne?"

"Yeah. I felt like such a jerk because he had a real reason to be upset." She shakes her head. "But it made me feel better knowing that he leaned on his best friend, too—that they ate junk food and watched movies and sometimes even laughed. The way we did."

"The way we *do*," I amend.

She smiles. "The way we do."

CHAPTER SIXTEEN

Baltimore

I'm still not totally sure how I ended up in a park so far away that Baltimore faded, turning into rural Maryland with each passing mile it took to get here. From our hillside perch, the view is encompassing—patches of crops, barns and silos, fresh produce stands lining the roads. Maybe it's the slightly heightened altitude; maybe my lungs are used to recycled tour-bus air, but I swear I haven't breathed so clearly in weeks. It feels so far from our daily lives—far from the stage's electronics and the hotel's modern amenities. Those things have no place here.

"It kind of looks like Tennessee, doesn't it?" Matt asks, looking over at me. He's lying on his stomach on the blanket, swaying his hands over the blades of grass.

I nod, crossing one leg over the other.

"It's nice, isn't?" He's baiting me, looking for a confession.

"It is."

"So you take back what you said?"

Smiling, I say, "No. It's just *also* nice."

"Whatever." He shakes his head, smiling. "You love it."

I called it "cheesy" when Matt showed up at the hotel room door with a picnic basket. I think I groaned, too, which seemed to delight him all the more. I knew we'd be hanging out while Dee's in Nashville for the day, but I didn't think it would be so . . . structured. I didn't think he'd plan something that involved a day trip. He announced that he was taking me on an official date, and therefore we are *dating*. I smiled, even as I shook my head.

I lie back all the way and reach for my film camera, which I haven't used nearly enough this summer. Holding the camera up, I can see sky filling most of the lens. At the very bottom of the shot, the topmost leaves of a tree line sneak into view. I press my finger decisively, capturing the space between land and sky.

Then I turn to Matt. He's still on his stomach, eyes closed and resting his head against his arms. The food is gone now, but it's nice to linger here. With a wicker picnic basket and the red-and-white checked blanket, I know I should be wearing a white cotton dress or a flouncy skirt. I should have long, glossy, cheerleader hair that swings when I make peppy movements—an innocent girl on a romantic date.

I don't fit with the idyllic setting or the 1950s date, but I think I fit with Matt just fine. The hem of his T-shirt is pulled up a bit by the blanket, and I can see two lines of his tattoo. I reach over, smoothing my fingers over the letters. His skin is warm beneath my hand, and he smiles at my touch. I turn so that I'm lying on my side, facing him.

"What's your middle name?"

"Carter—my mom's maiden name." His eyes move across mine. "Why?"

"Just curious. What kind of car do you drive?"

"Oh God." He buries his face in the picnic blanket. "Not that question."

I grin, thrilled that I've stumbled onto something interesting. Tugging at his shirtsleeve, I insist, "Yeah, c'mon. Tell me."

One eye peeks out at me. "Why do you want to know?"

"Because I think these are things I would know about you if we were dating in real life."

"Real life?"

"Yeah. Like, not in various locations across the US . . . mostly in a tour bus . . . while you were supposedly dating my best friend."

"Point taken." He sighs, rolling onto his side. "I drive a ridiculous-looking Porsche. That's what happens when you turn fifteen and a half and already have money."

I snicker at him, tipping my head back. "Why don't you just trade it in?"

"Haven't gotten around to it yet. What do you drive?"

"1971 Buick Riviera."

Matt blinks. "I don't even know what that is."

"It's an old muscle car—belonged to my grandpa. I love it, even though it's temperamental."

"I like that. Suits you."

I smile at him, lost for a moment in the collision of real life and *this*. This talking and kissing and the way he looks at me and how good he is, to me and to Dee.

"Hey." My voice is quiet. "Thanks for everything you did for Dee yesterday."

He spins a finger through a wave of my hair. "It was nothing."

He knows it was something, but I don't have to say it. Instead, I lean forward, pressing my mouth against his. I'm not always great at saying what I feel, but I speak make-out language very comfortably. By the time I remove my lips from his, Matt has a wicked grin on his face.

"So." He runs his hand down my arm as if to be persuasive. "Do you think you'd date me in 'real life'?"

"No."

"What! Why not?"

"Because of your douche-y car."

With a laugh, he says, "Okay. I gave you an open door on that one."

"So, how'd you know about this place?"

"One of my buddies is from the Baltimore area—I texted him."

"Saying what? 'Hey, dude, know any secluded places?' He probably thinks you're a serial killer."

"I think I said 'romantic and private.'" He says this with total nonchalance, but I'm charmed that he put so much thought into a date. Brenda would probably say he was "raised right." For some reason, this makes me think of Matt's mom. The thought makes the sides of my lips twitch, a frown nearly forming.

"What was your mom like?" I ask.

It's an abrupt change of subject, but Matt is unshaken. He smiles sadly, his eyes like fog over the Cumberland River. "She was happy. Kind to everyone. Kept our heads on straight during the Finch Four craziness."

As he usually does, Matt makes air quotes around "The Finch Four" like it's a touchstone of someone else's past. I can understand why. I almost never think of him as *that* Matt Finch, the one whose smiling, fifteen-year-old face was taped on the inside of every girl's locker in eighth grade.

"You told me before that you spent all your time trying to make her happy when she was sick. What kind of stuff did you do?"

"I don't know. A lot of things."

"Like what?"

"Okay. Um. The day before her first chemo treatment, she told me that she'd give anything to be one of those stiff-upper-lip women instead of being so emotional. So I printed out a life-size picture of Queen Elizabeth's face, cut out the eyes and mouth, and stapled some ribbons to the sides. I made a Prince Charles one for myself, and when they put her chemo IV in, I brought the masks out. We laughed so hard and just sat there wearing the masks and talking in these loud, offensively bad British accents." His mouth makes the slightest smile I've ever seen. If I didn't know him, I'd think it was a soft grimace, but his dimples tell me otherwise. This is a fond memory, if a painful one. "Everyone at the hospital loved it. At the next treatment, one little kid had a lightning bolt drawn on his forehead and a red-and-gold scarf around his neck. Eventually, we brought all my mom's fancy teacups and had a big tea party with everyone—all these people sitting around, hooked up to IVs, with nothing in common except cancer and the need to pretend they were stronger than they actually felt."

There's a pause when he's done, and I remember to breathe in again.

"Sorry—God, listen to me. Bumming you out."

"You're not. You're really not."

He looks at his hands. "I think the worst part is reconciling all the things she'll miss. She missed her first grandchild. She won't see whether or not I turn out all right. Never meet any girls I like enough to bring home."

He nudges my arm to suggest that I am one such girl, and I snort. "Nobody would take me home to their mother unless they were trying to piss her off."

"My mom would have liked you."

I understand why he wants to believe that, but I know better. Mothers don't like me, not even my own. They take inventory of my makeup, my tall heels, and, as Brenda puts it, my sassy mouth. They never get past it.

"No, really," Matt says, as if sensing my doubt. "My mom was sweet, but she could hold her own. She had to, with three boys. She liked anyone who could dish it out."

"Dee's mom is like that."

"Yeah?"

"Yeah. Even when I get myself in trouble, she never acts like Dee's too good to hang out with me. She's, like, the best mom ever." I can see Mrs. Montgomery in my mind, serving me chocolate milk in her kitchen late at night while Mr. Montgomery picked up my dad from jail. I was twelve, and he'd gotten into a fight at the local bar—the last night he ever drank. "I used to wish my dad would marry someone like Dee's mom."

"Do you think your dad will ever remarry?" Matt asks.

"He did."

"Really?" His eyebrows shoot up. "You have a stepmother?"

"Yup. Bren-da." I roll my eyes. Even my pronunciation of her name is mockery, puffing up my cheeks with the "B" sound and drawing out "da."

"You don't like her?"

I shrug. "I don't get her. And she doesn't get me."

"But she's okay? I mean, she loves your dad?"

"I guess." I pause, blowing a strand of hair off my face. "I mean, she's cares for him. She's good to him. But I think Brenda is too practical to *love* anything."

Matt looks surprised again, like I've said something unnecessarily mean. It's not mean; it's true. But now I feel like I have to defend my surliness. What comes to mind is the field of lavender Brenda planted as soon as she moved in. Before, the side yard of our farmhouse was a big, blank space. She went out every day, digging in the dirt for hours. It took two years for the plants to fully grow, green-gray stems and purple blooms. Now she spends hours harvesting the stalks, which she sells to a local soap company. I never see her standing on the porch, admiring the field the way I do, for its beauty. But she's devoted to caring for it. I'm not sure if it's something I can quite articulate to Matt. "I mean, I think she loves gardening, but she doesn't gush about it or seem particularly happy while she's watering her plants. That's how she is with my dad. She's not very affectionate, not like he is, but she's . . . devoted, I guess. She seems to enjoy taking care of him."

"And she makes your dad happy?"

"Yeah," I admit. "I'm not sure why, exactly, but she does."

I've never really given Brenda credit for that. She may not be warm or maternal, but she's reliable, a steady post for my dad to lean on. If my dad hadn't married Brenda, I never would have left him this summer. I'd be too worried that he'd get lonely and start drinking again.

"So what about your real mom? What was she like?" Matt asks, glancing up to gauge my reaction. "You don't have to tell me if you don't want to."

Of course I don't have to. I look straight at him, his eyes like choppy ocean water on mine. He told me about his mom, after all, and that counts for something. I take a breath, so deep that my stomach rises. "I used to think she was like magic. She pulled me out of school to go to the movies and woke me up late at night to catch fireflies. She let me wear the fairy wings from my Halloween costume to school whenever I felt like it."

Clearing my throat, I pause for a moment. I can't believe

how fast I recited those memories. Most of the time, I can only find traces of my mother, even when I search the furthest-back shelf of my memory. I'm not sure how I found them just now.

"For a while, I thought maybe she left because my dad wasn't fun enough." I sigh, running an edge of the picnic blanket through my fingers. "The older I get, the more I think she was immature and selfish. But I kind of miss it—believing that she was magical."

My mind flashes to my dad, asleep facedown on the kitchen table, as I got up by myself for middle school. By the time he got sober, I was so sick of being responsible, so sick of worrying about him. I wanted someone to worry about me, for once.

Last year, I overheard my dad and Brenda arguing as I walked by their bedroom door. The school had called to report that I'd skipped class. It wasn't even a class—it was my lunch period, but the vice principal blew it completely out of proportion. It's not like I left school to sell drugs. I left because I had the worst craving for a banana split. So I drove to Dairy Queen and was back before math class. Big deal.

"You have to be stricter with her," Brenda was saying to my dad. "That girl is begging for boundaries."

"Bren," my dad replied, and I could hear his exasperation through the heavy door between us. "She took care of herself all those years. You expect me to turn around and start micromanaging her life?"

He still beats himself up for it, still feels guiltier than I ever meant for him to.

"She's not in any real trouble," he insisted. "She's not putting herself or others in danger. She's a teenager, and she skipped her lunch period."

Ha, I thought at the time—*ha, my dad gets it.* I think he really believed what he said to Brenda that day. I think he believed it right up until I got arrested.

"You okay?" Matt asks after a few moments, and I shift back to our conversation.

"Yeah." I force a smile, trying to prove it.

"Do you ever think about trying to find her? Your mom?"

It takes some nerve to ask that question, and I like that he came right out with it. Shaking my head, I say, "No. I used to, but not anymore. We have our problems, but my dad and I are pretty great most of the time. If she couldn't see it, she doesn't deserve either of us."

Between us, his hand finds mine, and he pulls it toward his mouth. He plants a kiss on the back of my hand and says, "You *are* pretty great. Most of the time."

"Yeah, yeah," I say, rolling onto my back. Talking about my mom sucks the energy out of me. I rock onto my knees, changing the subject by pointing the camera at Matt.

"This is a no-paparazzi zone," Matt says. In an act of melodrama, he pulls his aviator sunglasses from the collar of his shirt and slides them on. The metallic lenses reflect my own image, the camera held up to my face and framed by my dark hair.

I smile at him. "Say 'cheesy.' "

"Oh, you think you're so funny." I start to take the picture, but Matt sits up quickly, grabbing me by the waist and tick-ling me with both hands. Since I was watching him move through the camera lens, I'm caught off guard, unable to wriggle from his grasp and unable to keep from giggling. The photograph captured will probably be nothing more than a blur of us.

"Stop!" I resent that he's making my voice sound like a girlish squeal. "Matt, stop, I don't want to drop my camera!"

I pull away, sliding myself off the picnic blanket, and I scramble to my feet. Just in case he tries to pull another stunt like that, I secure the camera's strap around my neck. The grass is prickly, but I take a few more steps, turning to take another picture of him on the blanket. "I shall call it 'Por-trait of a Jerk.'"

He shakes his head, and I turn to take a shot of the view around us. The view stretches like a quilt of colorful farmland, each patch growing new plants that will be whole by autumn. For reasons I can't explain, I feel the pull of home. Of Nashville. I've always thought of myself as a Chi-cagoan. Part of my identity is that I was raised a city girl—that I'm not *from* Tennessee. But that's changed in the past few months. Leaving home changed my idea of where "home" is.

When I turn back, Matt is getting up from the blanket, moving toward me.

"Put the camera down real quick," he says. "Stop docu-menting the moment for a second, and just be in it."

I look through the lens, snapping another shot of him, for

the sake of being contrary. The picture captures his trying-to-be-cute-and-persuasive face. "Why?"

Stepping toward me, he cradles my face in his hands, and I feel seen in such a specific way. It's like when Dee drags me antique shopping, the most grandmotherly of all her interests. I see a cluttered room of junk. But Dee is drawn to the tarnished silver teapots, the scuffed-up guitars, and, one time, a rusted blue bike with a wicker basket she insisted on giving me, to ride to her house. She gets this look on her face when she sees the object for how precious it is to her, despite banged-up edges and chipped paint. That's the way Matt looks at me as he ducks down and kisses me. He kisses me like he means it, in a way that feels anomalous with the great outdoors. It's an up-against-the-apartment-doorway kiss, a foot-of-the-bed kiss. By the time he pulls away, we both know he doesn't have to say it: *that's* why.

He's clearly pleased with himself, wrapping his arms around my waist. "See? Can't take a picture of that."

Cheesy. But true. I could try, but I know I couldn't take a picture that captures how I feel about him right now. Here, I've followed his ridiculous, romantic fancies, and I'm completely charmed by every bit of it.

He kisses me again, his lips parting over mine, and all of me feels bare. It's more than my feet against the cool grass, more than standing three inches shorter than I normally would be in my heels. I feel like every weak part of me is in broad daylight, like I'm asking to get hurt. No, I'm *begging* to hurt. But I simply do not care. I just don't.

The camera around my neck is pressing against his chest, and I adjust so that it's not digging into my stomach. Wrinkling my nose at him, I whisper, "You're squishing my camera."

Matt laughs, covering his face with one hand, but he keeps his arm around my waist.

"What?"

"Nothing." He shakes his head. "I like that you're not sentimental."

If he only knew that, at the moment he leans in to kiss me again, I'm taking pictures in my mind. I'm freezing each frame, trying to memorize the feel of his lips against mine. Because I know how fleeting feelings can be, and I want to remember him exactly, every touch. When this is all over, I'll revisit the mental image, turning it over in my mind, examining it from each angle.

If we could capture feelings like we capture pictures, none of us would ever leave our rooms. It would be so tempting to inhabit the good moments over and over again. But I don't want to be the kind of person who lives backwardly, who memorializes moments before she's finished living in them. So I plant my feet here on this hillside beside a boy who is undoing me, and I kiss him back like I mean it. And, God help me, with the sky wrapped around us in every direction, I *do* mean it.

CHAPTER SEVENTEEN

Baltimore

After stopping for dinner on the drive back, we arrive at the hotel ten minutes after my curfew. Yes. Curfew. The one that Peach gave me even though she'd flown to Nashville with Dee. This is mortifying, but it was her one condition for letting me stay here without her supervision. Of course, I want to blow off the curfew check-in, but Matt insists that we comply. This is the problem with dating a nice guy.

The elevator moves up to Matt's floor—the same floor where the band stays. Greg is my stand-in curfew monitor, which is so hypocritical that I could laugh.

"Hey," Matt says, turning to me. There are mirror panels on each side of the elevator, and I see him reflected back to me at every angle. "I had a great day with you."

I tilt my head up to him. "Same."

"Good." He leans in, and for some reason, it feels like

we're on the front porch of my house. That good-night-kiss feeling whooshes right through me.

When we reach Greg's door, Matt knocks, calling to him, "We're back!"

Greg pulls the door open and glares at us. "You're late. I had to avoid Peach's call to buy you some time."

We glance at each other, suppressing smiles. No way will either of us apologize, and Greg knows it. He's already dialed his cell phone, holding it to his ear.

"Hey." Greg pauses. "Yep, I'm here with both of them. Uh-huh. No, neither of them smells like alcohol."

I roll my eyes, and Matt laughs.

"Yes, I will walk up with Reagan to her room." Greg props the door to his room open and steps out into the hallway. He gestures for me to come with him.

"Oh my *God*, Peach," I say loudly, leaning into the phone. Matt squeezes my hand, and I follow Greg to the elevator.

"Good night!" Matt calls, and I roll my eyes at the situation. Honestly. So embarrassing. I cross my arms while Greg chitchats with Peach. When we reach my floor, Greg holds the elevator door until I've opened my own hotel door.

The hotel suite is eerily quiet and unmoving. On the one hand, I'm pleased to have the whole place to myself. I can sleep in the center of the bed, alone. But this just serves to remind me that, in a few weeks, I'm back to life in Nashville. No more spending every moment with Dee, and I can't even process how much I'll miss her, even her sleep-kicking.

I grab my phone, suddenly needy for best-friend contact. *Weird to be here without you.*

In a moment, my phone beeps. *I know. Weird to be here too.*

Things good at home though?

Yeah. Feeling much better.

Good. See you tomorrow morning.

Good night!

I change into a tank top and pajama shorts, and then slide on my slippers. I'm brushing my teeth when my phone beeps, and I wonder what Dee forgot to tell me. But when I glance down at my phone, it's from Matt. *Come down here?*

Don't have to ask me twice. I check my reflection in the mirror, only to see that I look giddy, my mouth in a can't-help-it kind of smile. I pull a hoodie out of my suitcase and zip it on. Then I unzip it a little.

I can't take the elevator, because it will beep when it opens right in front of Greg's door. So I take the stairs, texting Matt as I do. *On my way.*

One floor below, Matt's peeking out his door, and I scamper inside.

"Hey," he says, shutting the door behind me. "I need you to do me a favor."

When I turn around, I see a desk chair sitting in the middle of the room with a hotel towel draped across the back. Stranger still, he has newspaper spread out on the floor around the chair. On the desk, something small is plugged into the wall—an electric razor.

"Haircut," Matt says, in case I hadn't figured it out yet. I turn to look at him. "I don't know how to cut hair."

"It's not cutting. It's buzzing."

"You're buzzing all of your hair off?"

He nods. "It's time. No more boyish."

"We were only teasing you. I like your hair!"

"Me too. But it's time for a change."

"I don't know how to buzz hair, either."

"It's easy. I'd do it myself, but I can't see the back."

"Don't you and Dee have access to, like, trained hair professionals?"

He sighs, impatient. "Yes, but I want to do it tonight, right now, before I back out."

"You're insane," I say, but I still take my place behind the chair. He drapes the towel over his shoulders while I examine the razor, feeling its weight on my palm. I slide the On button up, and it vibrates to life in my hand.

"Oh God, oh God, oh God." I wince as I bring the razor near his hair.

"That's reassuring." Matt laughs. "Keep saying that."

I pull the razor through a piece of hair in the back, too nervous to start at the front. A clump of hair falls to the floor, and I consider clicking the Off button. I should leave him to his own devices and have no culpability in the results.

He senses my hesitation. "Reagan, seriously, you can't mess up a buzz cut."

I keep going until it's too late to turn back. My hands move methodically, without thinking too hard about what needs to happen, and it only takes a few minutes for most of his hair to be gone.

"Okay." I pause to examine my progress. With my arms raised, I can't seem to get enough control to steady the razor perfectly. "Can you move to the floor?"

I sit on the edge of the bed, and Matt settles himself in front of me and leans back. Draping my legs over his shoulders to steady myself, I examine an uneven patch, formulating my approach. Matt runs his hands up my bare legs, turning his head to kiss the inside of my knee.

"Stop that," I tell him. "Do you want me to mess this up?"

I feel his shoulders moving in laughter. I guess it's flattering, that he cares about kissing me more than he cares about having a bald patch on the back of his head.

I pronounce it finished, and he turns around to face me, on his knees and still in front of me. Without his longer hair, attention draws right to his eyes. His cheekbones look more defined, and so do the muscles in his neck. The haircut accomplishes its purpose: boyishness gone. I don't see Matt Finch of the Finch Four. I just see Matt.

I run my hands across the hair he has left. "Feels like a caterpillar."

"Feels good," he murmurs. "Lighter."

"I like it."

He steals a glance in the mirror hanging on the wall. "Me too."

When he turns back toward me, I start to gather the towel from around his shoulders. Though I try to be careful, there are still some loose hairs against his shirt. I set the towel on the newspapered part of the floor and begin to brush off his shirt. He glances down, tugs his shirt over his head and pitches it on the floor.

"You still have . . ." I trail off, pointing toward his bare neck. "Right here."

I lean forward, gently blowing against the side of his neck, where the remnants of the haircut are still lingering. When I sit back, he's closing his eyes, and I take the opportunity to kiss him. I mean it to be quick, but he kisses me back, harder, and I run my hands against the back of his head. The sensation tingles every inch of my palms and travels up my arms until all of me hums like a neon sign, electric. These few motions, and we've clearly pushed each other into new gear, into a faster pace, barreling forward.

Matt unzips my hoodie, smoothing it off my shoulders. I'd probably let him keep going, but his hands don't move in that direction. He presses my body against his with one arm, using the other to slide me onto the bed. I run my fingers over where I know his tattoo is, touching the words like deciphering Braille, trying to read his very person.

Time goes blurry as we lay on the bed, interlocked and mouth against mouth. There is a moment that I know we both sense—the one where it becomes clear that either of us could initiate more. This is an opportunity that most guys fumble for, greedy and even desperate to grasp it, but not Matt Finch. Instead, I feel both of us slowing ourselves down, and I'm oddly relieved.

Sure, I'm thrown by his restraint, but I refuse to let myself think too much into it. I don't want to regret Matt, and I don't want to stick him into the same formula I've used with every other guy. I've seen how that turns out.

By the time we lie still, it could have been minutes or hours or days. Our heads are resting on the same pillow, and I can't stop looking at him. I know it doesn't make sense, but the haircut makes him look *more* like Matt, more like who I know him to be. Lying here together, there's the sensation of being in a different world, like when you're little and can imagine lifting off into enchanted forests and starry galaxies, all from the comfort of your bed.

He stretches his arm out toward me, and I scoot closer, resting my head on his chest. His heart beats beneath my ear, with the low, steady cadence of a kick drum. Just a few more minutes.

I startle awake, disoriented. Blinking rapidly, I realize that I'm still in Matt's bed. Light is filtering in through the windows, but I have no concept of what time it is. Beneath the sheets, I'm still wearing my tank top and pajama shorts, and my bare feet are warm on his legs. I fell asleep here, and I slept through the whole night. Matt's eyes are still closed, and we've separated somewhere in sleep; his arm no longer curls over me. Good. Easier escape.

My instinct is to bolt. I don't want to think about whether I talked in my sleep or drooled or something. I don't want the awkward morning conversation. So I slowly inch one leg out from the covers, glancing over at him. His eyes are still closed, and I still like his short hair. To keep from shifting the bed, I hover my feet until they meet the floor. I reach for my hoodie, which got discarded last night, and start to stand up from the bed.

"Hey," Matt murmurs from behind me, his voice gravelly from sleep. I turn back to look at him. He notices my sweatshirt in my hand and his tired eyes widen. He gives a mock gasp. "You were trying to sneak out!"

I drop back down on the edge of the bed, trying to look less guilty. "No, I wasn't."

"Yes, you were!" He tries to look offended.

"No, I just . . ." My speech stalls out. I'm taking too long to find an excuse, and he reaches across the bed and wraps his arms around my waist. Making a growling noise, he pulls me toward him.

"No!" I squeal, trying to cover my bed-head. "Don't look at my hair."

"Your hair is so cute!" he squeals back, mocking me. "Promise you won't sneak out!"

"Fine!"

He sits up against the headboard, and I settle myself against his shoulder. Beside him, my rigid limbs relax. I slept here last night, and that's okay.

"Good morning," he says.

"Good morning. I like your hair."

"Why, thank you." His hand is on my leg, his fingers gently pressing one by one, like he's playing piano keys.

This stirs a curiosity in me. "Don't you play the piano?"

"Have you been watching old YouTube videos of me?"

I laugh. "No. But I thought you played it in the Finch Four sometimes."

"Yes, I can play the piano." He moves his hand to run it through his hair, but instead he winds up rubbing the short cut. "My mom taught me when I was little. I was the only one of my brothers who would sit still to learn. I haven't played in public in a while because . . . well, because it feels like too soon."

"I'd like to hear you play sometime." I'm inching across this territory, over a path of grief that is unknowable to me. "Not today or tomorrow. Just someday."

At this, his head snaps up, the flicker of a smile on his mouth. "Someday, huh? You're gonna give me a *someday*? Sounds serious."

He thinks he's so funny. I wrinkle my nose, then stay quiet for a while, teasing him with my silence. I'm sure my face looks thoughtful, as if I am summing his good qualities and dividing them by his flaws. Of course, I'm in no position to catalog someone else's faults, but I like to see him sweat it out. Finally, I tell him the truth. "I would like to know you for a while."

I'm not thinking about the details now—if we will know each other but in separate cities, if we will know each other as friends only, if we will know each other in the biblical sense. I just know I want him around for longer. Beside me, Matt looks as though he's been presented with a trophy, Grand Champion of Getting Reagan to Admit One Fraction of Her Feelings. "I would like to know you for a while, too. Especially with that kind of romantic sweet talk."

I make a face, swatting at his leg. He plants a kiss on the underside of my wrist, and then looks up at me. "So you broke your wrist after falling in your heels, but you keep wearing the heels."

I'm not sure why I didn't tell him the first time he asked. I could have told him, with blunt delivery, *My ex-boyfriend hit me.* The nonchalance would have had a certain shock value, which I usually enjoy. But in this case, I worry that it exposes how screwed up my life has been. Obviously, getting hit by Blake wasn't my fault. People have reminded me this a hundred times—my therapist, my dad, Dee, Dee's mom—but they don't have to. Believe me: I know. I have only a few hard and fast rules about how I live my life, and this is one: if a guy touches me in anger or if I wonder for even one second that he will, I'm done. Not done until he apologizes, not done until he promises it will never happen again, that he's changed. Done forever.

The part that embarrasses me is that I chose to date a self-professed mean drunk with a history of selling drugs. I knew he was bad news, but I liked that he seemed a little dangerous. It seems so naive now. But maybe it's time for

Matt to get a glimpse of that girl. See if it's enough to scare him off.

"There's kind of more to it than that."

"Oh yeah?" He sits up, face solemn, as if he can sense that there is nothing amusing about what I'm about to tell him.

"Yeah. But I don't want you to say anything, and I don't want you to look at me differently." I scoot away from him so I can see his face, and I wrap my arms around my knees. "My last boyfriend cheated on me, and I caught him." I say this quickly, reciting the facts from memory instead of reliving that night in my mind. "We fought, and he wound up hitting me so hard that I lost my balance. I fell on my wrist."

His eyes flare. "He *what?*"

"I said don't talk."

He presses his mouths into a flat line, the muscles in his jaw flexed.

"In the months that I dated him, he never drank. He stopped drinking after he got busted in a bar fight." I sigh. It sounds like I'm defending him, which I'm not—merely explaining him. "I have no idea why he had been drinking that night, but he was wasted, and he hit me." I glance over at Matt's face. The anger has melted into pity. "No, don't look at me like that."

"Like what?"

"Like you feel sorry for me. Like I need to be saved." My voice is huffy, defensive. "I can walk away all on my own— and I did. He's an asshole, and it shouldn't have happened, but

I'm not locked in some vicious cycle of abuse. I don't *accept* what happened."

He's quiet, and I can't blame him. What are you supposed to say to that?

"God," I groan, pressing my face into my hands. "I knew I shouldn't have told you."

"No," he replies, surprised. "I'm glad you did."

I give him my most disbelieving look, and I suddenly feel completely naked—not in a good way. I wish I could grab the words I said out of the air and cram them back into my stupid mouth. From the nightstand, Matt's phone rings, and he reaches over to turn it off without even looking at who it is.

"I really like you," Matt announces, which somehow makes me feel more embarrassed. "You're unpredictable and smart, and I basically want to spend all of my time with you."

I bite the insides of my cheeks hard enough to leave imprints. His words fall inside the scope of people describing me, which I hate even when it's complimentary.

"So you can understand why it would upset me that some asshole treated you like that. And how I want to hunt him down and kill him."

"If anyone's killing him, it's me. Or my dad."

"But I'm glad you told me," he repeats. "I feel like I know you better."

"Ha." I push my hair off my face. "Yeah. Now you know that I really am a wreck."

"You're not a wreck." Matt leans forward, kissing my shoulder. "You have a few battle wounds, like everyone else."

He runs his hand down my back, stopping in the place where my shoulder blades jut out. I could get used to it—to his touch, to the sound of his voice, to all of it. Maybe I am used to it, which is a realization that startles me. I don't know what we're doing here, and I haven't thought past the last tour stop in Nashville. I don't want to think past it, because I know how things end. I slept here last night, the whole night, next to him, and that was really foolish.

I sit up. "I should get back up there before Peach and Dee get back."

"Okay." His phone goes off again, and he frowns as he reaches for it on the nightstand.

"You're popular early in the morning," I comment, standing up from the bed. I slide my hoodie back on.

"No . . . ," he trails off, concerned. "I actually have to answer this."

Before I can say I don't care, he's holding the phone to his ear. "Hey."

I move toward the door, and he doesn't even look up. "Corinne, slow down, slow down. What happened? He what?"

Matt shifts, turning so that his feet are on the floor. His back is to me, hunched over as he rests his elbows on his knees. "Okay, just take a breath."

Now I feel like I shouldn't be here, like I'm intruding on Matt and another girl. I pad gently to the door; I don't even want to interrupt with my steps.

"Sorry," he mouths to me, covering the phone. He grimaces, trying to portray the seriousness of the situation.

Maybe her dad died. Or her dog. I should be more sensitive, to her apparent crisis, but I feel disregarded. This departure is all wrong. He couldn't possibly know that it's such a big deal for me—to stay here with him, to talk about Blake. But I did both of those things, only to be cast aside by his girl best friend.

Once upstairs, I'm startled to find Dee in our room. She's sitting on the bed cross-legged, unpacking the small bag of things she took home for the night.

"Hey! I didn't think you'd be back till later."

"Clearly." She smirks up at me. "And you are *so* lucky that Peach met Greg for brunch downstairs without checking in on you."

I play dumb. "Oh. Yeah. That's where I was, too. Brunch."

"Reagan O'Neill." Dee laughs. I notice that she looks better rested. Her complexion looks healthier, her skin clear of dark circles. "This bed did *not* get slept in last night."

"I didn't sleep with him." I pause, rethinking that statement. "I mean . . . I slept in his room, but that's it."

"*Really.*" Dee halts her unpacking process, frozen with a pair of jeans in hand. "Fascinating."

"Why? We haven't even known each other that long."

"That hasn't stopped you before."

"Hey." I grab a pillow and smack it against her arm. She laughs because she's right, and we both know it.

Dee keeps looking at me, shaking her head slowly. "You *didn't* sleep with him. Huh."

"Stop—you're making it weirder!" I squirm under the heat of her scrutiny. *"Anyway.* How was home?"

"Great. Much needed. My parents say hello." Her entire aura is lighter than it has been since the tour started. "I also floated the idea of getting my own apartment sometime in the next year or so, just to see how they'd react. They were really supportive."

"Oh yeah?" I confess: I'm surprised she'd mention this to her parents so soon. Dee doesn't adapt easily.

"Yeah. They know it's hard for me, the idea that I'll miss out on these huge life experiences by not going to college. And living on my own, near home, will still give me something similar." She tilts her head, suddenly looking shy. "And you really can live with me, if you want. If you stay in Nashville for school. You don't have to. You can live in a dorm. I won't be mad."

I laugh. There's the Dee I know—the one already obsessing over the details of the hypothetical. "Okay."

She smiles, loosening up again. "I'm so excited about the idea of it. Decorating a place so that it feels like mine, buying my own groceries . . ."

There's a knock at the door, and I glance up. "I'll get it."

It had better be Matt. My curiosity about his conversation is driving me crazy. In the fish-eye lens, I can see that he's changed into jeans and a T-shirt, and he looks distraught.

"Hey," I say, pulling the door all the way open.

"Hey. Sorry about that." He kisses me on the side of the

head. This action is completely dispassionate—a movement born of habit or obligation, not real feeling. I want to swipe my hand over my hair, brushing off the indignity of it. "Corinne's boyfriend just broke up with her, out of nowhere."

Great. I presume she needed to call Matt to let him know that she's now available, after his years of pining for her. "That's too bad."

"Yeah. She's really messed up about it."

"Hey Matt!" Dee says, emerging from our room. "Oh, wow. Your hair! When did that happen?"

"Last night." He runs his hand over his shorn hair.

"Looks great." Dee looks between our two faces. "Everything okay?"

Matt moves toward the couch, and I follow behind him. "Yeah. My best friend just called to say she got dumped."

"Corinne? You're kidding. Haven't they been together for ages?"

I knew Dee had met Corinne before, but I didn't know she knew her life history. Matt nods grimly. "Yeah—practically married."

That's how I felt when Dee and Jimmy broke up. I couldn't get used to the idea of them apart. Still can't.

"Oh my God," Dee murmurs. As a fellow victim of heartbreak, of course Dee would commiserate. "Is she okay?"

Matt frowns. "No. I don't think she is."

"You should invite her on tour," Dee suggests. "Get her mind off of it."

"I did," Matt says. "She's going to come, I think."

I close my eyes, almost a wince. Yeah, poor girl, breakups are rough, boo-hoo. But this is the same girl Matt said he loves. Used to love. Whatever.

"Who knows? Maybe they'll get back together before then, even. Maybe it was only a fight," I suggest, trying to sound cheerful. The sentiment is like an ill-fitting, frou-frou dress on me—too frilly.

"Maybe." Matt's voice is hesitant as he shakes his head worriedly. "I don't know. I don't have a good feeling about it."

Funny. Me, neither.

CHAPTER EIGHTEEN

Cincinnati to Nashville

We're standing in the lobby of an arena in Cincinnati, Ohio, and I'm soaking in my last few minutes with Matt and Dee. I'm already mourning the loss of our easy dynamic, the three of us. In mere moments, we'll have a fourth. Corinne is driving down from her college in Columbus. She'll be here for the show tonight, and then she'll follow the tour caravan in her car to Indianapolis. And probably Chicago and Lexington and Nashville. But dear *God*, I hope she leaves sooner.

I know I should be more sensitive, having watched my own best friend go through a devastating breakup, but I don't care. Corinne is barging in on my time with Matt, and I'm not the type of girl who shares—not food, not feelings, and certainly not boys.

Dee, Matt, and I have had more fun in the past three

days than in the entire summer. Before, Dee was mud-struggling, as her dad always says. When you're trying to walk a dirt path after a rainstorm, the heavy mud gloms on to your boots with each step forward. Your weight tacks you to the sticky ground, and there's nothing you can do to speed up your journey. But later, once you've struggled through, the mud dries on your boots. You can knock the clumps off like they were never there. Dee came home from Nashville with clean boots.

Now, Matt's girl best friend is barging in. I shove my hands in my pockets, annoyed.

"That's her," Matt says, nodding toward the doors.

Yep. It's her, all right, only she's wearing cute, square glasses that weren't in any picture I saw. As I suspected, she's not head-turning, Hollywood gorgeous. She's precious, take-home-to-your-mom cute. Marriage-material cute. Matt takes off toward her, and when she spots him, she relaxes into a full-body sigh, like a weary traveler relieved to finally be home.

He grabs her into a bear hug, and I can hear her squeal, "Ah, your hair!"

I can't make out what he's saying as Dee and I walk toward them.

"Reagan." He looks at me, but his hands stays on her arm. "This is Corinne."

"Nice to meet you," I tell her, but I don't extend my hand. I feel prickly. Almost jealous.

"You too." She's smiling, but I can tell she's sizing me up. "I've heard a lot about you."

"Hey." Matt knocks his elbow into hers. "Don't give away my secrets."

They grin at each other, and I can't ignore how comfortable they are together. The thought ignites a burner inside me, and my stomach rolls to a low boil. Her freckles, which I was hoping were somehow strange-looking in person, are adorable, and she has naturally rosy cheeks. She's wearing a cardigan, for God's sake.

"Hi, Corinne!" Dee says from behind me, leaning in to hug her. "Nice to see you again."

"Hey, Dee." She gives her a quick squeeze. *Stop hugging my people, bitch.* "Thanks for letting me tag along."

"Please." Dee waves her off. "We're glad to have you."

Speak for yourself. Smiling, Corinne wraps both her arms around Matt's waist, creating some sort of side hug. Oh, great. She's one of those affectionate types, like Dee. Only, on Corinne, it's not endearing. Worse yet, Matt looks completely at ease, like he is used to having this girl's arms around his waist.

She releases him as we walk toward the elevator, but Matt's attention stays on her completely. "How was your drive?"

"Not bad. I actually spent the entire trip listening to that mix you made after The Incident."

"Ah, yes." Matt turns to us. "The Incident is our name for my ex-girlfriend taking our breakup to the tabloids. I was in a very angst-filled place after that."

"*That's* an understatement," Corinne tells us. *We get it.
You know him.* "The mix has Janis Joplin on it."

"Hey," Matt says. "If memory serves, the mix is called
Angry Breakup Songs. It has to have Janis Joplin on it."

I'm going to suffocate in this elevator if she insists on
flaunting her historical Matt Finch knowledge. Fortunately,
the elevator doors open to our floor, and we step out toward
Matt's dressing room. Inside, Dee takes a seat in the armchair, and I sit at the end of the couch. Corinne keeps wandering, examining the room. She peers out the tall windows
at the river view below.

"Nice view. Totally reminds me of—"

"The room in Pittsburgh?" Matt finishes, grinning. "I
know. I thought that as soon as I walked in. I had flashbacks
to that security guard."

" 'Where are you kids supposed to be?' " Corinne's voice
is lowered into a growl, obviously impersonating someone.
She starts laughing, and Matt picks up where she left off.

" 'Um, onstage . . . ,' " Matt quotes.

Dee's smiling pleasantly at their inside-joke reenactment,
but I can't resist an eye roll. Matt sits down beside me, resting his arm on the back of the couch. For a split second,
Corinne's eyes follow his arm. She's startled, like this gesture
is unsettling proof of our closeness. She sits on the other side
of Matt on the couch.

Dee's politeness chimes in. "So, Corinne, you've toured
with Matt before?"

She nods. "A few Finch Four shows the summer after freshman year of high school."

I've been quiet for too long, and I don't want to let on to my annoyance. "Are you a musician, too?"

"Oh, God, *no*," Matt says. "She's completely tone-deaf. It is physically painful."

"Shut up!" Corinne grabs a pillow off the couch and smacks him with it. A corner of the pillow hits my side, which Matt doesn't notice. "That's a total exaggeration."

He grabs another pillow and hits her back, which sends her into a giggle fit. Now I feel like I'm at a middle school sleepover, which I hated even when I was in middle school.

Glancing at Dee, I ask, "How soon do you have to get ready for your meet and greet?"

She takes the hint. "Now-ish. I wish I could hang out, but duty calls."

Dee and I both stand. I can't stay here and play tug-of-war with Corinne, not without Dee to keep me on my best behavior.

"Hey." Matt encircles his arms around my waist. In my peripheral vision, I can see Corinne's smile dissipate. "You don't have to get ready. Stay awhile."

I'll be damned if I'm going to be the third wheel, and I'll be damned if I'm going to let Corinne figure out that I feel tetchy and threatened. "Nah. I want you two to have some time to catch up."

Matt looks completely enamored by my consideration for Corinne's feelings. "Careful there, O'Neill. Corinne's going to figure out how sweet you are underneath that hard-candy shell."

"Ha-ha," I say drily, but Dee laughs heartily. When I glance over at Corinne, there's an obligatory smile on her face. It takes all my effort, but I force my own smile. "Nice to meet you."

"You too."

I step back out of Matt's arms. I'm tempted to kiss him, to mark my territory, but it seems too possessive. Luckily, he catches me by the hand. "Come down before I go onstage, okay?"

"Okay." Then he kisses my hand. Corinne looks horrified, but only for the briefest moment. I suppress a triumphant smile. "You're embarrassing your friend."

"I'm embarrassing *you*." He plants one more smacking, overdramatic kiss on my hand. "Which is cute. Bye."

I roll my eyes. "Bye."

Before the door closes, Corinne and Matt start laughing about something—possibly me. Dee links her arm through mine as we walk across the hall to her dressing room, and I glance over at her. "Okay, that girl does not seem heartbroken about anything. Right?"

"She *was* kind of flirty with him . . . ," Dee trails off, considering this. "I'm sure she's just in the first phase of grieving the relationship."

"The phase where you want to sleep with someone else to piss off your ex?"

"No. The desperate phase where you're pretending to

be happy, as if that could somehow actually make you feel happy."

I sigh. "Maybe. But did you see the looks she was giving me?"

Even Dee, the nicest person on Earth, can't deny it. "I mean, she gave you a few once-overs. But Matt's her best friend. She's probably protective of him."

I get that. I even respect it. When it comes to my own best friend, my protective instinct belongs in a lion pride. But this is different. I'm not sure how, but it is.

"Besides, Matt is obsessed with you." Dee is trying to disguise a little smirk, and she's failing. "I've never seen you this jealous before. You like him."

I glare at her. "I'm not jealous. I'm . . . annoyed. I know girls who are like her. As soon as Matt's not around, the gloves will come off."

Dee pushes her dressing room door open, and I follow her inside, feeling totally stripped of control. "I just don't understand why she has to come running straight to Matt. Like, you'd think she'd have other friends, you know?"

"I guess," Dee says, sighing. She sets her purse on the makeup counter and doesn't meet my eyes.

I can't seem to stop ranting, even though I'm only getting myself more worked up. "She couldn't wait a little more than a week to see him? And why did he think this was, like, socially appropriate? He pursued me like an insane bloodhound, not the other way around, so I have no idea why he'd let her barge in."

"You know what, Reagan?" Dee huffs. "I know you got burned, okay? But Matt is not Blake, so stop making him into the bad guy. He's doing exactly what you would do for me. It's what best friends do. They pick up the pieces. Give him a break."

I can barely register that she's disagreeing with me. "But Corinne . . ."

"Had her heart crushed by her longtime boyfriend this week?"

My eyes bear into Dee, even though she's riffling through her purse and not looking at me. Her face is flushed, like it always is when she gets within spitting distance of a confrontation. She identifies with Corinne, having recently had her heart broken—I know she does. But that is *no* excuse for not taking my side. I *always* take hers. "I know you think you understand heartbreak, Dee, but you have no idea what it's like to have your trust repeatedly broken—to have everyone in your life eventually leave you."

Now she stands up straight, her brows furrowed. "Hey. I've *never* left you."

"Dee, you *literally* left midway through high school." My mouth snaps shut, like my own body is embarrassed that I'd give Dee such a horrible guilt trip. I didn't mean to say it—I mean, yes, I do feel sorry for myself sometimes, that my only friend left me to fend for myself. But I don't hold it against her.

Her lower lip trembles, but her eyes are unblinking. "I can't *believe* you would throw that in my face."

I try to make words come out—any words—but they refuse. My tongue is stuck against the back of my throat, and I have that shaky, feverish feeling that I get only in two instances: when I have the flu and when I'm a bitch to Dee.

"What was I supposed to do? Forget my music and stay in high school to babysit you?"

"*Babysit* me?" My chest fills with the heat of anger, pulsing so that I feel like I'm having an out-of-body experience. I hear my voice, but I can't control my mouth. "You can take your charmed life and *shove it*. Dee. Boo-hoo, everything is so hard, with your happy family and your dreams coming true and your piles of money."

"My life is not that simple, and you *know* it." Her face is nearly incandescent.

"Well, your life is much simpler when I'm around to make gas stations runs for you and act like your assistant."

We stand there, facing each other and shaking, like we're both shocked that we'd say these things. I can't do this; I need this to stop. I need to retreat. "Well, have a *great* show. I'll be riding to Indianapolis on Matt's bus."

"Of *course* you will," Dee shoots back. "I'm so glad you could use my tour to find a new boyfriend and parade him around everywhere."

My back is already turned, so Dee doesn't see my jaw drop. I have no idea where her backbone came from—her ability to have the last word instead of backing down and apologizing. How dare she? I've listened to *months* of her mourning Jimmy like he died. She can't be my friend the *one* time I vent about a guy I'm dating?

The door clicks shut behind me, and I want to run across the hall to Matt's room, bury my face in his shoulder, and sob because even my best friend thinks I'm a terrible person. My chest is rising and falling too fast, and I'm breathing through my nose like I'm asthmatic. I don't want Matt and Corinne to know I fought with Dee, and I especially don't want them to know what we fought about.

Instead, I pace around the arena for over an hour before the show, getting lost in the swarms of Lilah Montgomery fans. My phone stays in my hand the whole time, while I alternate between expecting an apology from Dee and deciding I need to say I'm sorry first. It's hard to say which I feel worse about: what I said to her or what she said to me. We've never torn into each other like that before, never intentionally tried to hurt each other.

I debate hiding out for the rest of the night, but I make the last-minute decision to show up backstage. Maybe we can work it out and be done with it.

"There you are," Matt says, sliding his hand around my waist. Dee's nowhere around.

"Here I am," I repeat weakly.

"Matt, two minutes!" a production assistant yells from behind him.

"All right," Matt says. He smiles down at me, kissing me on the forehead before he turns away.

Corrine has been standing here the whole time, but I almost forgot about her. She tells Matt to break a leg, and they hug for what feels like too long.

It was inevitable that I'd have to be alone with Corinne at some point. Any patience I might have had for her is long gone after my argument with Dee. For most of Matt's set, we exchange the smallest possible small talk. Standing on the side stage, I'm glad I didn't bring my camera to document tonight's show. I don't want to remember how adoringly Corinne looks at Matt onstage or her catcalls after each song.

There's a pause in between songs as he switches guitars, and I feel Corinne glance over at me. "I'm glad he had someone to keep him company this summer."

Past tense—"he had." As if that time is over because she's here now. And "keep him company," like that's all I am—a stand-in presence to keep him from feeling alone. Subtle undermining. Clever girl. Fortunately, I speak Passive-Aggressive Bitch as a second language.

"It's been *my pleasure*." There. Let her think about that. She's known Matt much longer, but I'm the one who knows the feeling of his lips, his hands, his bare skin against mine.

"You're really pretty." She says this with the blunt charm of a child, but I know what she's doing. Corinne is adorable; she's not intimidated by me. She's trying to ingratiate herself so I'll trust her. Unlikely.

"Expecting a troll?"

She laughs. "No. I don't know what I was expecting, based on what Matt's told me about you."

I shrug. I will *not* ask what he's told her, even though I'm nauseated with curiosity. From onstage, the next song begins, sweet and slow.

"Ah, there it is. Your song."

She looks startled. "He told you that?"

"Sure." As in: *Sure, he told me. He tells me all kinds of things.*

"Oh." She bites at the corner of her lovely pout. Her lips are not very wide, but they're full, perfect for making lipstick imprints. "Sorry if that's awkward . . ."

"Of course not. Everyone has a past—people they used to love. Matt's are just . . . better-documented than mine."

Her lips purse at the words "used to love." Good. I wish this banter would stop. I also wish she would stop looking at Matt like he's a puppy under the Christmas tree, like he's the most unbelievably delightful thing that has ever shown up in her life. But then her eyes move to the front row, which is comprised of all girls, as usual. "It must drive you crazy, all those girls."

"Not really. I'm not insecure." Just territorial.

"I'm sure you're not." I swear—I catch her eyeing my chest. *Bitch.* There's a part of me that wants to find Dee and tell her I was right about this girl—Matt's gone, and she unsheathed her claws.

"And I trust him." I'd never really thought about it until

now, but I do trust Matt—as much as I trust anyone I've known for a few weeks, I mean.

"That's good." Her smile at me is like a flickering fluorescent light. When she smiles at Matt, it's a sunrise. "Are you guys exclusive now? He hadn't mentioned it."

Of course we are. Matt didn't doggedly pursue me for half the summer so that I could be one of many. But I look at her like that comment is completely beneath me. "I'm not really the type of girl who insists on defining a relationship."

"Hmm." She's not even trying to disguise her judgmental expression. "That's good for him right now—something casual. He's got a lot going on."

"His mom. I know." That's right; I know he's still hurting. And I would never contribute to it.

She sighs. "She was really wonderful. It's still hard on everybody."

Even though we're chatting, we're both facing the stage, watching Matt with arms crossed. "He told me that your moms were best friends."

"Yeah." She's in flats, but my tall shoes make me eye-level with her, perfect for staring contests. "Matt's family moved to our neighborhood in Chicago when we were in preschool. I can't even imagine going home for Christmas without her. She was like my second mom."

"Yeah. Matt said that you were like a sister to him, so I got the impression that your families are close."

Her eyes cloud over at the idea that she and Matt are related. "We are."

"It must be hard to be so far away. Why did you decide on Ohio for college?"

"It's where my boyfriend was going. Ex-boyfriend." She closes her eyes for a brief moment, withholding a full-blown wince. "You don't have to say it—I know it was stupid."

Yep. "Nah."

Her tone becomes defensive, like she can sense my lie. "Well, I love Columbus, and I have my own friends there. So it's not like I'll transfer schools because we broke up."

"That's good. Do you think you'll get back together?"

Her arms tighten. "I don't know. I don't want to give him the satisfaction of getting me back. Besides, he was always really jealous of Matt, which was annoying."

Enough of this little heart-to-heart. "Well, guys are jerks."

The lights of the stage reflect back in her eyes as she watches on. "Matt's not."

Touché.

Dee never shows up to watch Matt's set, and I don't know why I'm surprised. I leave the wings before Matt's finished, moving into an area of the crowd that I know Dee can't see because of the lights. Even the fans' relentless noise doesn't drone out the words ricocheting around my mind: *stay in high school to babysit you, use my tour to find a new boyfriend.* Did she mean those things? I didn't mean what I accused her of—of not understanding real pain, of abandoning me, of using me like an assistant. What kind of sociopath says those things to her best friend?

By the time Dee makes her entrance, I feel ill. The girls

next to me lose all concept of personal space, sideswiping me as they jump up and down, screaming. Her shows are timed exactly, but this one feels a hundred times longer than any other as I simmer inside my guilt and the deafening crowd.

Just when I'm thinking that this night can't get any worse, Dee starts into the last song before the finale: "Open Road Summer." Everyone around me sing-yells the lyrics, and I wince as my name is among them.

"Riding top down with Reagan beneath the summer sky, and I swear this car could almost fly," Dee sings. *"School's back in September, but we'll always remem . . ."*

That's not what the crowd is singing.

She flubbed the lyrics—something I've never seen her do, not even in rehearsals. Her face registers the mistake for only a moment. The Lilah stage presence drops and, for a split second, it's just Dee and her horrified expression, magnified on the huge screens at either side of the stage. She self-corrects, but not before I know in my gut: this is my fault.

"Sunglasses, a country song, and a steering-wheel drummer, y'all, turn up the volume—it's an open road summer."

I press my face into my palms. It's too much—sweaty and claustrophobic among all these people—and I push my way out. In the nearest restroom, I rest my back against a stall door until the sick feeling eases. The groups of girls come and go, and I wait until they leave to splash some cold water on my face, which looks as bad as I feel. If I had a Sharpie, I'd write it on the stall door myself: *Reagan O'Neill is a bitch.*

My guilt overrides my hurt feelings, and I know I need to

apologize as soon as possible. Maybe Dee will be furious. Maybe she meant everything she said. Maybe I'll be riding with Matt for the rest of the tour. But I have to try. Outside, the venue has mostly cleared out, and I've obviously been hiding in the restroom for longer than I thought. I rush upstairs to Dee's dressing room, but she's not there and neither is her bag. She must have boarded the bus already. I doubt I'm welcome on it.

Matt's dressing room is at the other end of the hall, and I take long strides, trying to calm myself. I'll ride with him and apologize to Dee when we get to Indianapolis, in person.

"Did he go downstairs already?" I ask the guard near Matt's door.

The guard glances at my VIP pass and considers this. "Not yet."

I pull the handle, and the moment the door swings open, I can't believe what I'm seeing.

No, no, no.

I was right, I knew I was right, but I can't believe I was right. The world halts, suspending this scene for what feels like a lifetime.

This isn't real—Corinne's mouth pressed against Matt's.

I go cold. It starts in my core but spreads quickly to my limbs, my feet, my fingertips. I assume this is because my heart has stopped beating. My feet back up, stuttering against the carpet, and Matt's head jerks up at the sound of the door, caught. Of all the familiar impulses in my body—anger, jealousy, hurt—there is only one that prevails: *run*.

The door slams behind me as I take off down the hall. Reaching the elevator, I slap my palm against the Down button again and again and again, its plastic face red from my abuse. I don't have time to wait. The venue only has two floors, and I'd rather jump off the building than face Matt head-on. I duck down the stairwell, just in time for Matt to rush out of his room.

He calls out to me, but I'm already charging down the stairs. My hands clutch the rail, straining to keep balance as my heels clack like typewriter keys against the concrete steps. It feels like my legs are moving automatically, bending beneath me using only momentum.

"Reagan!" Matt's voice echoes from one flight above me. "Stop—please."

These words are meaningless to me. They're a foreign language spoken by a foreign person, someone I don't know at all.

"Reagan, please just hear me out! It wasn't what it looked like."

Oh, the hell it wasn't. How insulting, that he'd try to pretend like I didn't see something that was right in front of my face. I keep moving, putting as much distance as I can between us. He's undeterred; I can hear his footsteps quickening somewhere above me.

"She kissed me out of nowhere one second before you opened the door. . . . I didn't even kiss her back; I would have pulled away if I'd had another second to react, and . . ."

He keeps talking, but the sound sizzles in my ears like static. I don't care what he has to say about it. My feet fly faster and faster down the steps, to the rhythm of my only thought: *I can't believe I told him, I can't believe I told him.* I can't believe I told him about Blake, about my mom, about everything. I might as well have drawn a target on my own back, handed him a knife, and turned around.

As I reach the last flight of stairs—so close to the ground floor now—I can hear Matt catching up with me. "Reagan, please, this is a horrible mistake. Please."

Damn right, it's a horrible mistake—*my* horrible mistake for trusting him. As I hit the bottom of the stairs, I nearly trip. Pressing my palm against the side wall, I pause to steady myself. The last thing I need is another broken bone, another souvenir from another betrayal. When I turn back, Matt is a few steps away from the ground floor, a few steps from being close enough to touch me.

"Don't you *dare* come closer." I point my finger at him in an attempt to look threatening, but my whole arm is shaking. "And don't pretend like you actually care. I fell for your whole routine, so just go ahead and do your victory dance."

He takes a gasping exhale, as if I've jammed my fist into his stomach. "That's not fair."

I throw my arms out. "You want to talk about fair? Screw you, Matt."

Turning on my heels, I grab the door handle, but he calls out to me before I can open it. "Reagan, you have to believe me. It wasn't what it looked like."

"Bullshit." My heart is splitting like dry campfire wood, and I'm desperate to hurt him half as badly as he hurt me. "You know, I'm not even surprised. Mr. Celebrity thinks he can do whatever he wants with as many girls as he wants. Oh, don't give me that kicked-puppy look. You surrendered any right to have feelings about me when you . . . when you . . ."

He opens his mouth to speak, but I hold up my hand. With a deep breath, I stand up a bit straighter, trying for the illusion of composure. "You know what? It doesn't even matter—let's be honest here, Matt. We were messing around for a summer. This would have ended a week from now anyway."

"That's not true." His voice is quiet now. He's not fighting back. He knows he's done. "That is *not* true, not for me, and you know it. Reagan, I . . ."

"Don't bother," I snap. "Don't bother with more words, Matt, because I know how good you are with them. But they're just words. Your actions are loud and clear. I'm done."

My eyes feel itchy, and I turn away, suddenly embarrassed. The door has a small, square window, and I stare out into the parking garage that awaits me. Then I pull the handle in a quick gesture of certainty. Of finality. The door swings closed behind me, landing with a heavy thud and a metallic click, and something inside me closes, too.

A few paces from the door, I stop myself, fighting the urge to turn around. When I was little, I used to go to church with Dee's family, only because I spent the night most

Saturdays. I vaguely remember a story about a woman who looked back while fleeing a broken city. She turned into a pillar of salt. A harsh fate, but I got the point. You can't look back when you're escaping disaster. You can't hope that someone will come after you, either. I stopped expecting people to fight for me a long time ago, and I should know better. So I set my eyes straight on the course ahead of me, lengthening my strides. He's only upset because he got caught. He's nothing more than a bored, spoiled boy, and I'm Reagan O'Neill, the girl from the bathroom-stall graffiti. I'm not the cute little pastry of a girl you bring home to meet your family. I'm just a challenge to conquer, and he won. I lost.

As I blaze my way to the bus, my vision begins to blur, and I can't tell if it's fury or a precursor to tears. Hurt, regret, betrayal—I can't tell them apart, either, but each one is filling my lungs with pressure, like a dam about to burst open. I need to get to Dee.

I've reached the line of buses, but I can barely remember how I got here—what I walked past, who saw me tearing away from the door. I board, legs shaky against the steps, and Dee looks up at me. The space behind my eyes is swimming, and I can't even make out the expression on her face. She could be furious at me after our fight; she could kick me off the bus. I wouldn't blame her. It's been so long since I've cried that I barely remember how; I certainly don't remember how to stop. She's just a watery blur as a tear finally slips down my cheek.

"Oh my God, Reagan, I'm so sorry about what I said." Her cool hands clutch mine. One of us is shaking, and I think it may be me. "Please don't cry."

"No, *I'm* sorry. But it's not that. I have to go home." This comes out as a kind of gasp, and my shoulders fall in, trembling. Through the beginnings of a sob, my voice cracks like dropped glass. "I have to go home tonight. Right now."

The airport is more crowded than I expected. In O'Hare or LAX or LaGuardia, I would have expected chaos. But Nashville? I can't think of any reason why people would be flying into Nashville at one in the morning on a Tuesday. Maybe they're wondering the same thing about me—why would I be here? I bet they'd never guess I got cheated on by a former teen heartthrob and fled the scene. That I cried for the first time in almost ten years on a chilly tour bus, that my best friend called the airline, reciting her credit card number for a last-minute flight. That she stood at the base of the tour bus steps in the airport drop-off lane, hugging me so fiercely that I thought my ribs would break. They'd never guess that the single bag on my shoulder is full of essentials only, that a checked bag would have slowed me down more than I could bear, that my best friend promised to drop off everything else when her tour ends next week.

Crowds move past me on their way into the airport, and I don't recognize a single person. This summer, I've gotten used to the same stream of faces: Dee's band, the sound techs, the bus drivers. I miss life on tour already, but my heart just took a deathblow. It forced me into the Dorothy Gale School of Quitters: *There's no place like home.* Now that I'm here, it has to hurt less. Doesn't it?

I couldn't sleep the entire flight back, despite feeling tired all the way to my bones. I stared out the window, pressing my cheek against the thick plastic. The clouds looked like a whole kingdom, and I felt as small as I ever have.

Through the automatic doors, my whole body is met with warm, Tennessee air. It has that hard-to-place smell of home—is it the faint scent of water from the river? The surrounding grass and crops mingling with thick, Southern-lady perfume? I don't know, but it's comforting in a way I didn't expect. I could sink into the Nashville night like a plush lounge chair. Peering at the line of cars, I search for my dad's truck. He's at the end of the line, leaning against the bumper. No Brenda in sight, and I almost smile.

It's been over two months since I've seen my dad, the longest I've ever been away from him. His face is the most familiar sight in my world, but he looks different somehow. His hair and mustache are neatly trimmed, and he's wearing an old plaid shirt and work boots. For the first time, I can't even remember what he looked like before he got sober. It's like that part of him is so far gone I can't even make it out in the distance.

"Hi, Dad." I put my bag down by his feet.

"Hi, darlin'," he says, and I wrap my arms around his neck.

At the sound of the low rumble of his voice, I feel like I could cry again—out of comfort or relief or persistent, sticky sadness.

"Are you okay?"

I nod, pulling back from his embrace.

"Everything okay with you and Dee?" He's appraising my face, looking for hints of what hurt me enough to come home in the middle of the night.

I nod again. "We're fine. I was just ready to come home."

He scoops up my bag and puts it in the truck bed. "Good. Bren's awfully excited about the concert next week."

Less than one minute, and Brenda's a part of the conversation. I don't know what to say. We open our doors and climb in, quiet but for the planes roaring overhead.

"We sure missed you at home," my dad says, turning the key in the ignition.

I settle into the passenger's seat. "We?"

He smiles. "It was too quiet."

"Ha."

By the time we hit the highway, I've closed my eyes. I settle into the truck's worn upholstery, soft and musty, the faint hint of tobacco from before Brenda made my dad quit smoking. My eyelids fall, and the last thing I'm aware of is the low murmur of the truck, humming as it carries me home.

CHAPTER NINETEEN

Nashville

I fish another photo out of the developing solution. With a firm hold on the tongs, I give it a gentle shake and hang it up. It's a photo of the dry landscape in New Mexico, our first stop after LA—two days after the awards-show after-party where Matt and I danced, pressed up against each other and holding back. *No. No, don't think about that part. Think about the part where he cheated, where you walked in on him last night.* The thought splinters down my chest, threatening to crack my sternum and rib bones, and even a slow inhale aches. I dare myself to go five more minutes without resorting to a cigarette.

It was past noon by the time I woke up today. My first instinct was to unpack my bag, getting rid of any evidence of my life on tour. In keeping with that theme, I then decided to develop the rolls of film I took this summer. That way, I can dispose of the ones of Matt immediately—the proverbial, quick-ripped Band-Aid. Maybe I'll set them on fire; maybe I'll rip them to tiny pieces. Maybe I'll cut his face out of every picture and throw a handful of paper Matt heads into the trash or into the air—decapitated confetti. I pull the next photo out of the developing solution, and something about the photo catches my eye. Holding it up against the nearest red lightbulb, I examine the shot.

It's from just last week, on that Maryland hillside. The picture is a close-up of Matt's face, grinning with blue sky stretched wide in the background. In his sunglasses, I can make out my own reflection. Half of my face is obscured by the camera pointed at him, but below that, a smile—a wide, midlaugh smile.

In the bathroom mirror, my reflection is washed in the glow of the red light. My face looks too angular, and I look older than the girl I am in that picture. I hardly believe I existed as this girl, content and nearly carefree. Yet there she is, reflected back in Matt's eyes. *Stop documenting the moment for a second*, he told me. *Just be in it.*

I'm out of space to dry photos in the bathroom-turned-darkroom, so I stand on my bed, taping strings to my ceiling fan. When I'm done, I hop off the bed to grab some clothespins, pausing at my laptop to blast my favorite angry music so loud that I can't hear my phone. Matt has called me a dozen times in as many hours, and I've ignored them all, deleted every voice mail. He's texted me, too. I tried not to read them as I deleted them, but a few words stood out—*I'm so sorry* and *call me* and *misunderstanding* and *talk about it.* Maybe I'll eventually respond: *don't care* and *no* and *yeah right* and *no.*

Dee called not long after I woke up, wondering if I was okay. My crying freaked her out, I think. Freaked *me* out. I told her I was fine and happy to be home. Then she got quiet and said, "Listen, Reag. I talked to Matt. . . . He really—"

"Don't you dare take his side," I said darkly. "He has no right to put you in the middle."

She cleared her throat, which she does when she's trying to regain composure. "You're right. Sorry. I just hate that you're hurting."

"I'm fine," I lied.

I spend the next hour developing photos and clipping them onto my fan. Obviously, no pictures of Matt are allowed in my presence, and I leave them to dry in the bathroom, awaiting their assuredly violent fate. When I'm done, I turn the fan on low and lie down on my bed. The pictures circle above me, looping images of my summer: Dee on our tour bus, Poet's Walk in Central Park, the southwestern architecture in Santa Fe and Dallas, pictures of the crew backstage. It's what my summer would have looked like without Matt. Still good, I remind myself. Still so good.

A little after five o'clock, there's a rap on my door.

"Can I come in?" Brenda's soft drawl asks through the door. At least she's learning not to come in without permission.

"Sure."

Brenda was asleep when we returned from the airport last night and has been at work all day. The door opens to her predictable form—a dowdy skirt and soft brown hair, grays sneaking in around her part. She smiles hesitantly. "It's good to have you back. How are you?"

I shrug, sitting up against the pillows. "Okay, but tired."

"Is there anything in particular you'd like for dinner?"

After two months of room service, hotel bar food, and gas station snacks, my mouth waters at the idea of home-made food. "I'll eat anything."

She nods, backing out of the room a bit. "I'll give you a holler when it's ready. Should be about the time your daddy gets home."

"Thanks, Brenda." I roll over to my side. Even though it was an exchange of a few simple sentences—not affectionate or deep—it's the most benign interaction I've had with Brenda since before my arrest. She didn't prod me to get out of bed or ask if I'm upset and why. I didn't push her buttons in retaliation. It's a small victory for both of us.

I stay there in my quiet room, and my thoughts jerk toward Matt. I force them away, thinking about new photography projects, of how to structure my portfolio for college applications. I huddle my thoughts under college—my fresh start, a year away—until I hear Brenda call from downstairs.

By the time I hit the base of the staircase, I smell maple syrup. Heavy, savory bacon and fresh pancakes. I follow the scent into the kitchen, where Brenda's standing over a skillet.

"Breakfast for dinner." I survey the spread. "My dad used to make this every Friday night."

Brenda smiles. "He mentioned that."

Before Brenda came along, breakfast-dinner was a ritual. Eggs, bacon, pancakes, and anything else we could think of. My dad always said that meal was a celebration that the weekend was here, and it was years before I realized that he didn't know how to cook much else back then. Even as we both learned how to make other meals, breakfast-dinner stayed. When Brenda moved in, she took over all the cooking. My dad was grateful, and I guess I mostly was, too. I didn't realize how much I missed it until now.

The garage door opens, followed by my dad's grinning face. "Smells great in here."

He kicks off his boots, and I take a seat at the kitchen table. My dad kisses Brenda on the cheek as he moves toward the sink. "So good to have both my girls home."

I don't know if I like being lumped into a category with Brenda, as if we matter equally to my dad. He's only known her for four years. Still, Matt Finch's stupid voice sneaks into my mind—*And she makes your dad happy?* Yes. She does. When I look up at Brenda, she's shuffling pancakes onto my plate. I waste no time smearing butter on each layer of the stack. My dad and Brenda join me at the table, and she closes her eyes to say a prayer. I stare at the table's centerpiece, counting the stalks of lavender until she's done.

I press the side of my fork into the tower of pancakes, sliding off a big, fluffy bite. It tastes like my old life—the one after my dad sobered up and before Brenda barged in. It reminds me of a time before I was sneaking out and pissing everyone off and compiling a police record. It tastes like being a kid, and I could cry again. I really could. But I won't.

I stay quiet while Brenda and my dad chat about their work days. Not once do they ask about the summer or why I came home early, and I eat my whole dinner in peace. Of course they know something happened, but they also know I won't tell them unless I want to. It's a relief to feel privacy in my own life.

"Well," my dad says finally, putting down his fork. "That hit the spot."

I nod. "It was really good, Brenda. Thanks."

Her smile is tentative, like she's waiting for a sarcastic comment. I don't have one, so I clear my plate from the table without another word. From the front of the house, the doorbell rings, and my dad rises to answer it. After a moment, he calls into the kitchen, "Reagan, darlin', you got company."

My first thought is Matt. Maybe he's ditching the Indianapolis concert tonight; maybe he drove all this way to apologize. I'm going to slam the door in his face a million times. But when I step into the foyer, it's clear that the person at the door is a girl. My fury must be obvious because my dad looks confused. I step past him and close the front door behind me.

Corinne is on my front porch. This has got to be a joke.

"What the *hell* do you think you're doing here?"

Her face looks remorseful, but her mouth can't seem to find the apology. Finally, she bursts out, "Look, I'm sorry, okay?"

She says this like I'm holding a knife to her throat and making her apologize in exchange for her life. I don't need her apology. I cross my arms, leaning back against the storm door. My glare must be bearing into her because she looks down at her feet. "I just got dumped, and I'm . . . I'm used to being the girl in Matt's life. I got jealous."

"Well, I hope you two will be happy together." I spit the words out like venom. "Get off my property."

"It's not like that. He doesn't have feelings for me anymore."

I confess: this was more believable coming from Corinne than it was from Matt. But it's still a seconhand lie, passed from him to her to me.

"Poor you."

"Look." Her voice is firm. "I only kissed him to try to get his attention, and it was petty and mean, and I'm sorry."

She really does look remorseful, her eyes turned down at the sides. If I were in a more forgiving mood, maybe I could admit that I know the feeling of a best friend slipping away. Or how easy it is to grasp for validation after someone has rejected you. But alas. I'm a cold, hard bitch, and so is she.

"Reagan, he didn't even kiss me back. He froze like he was too horrified to even move, and then you walked in." I hate that she used my first name, as if she knows me. I hate that she's covering for him. "It was actually really mortifying for me. And I understand if you hate me. But please don't hate Matt."

I grind my toe into our welcome mat, trying to rescind its message. I don't want her relaying to Matt how upset I am, so I look at her head-on. "It would have ended anyway. You just pushed our expiration date up a week."

A look of surprise registers on her face. "I didn't realize that. Matt made it seem like . . ."

"I'm going to college next year. And I'm not the kind of girl who follows a guy around."

The hit lands. She bites at her lips, which are still annoyingly full and a pouty. I hate her for pressing her pretty mouth against Matt's. Right when I think I've had the last word, she blurts out, "He starts at Belmont this fall."

"In Nashville?"

She nods. "He moves in two weeks from now. They have a music-business program. He decided to go before he even left on the tour."

"Well," I say with a sardonic laugh. "That goes to show you how disposable I was. He didn't even tell me that."

"I know he didn't. He didn't want to spook you."

"Spook me?"

"He didn't want you to think he was moving to Nashville for you. Too serious or too fast or something."

Spook me. Like a wild horse, too wild to get close to without the risk of bucking or fleeing. Like my mother.

"Well, good for him. I'm sure there will be plenty of

Nashville girls who fall for the charm. But not me—I see through it now."

Corinne rubs her temples, closing her eyes. "Well, I had to try."

"How'd you find my house, anyway?"

"There are only about a dozen O'Neills inside city limits. Your house was the fourth I knocked at."

This impresses me, however begrudgingly, as she turns to go. She pauses at the base of the porch steps and turns back. "You should know . . . I haven't seen him happy since . . . well. A while. His mom was so sick, and then she died, and he was in such a bad place. Like the real Matt was in a coma. When he started touring this summer, even his voice on the phone seemed alive again. Any time he talked about you, it sounded like he was . . . waking up."

This comment feels like a hammer straight to my heart. But I can't even process what she's saying. I want her gone. "Too little, too late."

She retreats, finally giving up, and I want to pick up one of Brenda's clay flowerpots and heave it at her. As her car peels out of the dirt driveway, I rake my hands through my hair. What *was* that? Here at home, my life on tour feels surreal—like a summerlong dream I finally woke up from yesterday. Corinne's presence proves that it was real, which only makes me miss Dee and the ever-changing cities more. But the person I thought Matt Finch was? I think I'll miss him most of all.

CHAPTER TWENTY

Nashville

The world is in grayscale today. The sky looks like mercury glass, translucent with silvery clouds. Even the trees look sullen, drooping under the weight of gloominess. I hate when the weather is indecisive. If it's going to be anything less than sunny, it might as well thunderstorm. Don't drizzle, kind of, some of the time.

My heels splash against shallow puddles, making empty thuds on the sidewalk. After Corinne's little surprise visit, I've spent the past two days in bed watching reality TV. Those morons make me feel better about my life by comparison. But not today. Today is the day for action.

I'm getting a tattoo. I woke up this morning with a desperate itch for change. It made me restless all morning, too much energy for my body to contain. Most girls change their hair after a bad breakup—a different color, a shorter cut—but that's not enough. So I drove to downtown Nashville to visit Archangel Ink.

From outside, I can see Gia perched on a stool, her feet propped up against the padded chair. Gia's in college, and she runs in a circle that occasionally overlaps with Blake's. I wouldn't say that we're *friends*, but we're friendly. She looks a bit intimidating, with her long, tattooed arms, but she's soft-spoken and genuinely passionate about art. Her tattoos themselves are like paintings—curling blue waves inspired by a Japanese artist, blooms of white flowers, black-ink branches peeking out from her black tank top.

"Hey, Gia." I lean in without opening the door all the way.

She looks up. "Reagan. Hey. Come in."

Gia wears even more eye makeup than me, with Cleopatra curls of black eyeliner. She stands as I get closer, leaning against the chair. "I haven't seen you around."

"Yeah. I've been gone this summer."

"I, um," she begins, toying with the ends of her waist-length hair. "I was sorry to hear what happened with Blake."

"Thanks."

Her smile is genuine behind heavy red lipstick. "Can I do something for you?"

"Yeah," I say, and I'm surprised by how determined I sound. "A tattoo, actually."

Her eyes light up. "You're finally caving?"

Gia and a few of Blake's other tattooed acquaintances have often tried to persuade me to get inked. People with tattoos are like evangelicals, ever-eager to spread their gospel. What can I say? I've never been a joiner. It seems to surprise people that I don't have tattoos already, though I'm not sure why. And, really, I prefer to *not* be who people expect.

"Yeah."

"Exciting! Do you know what you want?"

"Actually, I was hoping you had a few examples of birds."

The second night I had the cast on my arm, I was sitting at the kitchen table with Dee and her mom, and I laid my head down on my good arm. *I'm such a disaster of a person,* I said. Mrs. Montgomery smiled. *Nonsense,* she said. *You're just a broken-winged bird. And there are two things you can do with broken wings: you can roll over and die, or you can lay low, heal, and start fresh.*

I joined the tour as a broken-winged bird. Even as pain throbbed in my wrist and in the left side of my chest, I didn't roll over and die. I'm made of tougher stuff than that—of leather and suede, of railroad steel and Tennessee soil. This tattoo will be my reminder. Like Darwin's tiny birds, I can evolve, slow but sure.

"Birds . . . yes." Gia pushes off the counter. There's a pile of binders, and she digs through them, studying the titles on their spines. "Here."

She hands me a white binder, open to a few pages of birds. "Mind moving to the back room for me in case anyone walks by?"

"Not at all."

I follow her behind the back curtain, where there's an

identical setup—a padded chair that looks like it belongs at the dentist's office, an array of tattoo tools, a stool for the artist. I guess this room is for people getting tattoos in below-the-belt areas. And, apparently, people like me, getting tattoos underage.

Sitting down on the chair, I set the open binder on my lap. A fleet of birds spans the page. Some are more cartoonish; some are meant to be realistic. Some are perched, others in flight.

"Where are we doing this?" Gia asks.

"My wrist," I say, flipping over my left arm, which is still thinner than my right. I point to the pale underside of my wrist, where I imagine the break in the bone once was. "Here."

"Okay—be right back. You'll have to sign a few papers."

My attention settles on one bird in particular—the smallest one. She's not like the others, who are either colorful or solid black shadows. She's somewhere in between, her body an outline, waiting to find definition. Her wings stretch wide, but she's not soaring; her clawed feet are not tucked up against her stomach. She seems . . . ready. Like she's getting there.

Gia returns, and I tap the picture of the bird. "This one."

"The finch?"

My heart stops. "What?"

"The finch." She looks up again, pointing to the bird that I have my finger on. "This one, right?"

I cover my eyes with the palm of my hand. "You have *got* to be kidding me."

"No? Everything okay?"

Tilting my head up to the ceiling, I sigh exaggeratedly. "Yeah. It's nothing. A weird coincidence."

Maybe the tattoo is meant to be. The finch will symbolize the summer's spectrum, from the shattering moments to the parts where it felt like I could almost sprout wings and fly.

Or maybe it means: Don't change your body when what you actually want to change is the way you left things with Matt. I hate that he's sneaking back into my life like this, where I least expect him.

Gia crosses her paint-palette arms, and her red lacquered nails look startling against her pale skin. "I know it's none of my business, but can I give you some advice?"

"Sure."

"As a tattoo professional, I should probably tell you to go for it." She says this gently, as if trying not to offend me. "But as someone who knows what it's like to get hurt, I'm going to suggest that you give this some more thought. Maybe try something temporary first, to see if it's really what you want."

Given the circumstances, this suggestion feels like a great kindness. I nod.

"Let's do *mehndi*—henna," she says, pulling a drawer open. "Do you know what kind of design you'd want to try?"

"Something simple. Small." I sigh, leaning back in the chair. "Anything but a finch."

I leave with a henna tattoo on the inside of my wrist. Gia's been studying Eastern art, but instead of the elaborate, traditional designs that Indian women use, she gave me a delicate constellation—Ursa Minor, the Little Dipper. She moved her hand slowly, explaining as she connected the stars with thin lines of wet ink. *The star at the end of Ursa Minor is Polaris, the North Star,* Gia said. *The guiding star.*

Outside, the atmosphere has fulfilled my wish for decisiveness. Rain pours from the sky, smacking against the awnings of nearby shops. It smells like summer—the scent of hot asphalt rising into wetness. Once inside my car, the rain beats on the roof, and I pull onto the puddled street. I'm not usually a nervous driver, but my ancient windshield wipers can barely keep up with the streams of rain. By the time my exit sign becomes visible, I have a talon-grip on the wheel. A few precarious turns later, and I've never been so glad to see the wooden fence that runs the perimeter of my house.

I park on the dirt driveway that has turned into a mud driveway and cut the engine. Raindrops drum down above me, and I can't help but admire how beautiful the farmhouse is, even distorted by panels of rain. The wide front porch is half wet, and Brenda's potted plants look shiny and slick. The field of lavender makes a hazy purple backdrop, a blur of color in the distance. I stare up at the house, watching the weather vane rooster dance. The storm seems to slow, however slightly, and I make a run for it. I tuck my left wrist under my shirt, protecting the henna tattoo from harm. The mud clings to my shoes, trying to slow me down, but I pull my legs up fast enough to get to the porch.

Once upstairs, I remove my damp clothes and wrap myself in a robe. I flop onto my bed, staring up at the ceiling fan. The pictures spin above me—no starting point, no ending point, my summer circling around infinity. As if on cue, my phone beeps. I brace myself for another text from Matt, but they've tapered off considerably in the past two days. The text is from Dee, with a video attached.

Look what I did! Wasn't the same without you.

I sigh. She called last night to see if I'm coming to her final show in Nashville tomorrow, and of course I'm not. I don't want to be in the same room with Matt, even if that room is an auditorium. The whole situation is unfair to Dee and to me. We started the summer together; we should end it together.

I click the attached YouTube video, which is titled "Lilah Montgomery MY OWN Live!" She did it, performed a song that is finally starting to be true. The video starts with only Dee onstage, the camera pointed up at her from a few rows back. She's in a blue dress that she wears at the end of the show, with her guitar strapped over her chest. Sure enough, she nails it—the grit and grace in every lyric—and she means them all. On her own, she's doing pretty damn well.

When the song ends, I want to text her back right away, but I feel like I've had the wind knocked out of me. I had an entire summer away to get control of my life, to be a better version of me, on my own. Instead, I got tangled up in guy drama. I let myself get cheated on twice in a four-month window. I'm so disappointed in myself, for knowing better but doing it anyway.

Desperate for fresh air, I shove my bedroom window open. Outside, the rain has slowed to pattering, but I can't tell if the worst of the storm is yet to come. The dark clouds are shifting overhead, wrestling against the patches of blue sky in the distance. It's the improbable halfway point between two places—gray and blue clashing, and there's no way to tell which will yield.

CHAPTER TWENTY-ONE

Nashville

I'm driving well over the speed limit, foot tense against the gas pedal.

The text I got said: *Can you come down to Ryman Auditorium? Something's going on with Dee. Thanks - Lissa St. James.*

Two things shocked me about this message. First, Lissa said "Dee" and not "Lilah." She's never called her that in my presence—because she represents Lilah Montgomery: country star, not Dee Montgomery: normal, human girl. Second, if Dee is upset and hasn't called me, then she must be mad *at* me. I've tried calling her six times since, but she won't answer. As I pulled off the exit for Ryman Auditorium, I caved and called Lissa.

"Look, I didn't know what else to do, okay?" she snapped, as if I had demanded an explanation by returning her call.

"Dee's upset about something, and she won't snap out of it. She's quiet, withdrawn, and I need her to get it together for the press conference in half an hour. Can you come down and try to fix her?"

I hope I can. My tires squeal as I pull into a parking spot outside the auditorium. I rush to the door Lissa told me to meet her at, and sure enough, she's standing there in a skirt suit.

"Thanks for coming." She gestures for me to follow her inside.

"Yeah, well," I say. "I didn't come for *you*."

We're at the bottom of an unadorned set of stairs—all concrete and unpolished metal rails, clearly a service entrance. I start to follow Lissa up the stairs, but she turns when she hears my footsteps stop. It's my one chance to know for sure. "Did you leak that photo?"

"I certainly did not."

"Then who did?"

"It was a girl in your grade at school. She sold it to the tabloids."

I blink. I meant that question to be rhetorical. I didn't think Lissa actually knew. My fingers bend into claws. "Who? Tell me her name."

"The girl's father lost his job months ago. Their house was getting foreclosed on."

It takes me a moment to process this. Would I sell someone out to save our home? To save my dad's pride and the life that I know? I might. I hate to say it, but I really might. Not Dee, of course, but . . . someone else? Maybe. "How do you know?"

"I wrestled it out of one of my tabloid contacts."

"Why didn't you tell Dee?"

She sighs. "It wouldn't have changed anything."

I consider this as we reach the second floor. Lissa gestures toward a room with Dee's name on it. For some reason, even in the fluorescent hallway light, Lissa's face doesn't look so pinched.

The door is open a sliver, and it doesn't creak as I slip inside. Dee is in full hair and makeup, laying faceup on the couch with no expression whatsoever. Her posture is stiff, like a mummy or a nervous patient in a therapy session. I shut the door behind me, and she sits up, startled. "Dee, you should have told me you were upset."

Her brows furrow. "How did you know?"

"Lissa texted me." I sit beside her on the couch. "I had no idea you were still mad at me. I know we never really talked about the fight, but I didn't mean *any* of that, you know, and—"

"What? No. It's not that." She stares into her lap. "I know you didn't mean it. I didn't either. I'd basically forgotten the whole thing."

"Then what did I do? Is it that I'm not coming to the show tonight, because—"

This time I cut myself off. The real problem is so obvious that I can't believe I didn't see it the moment I walked in.

There's a huge bouquet of irises and wild daisies on the side table nearest the couch. Only one person in the world has ever given her such a bouquet: Jimmy. And he would never send her those flowers without an accompanying card.

I place my hand on her knee. "What did the note say?"

She flashes the card at me. Handwritten, five letters, no signature: *IWLYF*. Dee and Jimmy used to write each other notes during class using almost all acronyms, and Dee and I would spend our lunch period laughing and trying to guess them. *IASB*: I am so bored. *WDYWTDTW*?: What do you want to do this weekend? Eventually, he started signing *IWLYF* to all of them, in every note, every card, every e-mail. *I Will Love You Forever.* Cheesy, sure. But I envied it all the same. It seemed more powerful to me than "I love you" or "love always" or "love." I will love you forever. Simple, declarative, infinite.

Dee reexamines the card in her hand, like it will reveal a hidden message. "Did I ever tell you why he came up with it?"

I shake my head. It's easy to forget that there are so many pieces of Dee and Jimmy's relationship that I don't know— that I'll never know. "We were thirteen. He'd heard you and I say 'infinity' to each other, and he thought we should have something like that, too. The first time he wrote 'IWLYF' in a note, I knew what it meant. It probably sounds really dumb to you, but I also knew he meant it, and I did, too."

"It doesn't sound dumb at all." I'm trying to understand why Jimmy would send this note. It seems like a specific kind of cruelty, like lobbing a brick of your love through someone's window and running off. "So what does this even mean—sending you flowers with this note and nothing else?"

Dee props her chin against a cupped hand. "I think . . . I think it's all that's left, you know? He doesn't know how to do this. I don't know how to do this. But we'll love each other forever."

With her free hand, she's twisting her necklace. "I keep thinking about how he wanted an acronym because you and I had 'infinity.' You and I had a friend thing, and he wanted a friend thing, too. Other than you, he's the best friend I've ever had in my life. And I think I've been missing that more than I realized. He was my friend."

It takes a long time to learn someone. It takes a long time to see a person as a whole spectrum, from worst to best— from the mismanaged heartache that lands them in AA to the pancake dinners, from the hurtful things shouted in a dressing room to the huge-hearted strength that only a best friend can understand. Once you get there, it's forever.

"So . . . does this mean you're getting back together?"

Dee looks up at me, seemingly ignoring my question. "Do you remember when Ginger had her foal, when were in junior high?"

Of course I remember it, how Dee's mom drove us to the Colliers' barn in the middle of the night so we could watch a baby horse come into the world. But I have no idea what that has to do with this. "Um, yeah?"

"Do you remember the way she couldn't stand up at

first? How her knobby little legs buckled beneath her? How helpless she was?"

"I remember."

"That's how it felt after Jimmy ended it. I felt like I knew nothing about myself or the world. I felt like I couldn't even stand on my own." She twists her necklace, looping it around her pointer finger. "But I'm doing it now, and I want to see where it takes me."

I open my mouth, but no words come out. In all the scenarios that Dee and I have talked about this year—all the ways that her relationship with Jimmy could go—never once did it involve Dee pushing him away. "But . . ."

"I *know*. I can't explain it, but ever since the flowers showed up, I've been thinking: *I'm not there yet*. I don't even know what that *means*. And I'm freaking out because, like, this is not how I expected to feel, and I don't know what to do. . . ."

I pose exactly this question to Dee. "Well . . . what do you *want* to do?"

She takes a deep breath in. "I don't *know*. I guess I want to have my own life, too, here in Nashville, and my own apartment. I *don't* want him to come home from college every weekend that I'm home so we can be together. But I want to be able to go get coffee with him when he's home from school and hear about his life. I want to text him when I see something that reminds me of him. I want to leave that door cracked open, because what if we do decide we want to walk through it someday?"

At first, I don't disturb the silence as it falls around us.

It's like Dee has dammed up her truest wants this entire summer, and now she has flooded the room with them.

"You need to talk to him," I say. "I know you guys haven't seen each other since you broke up, but it doesn't have to be like that. You can be friends. It doesn't have to be all or nothing."

"That's funny, coming from you," she says, smirking at me, and I smile back. "But you're right. We don't need a plan."

"Exactly."

She nods, letting out a sigh, and she clutches her hand over mine. "I think I knew that, deep down. I just needed to hear it from someone else."

There's a gentle knock at the door, and the blood halts within my veins. If it's Matt, I'll shoot through the ceiling, a rocket fueled by scorn. But it's not him. The makeup artist peers in. "Lissa said you may need a touch-up."

Dee gives a bitter laugh. "She's correct. Come in."

"I should go," I say. "You're okay, right?"

She hugs me tightly. "I will be."

"I'll see you tomorrow for dinner at your parents' house. Break a leg tonight."

Dee gives me the eyes. "You *could* come to the concert. . . ."

I flash a grim smile. "Not if he's here."

"Yeah, I know." She sighs. "You should get going, then. He'll be done with his sound check any minute. Don't want you to have an awkward run-in in the hallway."

With one last squeeze, I duck out the door. I don't want to see Matt in the hallway, and I certainly don't want to see him onstage—at least, not without a basketful of rotten tomatoes in tow. I'd really love to peg him right in the face with one, to watch the thin red juice splatter across his skin. Or maybe tomatoes aren't the best choice. Maybe I'd prefer a cooked red potato because no other vegetable looks more like a human heart. The soft, starchy insides would break apart on impact. I bet Matt would know it was from me, too—a broken heart smashing into him.

Still, I'm nothing if not a masochist—a willing victim to the things that might hurt me later. My feet steer me toward the auditorium, even though my heart tries to back up. I'm weighing regrets—which will hurt more? The pain of seeing him one last time or the pain of denying myself the chance?

I enter through the farthest-back door. Matt stands alone on the historic stage, faced by hundreds of empty, wooden seats in a semicircle. When Matt and I talked about this concert earlier in the summer, he said he didn't deserve to perform here. Dee feels the same way—hesitant to believe that her feet belong on the hardwood stage, on top of Patsy Cline's footprints.

But here he is. I don't want to throw tomatoes at him, as it turns out. I'm not sure why.

"That was good, Matt," a voice calls from the sound booth. "We'll keep that bass lower for tonight."

"Thanks," Matt calls, shielding his eyes. "Can we close out with the new song one more time?"

"Sure thing. Ready when you are."

He's wearing a baseball hat, jeans, and a white T-shirt. He looks like the Matt I thought I knew. But he's not. I have to remember this because he's moving toward the baby grand piano onstage, sliding onto the bench. His fingers move in slow, sad chords as his foot pumps the pedal.

Like a wounded soldier
Trudging the old road home,
But I ain't the old me,
And I walk this path alone.
I'm battle-worn, I'm battle-torn
With these scars inside my chest,
Kept up that happy face for you,
To hide that I'm a mess.

But I gave you every ounce of fight in me,
And I have no regrets.
If I was going to lose you,
At least I lost you to my best.
But it felt so wrong,
So tangled up in blue,
Like that old Dylan song,
Like I don't know who I am,
Now that you're gone.

I try to swallow, but I can't. Raw honesty finds you right where you are, even at the back of an auditorium, and it takes you by the throat. It asks you if you can be honest, too.

I never want to be asked, because the answer is no. He finally did it, wrote the song about his mom, and on the piano, no less.

During the second verse, the tears overflow my lower eyelid. My face doesn't crumple—I don't fall apart—but the tears dribble downward nonetheless. I don't wipe them away.

But I lived through the pain.
Now I see the other side.
Now I know that life's too short
To shut myself down and hide.
I'm battle-torn, but I'm battle-born.
These scars are part of me.
I got nothing left but what I've learned,
And I'll use that, and you'll see,

I can still give every ounce of fight in me,
Till I have no regrets,
Because if I'm going to lose someone,
I'm gonna lose her to my best.
And I'll be strong,
When a hard rain's a-gonna fall,
Like that old Dylan song,
You're the reason I stand tall,
And that will never be gone.

When his new song fades out, Matt stands from the piano and grabs his guitar. He breaks into a slow, acoustic version of

"You're Gonna Make Me Lonesome When You Go." The guitar chords are stripped-down and simple, and the soft rasp in his voice wrecks me. It wrecks me right there in the drafty back seats of the former Grand Ole Opry. How many people have shed tears in this place, backlit by stained glass and the amber glow of generations gone by? Now I'm among them, drops of holy water on the church floor.

He doesn't deserve me; that became clear last week. But Matt Finch deserves his place on this stage. In his simple blue jeans with a simple guitar line behind him, he's exposing every scar across his soul. He just told the most painful story of his life to a bunch of sound technicians and lighting professionals. Tonight, he'll tell it again to hundreds of strangers.

It's more than I could ever do, for him or for anyone else. Somehow, this makes it easier for me to slip out the door, wiping the wet streaks from my face.

I collect myself as I walk to my car and then inspect my makeup situation in my rearview mirror. When my phone buzzes, I half expect it to be Matt, but it's Dee: *Can you come back????*

I text back as fast as my fingers will move: *I'm still here, in my car.*

She doesn't text me back right away, and worry gets the best of me. I hurry toward the back entrance again. Before I can reach it, Dee bursts out the side door.

"Hey," she says, breathing hard. "I have *got* to get out of here."

It takes me a moment. "But . . . the press conference. Lissa's gonna *kill* you."

Dee shrugs. "So they wait an extra half hour. Can I drive?"

Unable to form words, I toss her the keys. There's an easy confidence in the way she catches them and then spins them around her finger. We hurry back to the car, both spurred on by the present threat of Lissa chasing after Dee.

"Okay." She turns on the engine. "I need you to text Jimmy and find out where he is."

My head pivots toward her. "Okay . . . what, exactly, are we doing?"

She smiles as she presses the gas pedal—hard—and the tires squeal on our way out of the parking lot. "I need to see him or I won't be able to think straight. Because you're so right. Jimmy and I don't have to scrap all our years of friendship over a breakup. We can still be a part of each other's lives. And I just . . . I need to see him."

A small smile creeps onto my face. "Well, then, let's find him."

Hey, I type, hands jittery. *Where are you right now?*

Dee's passing the cars beside us so quickly that I don't have to look at the speedometer to know we could get pulled over. I'm not sure when she last drove a car, but it seems like she's making up for lost time in this one trip. She drums her hands against the steering wheel, anxious for his reply. It comes quickly.

Running some errands. Why, what's up?

"He's running errands."

She groans. "Like, where specifically?"

My phone vibrates, but it's Lissa's number, so I click Ignore. Then I type Dee's exact words to Jimmy. *Like where specifically?*

*The BP on 8*th*. Why?*

"He's at a gas station by Belmont. Get on the outer belt right here," I say, pointing. "We're still a few exits away."

"Okay, tell him not to leave," she says, speeding toward the on-ramp.

I return to my phone. *Stay where you are, OK?*

Then the inevitable reply: *OK, but what's going on? Are you involving me in some kind of police chase?*

Ha. Ha. Jimmy's allowed to give me grief because he actually knows me. And besides, it is a kind of getaway—from Dee's gilded cage. Meanwhile, my phone is beeping with text messages from Lissa, the cage master herself. *Where are you? Get her back here. Reagan, I know you're reading these. Tell her to call me.*

"Lissa's freaking out." I say this out of amusement, not as a warning.

Dee rolls her eyes. "Yeah, I figured she would be. But my career isn't going to end over one delayed press meeting, is it?"

She rolls down her window a bit. The wind rips past the windows, and it tousles her hair.

"Dee, you know there will probably be people at this gas station. . . ."

She maneuvers around a car that's not going fast enough

for her taste. "Oh well. I don't really care today. I mean, I can't live like that—not doing things I want to do for fear of being photographed."

"Okay, I feel compelled to ask you this: are you drunk?"

"Shut up." She laughs, glancing over at me. "*No*. I'm just . . . ready."

This hell-if-I-care attitude suits her like one of my too-tight skirts: it may not be her normal style, but disobedience looks good on her. When I glance over, she's breathing in deeply, inhaling the fresh air like she's been trapped indoors for weeks on end. Outside, we're heading away from the skyline, but the edges of Nashville are still nothing like our hometown. The sky is as blue and the grass as green, but the rest is all asphalt and car exhaust and billboards.

"What are you going to say?" I shouldn't be so nosy, but I can't help it.

"I don't know," she admits, but a smile creeps onto her face. She uses one hand to try to tame her hair, but it still flies around wildly.

I stay quiet, leaving her to her thoughts until I see our exit. "Take this one. Then turn right."

She obeys, and we zip through the only stoplight standing between us and the gas station. Dee turns the wheel harder than she needs to. The tires veer sharply into the gas station, and my eyes find a spot toward the back edge of the parking lot, out of the way of other people.

I see him before she does—a tall figure leaning against the tailgate of a black truck. I haven't seen him all summer, but, even from a distance, he looks like the same old Jimmy. That's part of his charm—he's steady. He's always had the same haircut, and he always wears the same kind of Levi's with the same simple shirts. But it's not boring, not on him.

When Dee spots him, she brakes hard, stopping dead in a vacant area beside the gas station. She slams the car into park and fumbles for the handle and bounds out. She shuts the door hard, almost tripping over her shoes as they collide with the asphalt. Blond hair bouncing around her, Dee heads straight toward Jimmy.

When he spots her, he steps forward, looking concerned. Dee slows to a determined walk, and I see his mouth moving. It's clearly "What are you doing here" and "Is everything okay," arms held out as if ready for action. He's still asking questions when Dee gets close enough to throw her arms around his neck. He holds her there, with her feet suspended off the ground and pointed like a ballerina's. They hang on to each other for dear life, the girl on the magazine covers and the small-town cowboy—my best friend and her other best friend. After a few moments, Jimmy moves his feet from side to side, and Dee's feet swing like a clock's pendulum. It's a strange kind of slow dance, a hold-tight at the edge of common ground.

My view of them is framed by the car windshield, and the picture also includes a sidewalk littered with cigarette butts and old gum, a rusted Dumpster, and a gas station employee yelling into his cell phone outside the convenience store. Beyond them all, Dee is planting her flag—claiming the territory she's willing to fight for.

My therapist once told me: you are the only person who can build emotional barriers, but you're also the only person who can topple them. Other people can't knock down the walls you've built, no matter how much they love you. You have to tear them down yourself because there's something worth seeing on the other side.

I thought it was stupid then, staring back at my therapist across her coffee table, but maybe I was wrong. Maybe I just saw it with my own eyes.

A loud honk makes me jump in my seat. Glancing back, I see a pissed-off woman gesturing that my car is blocking her path. I slide over to the driver's seat and move the car to a real parking spot a few yards to the right. Before I can even shift into park, Dee's back in my line of vision, headed toward me. Over her shoulder, Jimmy's smiling and shaking his head. She jumps into the car and says, "Back to the Ryman!"

I pull around to the exit, giving Jimmy a wave as I do. "What did you say to him?"

"Nothing. Not a word. Oh, wait! Stop!" She's tearing through her purse, and she pulls out one of the black Sharpies she always carries for signing autographs. She scrawls something across the palm of her hand. Then she climbs into the backseat and presses her hand to the window. I don't have to see her hand or even see Jimmy nodding from behind us, looking overcome. I know what she wrote across her skin: *IWLYF.*

Dee can create whole songs out of her feelings. She can turn those songs into concerts, into music tours. But sometimes all you need is one true thing that you're brave enough to write in ink. She doesn't even know what this one sentence will mean for them—will they get back together now or later or never?—but that doesn't matter right now.

She crawls back to the front seat as I steer us onto the highway. Wind gushes through the windows, and Dee flings her arms open wide.

"Woo-hoo!" she screams at the open road before us, vowels pushing against the summer air. "Wooooooo!"

The rest of the world will never know why Lilah Montgomery showed up late to the Middle of Nowhere Tour press conference in Nashville or why she didn't look as polished—breathing fast, with wind-tossed hair and an extra glow about her. But I'll know. I know these secrets of Dee's life like I know the constellations, like I know the road home. I'll know why she gave a new answer to the standard press conference question about what advice she has for her young fans, as quoted in the Arts section of the *Tennessean:*

"I don't know! I'm seventeen!" Ms. Montgomery replied with a laugh. "This past year has been a lesson in letting go and holding on, and I still don't know what to make of it. I guess I do know this: find a best friend, and hang on tight."

CHAPTER TWENTY-TWO

Nashville

I awake to a soft knock on my bedroom door. Through sleep-blurred vision, I see my dad peeking in. "Hey Dad."

"Hey darlin'—sorry to wake you, but I was starting to worry you'd stopped breathin'."

Not quite. Just exhausted from yesterday. It was too much for one day, especially for someone as emotionally stunted as me. "How was the concert?"

"Well, Dee was marvelous. Shined like a star. I couldn't believe how big that crowd was—all those screamin' kids— just crazy. Brenda enjoyed it very much."

"Good." I sit up, propping myself on my elbows. There's music coming from somewhere, and I reach for what sounds like my phone alarm going off. I punch a few buttons, but the faint sound continues. "Do you hear that?"

When I glance up, my dad has disappeared from my

door. I put my bare feet on the carpet, looking around. For a moment, I think I've left my iPod on somewhere, but the sound is clearer than that. Straining to hear, I can make out something acoustic. Coming from . . . the backyard?

I glance down from my bedroom window and feel my jaw fall open. Matt Finch is standing below my window, guitar strapped across his chest. I pull my window up, and I expect the song from that old movie—the one about a guy with a trench coat and the big radio and his heart on his sleeve. But it's not that. It's not anything I recognize, and I strain to make out the lyrics: *Stop being ridiculous, stop being ridiculous, Reagan.*

What an asshole. The mesh screen and two floors between us don't seem like enough to protect him from my anger.

"Nice apology," I call down to him.

"I've apologized thirteen times," he yells back, "and so far you haven't called me back."

I open my mouth to say it doesn't matter, but he's already redirecting the song.

"*Now I'm gonna stand here until you forgive me,*" he sings loudly, "*or at least until you hear me out, la-la, oh-la-la. I drove seven hours overnight, and I won't leave until you come out here.*"

He had a flight home to Chicago right after the final show last night. He drove straight back here?

"This is private property!" My throat feels coarse from how loudly I'm yelling. "And that doesn't even rhyme!"

The guitar chord continues as he sings, *"Then call the cops, call the cops, call the cops. . . ."*

I storm downstairs, my feet pounding against the staircase. When I turn the corner, my dad looks almost amused from his seat in the recliner. Noticing my expression, he stares back at his newspaper, as if I won't notice him.

"Can you get him to leave?" I demand, pointing toward the back of the house.

"Oh no." He moves the paper so that it obstructs my view of his face. "I am *not* getting involved in this."

"Dad, come *on.*" There's begging in my voice. "He's disturbing the peace. It's a noise violation! And trespassing!"

He shrugs, and I turn back toward the stairs in a huff. But then something occurs to me. I spin slowly on one heel, my eyes searing through the newspaper like a magnifying glass in the sun. "Dad. How did Matt know which window was mine?"

"Well . . ." He peeks over the sports section. "I reckon I told him."

"You talked to him?" My voice is no longer a voice. It's a shriek. "God, Dad!"

He juts out his chin, defensive. "How was I supposed to know you had some sort of drama with him? He shows up, lookin' to serenade my daughter. Thought it seemed innocent enough. Sweet, even. Old-fashioned."

"It's not any of those things! I *hate* him!"

At that moment, Brenda opens the front door, balancing

two paper bags of groceries. My dad jumps up to help her, and she sets her keys on the entryway table.

Pausing to look at me, she says, "It seems like someone or another is here every time I get home. Who owns that fancy car?"

The flashy Porsche that he told me about is in my driveway. My summer life is infiltrating my real life again, and it's too strange to handle. I roll my eyes, tilting my head up toward the ceiling. My dad answers for me. "Matt Finch."

"The boy who played in Dee's concert last night?"

"The very same."

"Well, that's fun. He seemed like such a nice young man. And that voice!" Brenda looks delighted, glancing around. "Where is he?"

"He's in our backyard, singing up at Reagan's window."

Brenda looks amused, too, and I pound my feet against the hardwood floors of the dining room, which is right below my bedroom. When I yank the window up, I'm almost eye level with Matt through the screen. It feels weird to see him so close, from inside the house I grew up in. I'm suddenly self-conscious of my makeup-less face and wild hair.

"I am seriously thinking about calling the cops."

He continues to play and sing. *"I hope you do, yes, I hope you do. Because maybe the sight of police officers will remind you that you've made mistakes, too, you've made mistakes, too. . . ."*

With a screech of anger, I slam the window down, and it rattles Brenda's china hutch. How *dare* he turn this on me; how dare he use my past to make a point. I whirl around, and my dad has clamped his lips together, trying not to laugh. Thanks for the backup, Dad.

Once up the stairs, I grab my phone. I need a plan of action. I'm not exactly on friendly terms with local law enforcement, so I can't actually call the cops to get rid of Matt. If I took a baseball bat to his Porsche, I'd probably get a misdemeanor, so that's out, too. I have one last idea, so I dial Beau Morgan. He's a few years older than me and a rare combination of both nice and seriously hot. The latter is why I made out with him a few times during my freshman year. I only kept his number for convenience—because he works at his dad's car-repair shop.

"Hey, Beau." I struggle to maintain the calm in my voice. "Reagan O'Neill. Listen, I need a favor. One of my friends parked his car here last night, and it won't start. It's in the driveway, and we really need a tow."

By the time Beau arrives, I've put on a cute outfit—a summer dress and heels—plus a full face of makeup. If I'm going to confront Matt, I need all my armor. The tow truck rattles into our driveway, and I wave at Beau from my seat on the porch. Brenda is off toward the left of the house, wearing a wide-brimmed sun hat and weeding her precious geraniums. Matt's still standing at the back of the house, singing below my window, and I doubt he can see Beau backing the tow truck up to his shiny Porsche.

Beau waves, shooting me a smile. Out of the corner of my

eye, I can see Brenda sit back on her legs and stare at Beau confusedly. I ignore her, walking toward the tow truck.

"Hey," I say. "Thanks for doing this. My friend will pick it up shortly. I'll let him know where your lot is. He'll pay you, of course."

"Great," Beau says, still smiling as he turns to rig up Matt's car. "It's good to see you. You look good."

"Thanks."

"Nice car." Beau nods toward the Porsche.

I smile. "It's actually a piece of shit."

I have to strain to hear Matt's guitar-playing over the tow truck's rumbling engine. Last I could hear, he was playing a dramatic Johnny Cash duet, complete with June Carter's parts in a campy falsetto. There's no particular theme to his selections, from what I can tell.

I wave to Beau as he pulls out of the driveway in his tow truck, with Matt's ludicrous car dragging behind it. As he turns onto the main road, he honks in good-bye, and I curse under my breath. Matt probably heard that, but it's too late now. His car is gone.

Sure enough, the guitar-playing has stopped and, next thing I know, Matt's running up from the side of the house. He has his guitar spun around, so it hangs behind him like a backpack. I cross my arms, ready for a fight. It's been less than a week since the last time I kissed him, but the memory of him feels farther away than that. He doesn't belong in the front yard of my house. Here, he looks like an old memory come to life, a ghost of the person I thought he was.

"Damn it, Reagan! Are you kidding me?!" A shudder runs down my back at the sound of his voice saying my name. But he knows that I mean business now, which was exactly my point when I called the tow truck.

"It was either the tow truck or the cops," I say, glancing down at my nails impassively, just to piss him off more. It works.

"You had my car towed," he repeats, like saying it out loud will change it.

"Well," I say thoughtfully. "Pretend like, instead of your car, it's all of your trust being hauled away unexpectedly. Then maybe you'll feel a *fraction* of how mad I am at you."

I figure this—a reminder of what kind of hurt he caused me—will make him start apologizing. But I'm wrong. In fact, he looks mad, his brows creased and mouth in a hard line.

"I've gotta tell you," he begins. His voice is a growl, fully pissed off. Good. "It feels like you've had a telephoto lens on me from the first time I looked at you. You've been waiting for me to screw up, and I found myself in a bad situation. But that doesn't prove that I'm a bad guy. It proves that people make mistakes. I'm a good guy, and I'm good for *you*."

He points his finger at me, directing his words like an accusation. I feel my cheeks flush, and I wish Brenda would go back inside.

Before I can drum up a comeback, he continues, calmer now. "What happened last week was messed up, but I didn't initiate it, and I think you know that somewhere deep down.

That's the confusing part. It's like you're relieved to have an excuse to push me away."

Brenda is still gardening somewhere in the periphery of Matt's tirade, and I am so mortified that I want to sink into the ground. Matt's so close to me that I could physically push him away, and I consider it. "And when I come here, you get my car towed, trying to piss me off and push me away *more*. But I'm not biting, Reagan. Maybe it worked on other guys, but not me."

My arms stay crossed, and my mouth stays closed. I have nothing to say to him.

He looks defeated, shaking his head at me. "Forget it. You're too mad to even see me."

He's right. I'm so mad that it stands like a shield between us. I can't remember Matt before Matt-and-Corinne. The feeling of betrayal frames his face in my mind. So maybe he didn't initiate it—big deal. He did something worse: he reminded me how much I stand to lose, how easy it is for someone to hurt you once you let them in.

"If you could see me, you'd see that I'm sorry," he says simply. "And that I'm right."

With those smart-ass final words, he heads toward the front gate of our house. The guitar bounces against his back, and he looks like a sad, vagabond minstrel.

"Matt," I call. "Wait."

He glances back at me, willing to turn around if I have something worth saying. I sigh. "At least let me give you a ride to the tow lot."

Matt looks surprised for a moment, like he thought I'd say something else. He shakes his head. "No way. I need to walk this one off anyway. Cool down before I start saying things I'm gonna regret."

"Fine!" I shout. I tried to be the bigger person, and he turned it down. "See if I care. Have a great life!"

At the sound of me yelling again, his pace toward the main road becomes quicker, with heavy, angry footsteps. Then he pauses, turning around to call to me, "This isn't over!"

"Not over my ass!" I yell back. "It was over last week and still is!"

He spins back around, flinging his arms in frustration. Fine. If he's going to storm off, then I am, too. My cheeks are burning with anger, my whole body flushed with pent-up everything. I turn on my heels, thundering back toward the house, where I intend to slam every door in the whole place. Brenda glances up at me from the patch of garden nearest the porch steps. I know what she's thinking. I went away for the summer and still brought a huge mess home with me. Same old Reagan, wreaking havoc on everything she touches.

"Having his car towed, Reagan?" Brenda asks. She's using her favorite, holier-than-thou tone of voice, scolding me in the midst of a situation that is none of her damn business. "I don't think that's how your daddy raised you."

"How would you know? You're not my—" The words leap from my mouth out of habit, before I can stop myself. I don't even mean to say them, but they're my knee-jerk reaction to Brenda. Especially when I'm this worked up.

"Damn right, I'm not your mother," she says loudly, standing up to her full height. My eyes widen, surprised to hear a swear word out of her mouth. "Your mother is a selfish child who doesn't know a good thing when she sees it."

My mouth falls open, and Brenda gives me a moment to react. She pulls the garden gloves from her hands and drops them to the ground. I should feel mad that she insulted my mother, but I don't. In fact, studying Brenda from the top of her ridiculous sun hat to the hem of her full-length skirt, I can't feel any of the resentment that I normally do.

"I never met your mama," she says, stepping closer to me. Her voice is quieter now, as if she's trying not to startle me. "And I shouldn't talk bad about her, but here's the thing."

I blink, taking in Brenda's strong features, the firm lines of her jaw.

"She left a sweet little girl and a good man who loved her, and I'm not gonna pretend like I know why she did that. What I do know is that you're right on the money. I am certainly not your mother, and she's the last person I ever want to be."

I swallow hard. Brenda's brown eyes are locked on mine, waiting for me to understand her words. For once, I do. "I don't want to be like her, either."

"You're not," Brenda says simply. She puts her hand on her hip and examines me. "So I'm not sure what you're doin' standin' around here."

I dig the toe of my shoe into the dirt. "It's complicated."

"Is it? Most complicated things in life are actually pretty simple at the core. We put so much extra nonsense in the middle that we can't even see how easy it really is."

I cross my arms, squinting at her in the sunlight. "You mean you think I should forgive him?"

"No, darlin'," she says, picking her gardening gloves back up. "I think you already have."

Her words land like darts to my core, smack into the bull's-eye of myself. She's right, dammit, she's so right, and I hate her for it. No, I hate me for it. I hate Matt for being right, that it seems safer to be mad and alone than together and bare-hearted.

"Shit," I mumble, combing my hands through my hair. I hate being wrong, and I hate having to eat my fighting words.

Brenda doesn't reprimand me for swearing; she doesn't even look back up at me. She's already crouching back down, popping the last weeds out of the dark mulch. Maybe she assumes I've left, but I can't seem to make my feet move. I know what I have to do, but my legs feel paralyzed beneath me. Instead, I'm working through something in my mind, spinning it around and around like the photos dangling from my ceiling fan.

"Hey, Brenda?" I say quietly. She sits back on her legs, wiping her brow. As she glances up at me, something hits me. My one true thing—something I believe enough to write in ink: I don't want to operate from fear. I'm not my runaway mother, and I won't bolt in the other direction just because I'm scared.

Brenda looks at me expectantly, and I realize that I've been quiet for too long. So I look my stepmother square in the face. "Thanks."

And then I take off running. My shoes hit the dirt driveway hard, and it'll take me forever to catch up with him at this rate. So I tug them off and toss them by our mailbox. Uninhibited by four inches of leather beneath my feet, I'm striding now, my legs pushing beneath me. I tend to skip gym on the days they make us run, so I haven't moved this fast on foot since the last time I ran from the cops. Which is to say: I'm usually running away from trouble, not toward it.

The dirt road stretches out in front of me, lines of cornfields on my right and thick forest on my left. I stick to the cool stretch of grass between the road and the cornfield, where the ground is still soft from the storm. In the distance, disappearing toward the horizon line, I can see Matt walking down the road, guitar still bouncing against his back.

"Matt!" I yell. "Matt!"

He turns, seeing me, and I can't make out his expression. He doesn't move toward me, and it's enough to make me wonder if I'm wrong. I slow myself to a walk, but Matt won't budge. He stands his ground, making me walk all the way to him. Without the veil of irrational anger, I can see him again. *My* version of Matt, the one who is funny and sweet and . . . looking seriously pissed at me. I'm breathing hard, and I can feel how filthy my feet are beneath me.

"You got something to say?" When he tilts his head at

me, his expression stays unrelentingly stony. Okay, so having his car towed was a dick move. I admit it.

I put my hands on my hips. "No. You said you wanted me to hear you out. So fine. Let's hear it."

He takes a deep breath, gathering enough air to raise his voice in exasperation. "You are *infuriating*; do you know that?"

I glower at him as he runs a hand over his short hair. Suddenly, I'm remembering the night I cut it, in the hotel room, and that familiar emotion creeps into my chest. I'm not a songwriter, and I'm not sure how to describe that feeling. It's the one I've come to associate with Matt—the swell of newness and infatuation and trepidation. Together, they're enough to make you feel high, like you're living life right on the edge of something good.

"*Infuriating*," Matt repeats. He gestures angrily, his arms flying at his sides. "It honestly keeps me up at night. You're complicated and hard-shelled and impossible."

I cross my arms, rocking myself slightly. Without my shoes on, I'm thrown off by how much taller he is than me. "I ran all this way so you could insult me?"

"I can't stop thinking about you," Matt continues, ignoring me. "We're good for each other. I know we are. I had a seven-hour drive to think about it. This summer, you made me face up to a lot of stuff I was hiding from because you don't see me as that guy from the Finch Four. I don't have to keep any shields up, because you see right through them anyway. And I see you, too, Reagan—you know I do—and I like all of it, even the parts you try to hide."

I look down at my feet, embarrassed because I know exactly what he means. We both had terrible things happen to us before the tour started. Being together didn't make his mom's death or my casted arm okay, but Matt's brokenness gave me silent permission to be broken, too, to feel comfortable even in my not-okay-ness. And it's so much more than that, too. I'm addicted to his confidence and kindness; to his stupid, cheeky comments; to the dimples that show up only when he's really amused. But if he hurts me again, if he leaves, then what happens to me? Withdrawal? A new addiction? Or just the same brokenness as before.

"And the thing is," Matt says, taking a step toward me. His voice is quieter now, watching my face. "I could have sworn you felt the same way."

I open my mouth to say "I don't care." It has to be the biggest lie in the English language: *I don't care.* We say it with a scoff or a snort, like caring is so beneath us. I don't care that my mom left—*her loss; I don't care.* Those girls who tormented me in school—*whatever, they're tragic bitches; I don't care.* Some people do, though. Dee cares about everything, with no apologies or irony, and I admire her for it. Maybe I'm sick of not caring, of saying "I don't care" so fervently that even I believe it.

I feel my eyebrows crease, and I know I'm going to give myself away. I do feel the same way—of course I do. I'd never get this mad at someone I didn't care about. It's the damnedest thing, how you're most vulnerable to the people you care about most. He looks vindicated by my expression, surer of his claim.

"So I'm going to keep showing up here until you can say to my face that you want me out of your life," he says. "Not because you're protecting yourself from getting hurt, but because you really don't want me."

Maybe I want you out of my life because you betrayed me. But the thought is a lie, top to bottom. I don't want him out of my life, and I don't even really believe he betrayed me. I know now that he was in the wrong place, and I walked in at the wrong time. It doesn't change the fact that recalling the two of them together feels like getting my heart run over by a lawn mower.

"This all sounds really nice, Matt." I sigh, filling each syllable with sarcasm. My mind finds Corinne's face, the face of the girl I found in Blake's bed. "But what happens when you meet another girl you'd rather be with?"

He looks at me hard. "What happens if you meet some guy you want to date? Or get sick of me or sick of being in a relationship? We talk, we fight, maybe we break up. I can only tell you that I'll end it like a man—no cheating or getting mean and distant."

"Why bother, Matt?" I give a bitter laugh. "Why should we bother when we're standing here negotiating the terms of our likely breakup?"

My eyes meet his, that steely color not backing down. And the thing is: it's not a rhetorical question. I want him to give me a reason—a reason worth risking it for. When he opens his mouth to reply, his voice is quiet but determined.

"Because I've recently learned, in a very painful way, that life is short. And I don't want to waste my time with anyone who would make me feel . . . happy *enough*." He pauses, searching my face. "I'd rather duke it out with someone who makes me feel everything." A thick lump is rising in my throat, and I swallow it down, like I always do. But hell if my lip isn't quivering ever so slightly, right beyond my control. He's defrosting me, and he knows it. "Wouldn't you?"

"I might hurt you," I blurt out. I can be selfish and insensitive, and I have a mean streak that compels me to do things, like have someone's car towed. He's no safer from me than I am from him. Without particularly meaning to, I uncross my arms, clasping my hands together. "Honestly, I might."

"I know that."

"And you might hurt me."

"Maybe." He keeps his eyes on mine, but his hand finds my still-scrawny wrist. He lifts it up gently, exposing the pale underside and the hand-drawn stars. "But never like this."

It's hard to think straight when I feel his skin on mine. "I know that."

"I would like to know you for a while," he says. "And if that means we're just friends, so you have some time to work things out . . . I can do that."

"Hey. You've got a lot of baggage to sift through yourself. Maybe *you* need some time to figure things out."

He smiles now, hesitantly. "We'll just have to go easy on each other at first."

You'll just have to go easy on it at first. That's what they told me at the doctor's office, the day I was freed from my cast. Matt's trying to remind me that I let him into my life for a while, and, when I did, he made himself at home. When I let him in, he belonged.

He still has a loose hold on my wrist, so careful not to hurt me. He'll get into a screaming match with me and take off in a huff when I push him too far. But he's gentle when it matters, when the difference between past and future is a few inches of Tennessee soil between us.

Despite the doubts that remain, despite a past covered with black marks and missteps, I slide my healed arm up so that my fingers lace between his. I know my mistakes like the back of my hand, but I can chart my future by the underside of my wrist. The henna constellation marks my skin, a reminder to guide me. After all, the night sky is a mess of stars—a million fireflies crammed into infinity. But the mess becomes a map once you know how to use it.

Hanging on to someone's hand—it's such a simple act, but it's harder than it looks. I keep my eyes on his, not even blinking, and all I can think to say is, "Okay."

"Okay," he says, smiling, and this is our deal—a quiet understanding after a summer's worth of slow learning. I know our days of bantering and struggling to get through to each other are far from over. Sometimes I'll push him away and need him to pull me back in. Sometimes he'll try to shut down, and I'll climb in and hot-wire him if I have to. We'll fight with each other—I know that, too—but we'll also fight *for* each other. That's the difference, the one that keeps me standing here with his hand in mine.

He adjusts the guitar against his back, and we start down the path back home. Matt pulls his hand away, but only to sling his arm around my shoulder. I wrap one arm around his waist so that we're moving forward but hanging on at the same time.

"So when were you going to tell me about moving to Nashville?" I glance up at him.

"Oh, that." He gives me that rascal of a grin, complete with dimples. "I wasn't going to, not directly. I thought it would be more fun to write it into a song, then perform it in a concert."

I roll my eyes, tugging my arm away to give his shoulder a push. He pulls me closer, sliding his hand around my neck so that his thumb is right on my pulse. We stand there for a few moments, just looking at each other. My eyes are puffy from nearly crying—I know they are—and my feet are bare and filthy. I've been arguing on the side of a dirt road with a petulant singer who's wearing a guitar on his back. This entire scene is a mess, and maybe we're a mess, too. But it's still him and still me, and there's still that feeling of possibility—the one that sparks like a Roman candle inside me as his lips touch mine. And it's a start.

ACKNOWLEDGMENTS

I'm grateful to my parents every day for giving me a child-hood full of books, a college education, and their unwaver-ing support. Please consider this a public apology for ages 14–16 and that one time with the cops and for a few other things you hopefully still don't know about. Thanks also to my brother and entire family, including the Dudley clan, for being the kind of people I both love and like.

Thank you to my incredible friends; I could never write a cast of characters even half as warm, funny, supportive, and weird as you all, but you sure inspire me to try. To my fellow 2014 debutantes and fabulous kidlit publishing friends: I couldn't ask for better company on this road.

My bottomless gratitude to Bethany Robison, dear friend and every-step-of-the-way critique partner, whose appearance and continued presence in my life are the reason why the word "godsend" exists.

So many thanks to my wonderful agent, Taylor Martindale, for handling my career with grit and my craziness with grace.

To Mary Kate Castellani, whose considerable skill and instinct shaped this story into a book, and the whole Walker/Bloomsbury team: thank you for your hard work and for being the kind of publishing house that actually feels like a publishing home.

And finally, thanks to J, for the thousands of small moments that make up the biggest love.

MAY 2 0 2014